# SALTBLOOD

# ALSO BY TC PARKER

*Hummingbird*
*A Press of Feathers*
*Salvation Spring*
*Maiden (with Ward Nerdlo)*
*The Long Con: An El Gardener Omnibus*

THE EL GARDENER TRILOGY
*The Debt (Book 1)*
*The Push (Book 2)*
*The Remembrance (Book 3)*

# SALTBLOOD

# TC PARKER

PUBLISHED BY NEFARIOUS BAT PRESS
2022

SALTBLOOD
Second Paperback Edition

Published by Nefarious Bat Press

*For my Mum*

# PROLOGUE

**From:** c.lee@specialprojects.vanderhalden.com
**To:** l.webber@specialprojects.vanderhalden.com
**Re:** Project Fortress

Hi Lucy,

Awesome to see you at the planning session last week – and hope you had a great flight out to England. The weather there looks pretty good from here right now – it's still hotter than hell in Austin. We've got the coolers on full blast at home, and I *still* can't get my daughter to sleep through the night!

Not sure when exactly you're due back Stateside, but I know you wanted updates on possible locations for Project Fortress as soon as they landed, so thought I'd send them through now rather than later.

So here it is: we've had all 3 of the scout reports in (see attached), and it looks like we might have a winner! It's not the one we were expecting, either.

I'll fill you in on the specifics next Friday (I'm guessing you'll be back for the team meeting then?), but here are some of the highlights to tide you over in the meantime...

First, the bad news: Newfoundland is a bust. I know you had high hopes for Fox Point, but it looks from the report like it's barely even an island – you can wade across it from the mainland when the tide is low. Obviously not ideal for our purposes!

Also: I spoke to our Acquisitions lead in Toronto (a guy named Brian Fenton) and he thought there might be some issues with the Canadian government. Nothing we couldn't smooth over if we needed to, I'm sure - but apparently they've been a little less cooperative since the last election, which is annoying.

Tasmania is better, but not by much. Kookaburra Island is definitely remote enough – nearly 50 miles off the nearest coast. Though I wouldn't want to take a guess at how you pronounce it!

(It's the name of a bird, right?)

Trouble there is the people: I don't think we realized when we sent our guys out there just how populated the place actually was. And the Australian scout doesn't seem to think the locals would be amenable to working with us. Plus there are a lot of research scientists in the surrounding areas – zoologists and ornithologists on the other islands, marine biologists out in the water – and I'm pretty sure they'd have something to say about us rocking up in their territory, too.

Which just leaves Scotland. And here's the good news: the spot there is perfect. Away from the mainland, but not *too* far away. Populated, but not *too* populated. The scout there says there are maybe 100 people, 150 tops. Climate reasonably temperate, for that bit of the world - not too hot, not too cold, so nothing's likely to freeze or melt if we don't want it to.

There's one watch-out, to do with the water of all things. The Scottish scout says there are "excessively" high levels of sodium chloride (!) in the sea around the island - high enough that we run the risk of it corroding the metals when we put up the pen.

R&D think we'll be fine, though. And they seem to know what they're talking about, so we probably don't need to worry too much. It's just salt after all.

Even better news, on Scotland: it looks like the locals there might be happy to have us. The scout was a little sketchy on the details, but it seems they might be in the market for a corporate partner - someone in their corner with the firepower to help them deal with some longstanding livestock dispute they've got going on with one of the neighboring regions.

(I'm thinking it's livestock, anyway - but I guess it could be an import/export problem. Like I said, Tristan was pretty vague, so I'm putting words in his mouth here. Take a look at page 31 of the report and see what you think).

And obviously, if we help them out... they won't mind helping us.

I'm going to pull together some more specifics ahead of next week, so I should have something concrete for you by then. Maybe we can get this thing going quicker than we thought!

Hit me up if you need / want anything in the meantime.


Take care,
Carl

# WHAT SEAS, WHAT SHORES

# CHAPTER 1

There was a cage over the boat - a thin wire mesh, tightly-woven, running from one side of the deck to the other, ten feet high but dense enough to block Robin's view of the sea around them and, she had to assume, the island ahead.

"Think it's to stop us jumping out?" said the man next to her.

"Not me," said Robin. "Pretty sure I'd get swept away."

"In this?" said the man. "No way. It's not even that cold out there. A half-decent breaststroke and you'd be back on land in an hour. Trust me on this."

"You know a lot about the North Sea?"

"Is that where we are?"

"I thought so. But who knows right now? It's not like we can navigate by sight, with whatever that is hanging over us."

She gestured up at the cage, which shook very slightly in the breezewater.

"It's like they don't trust us at all," said the man, grinning.

She smiled.

"Jack Perry," he said, extending a hand.

"Robin," she said, shaking it. "Are we allowed to do last names?"

"I guess we'll find out soon. But I'd rather err on the side of good manners in the meantime."

She took him in, properly: white, brown hair in a number 4 cut, with a strong jaw and a boxer's nose. A few years older than her, maybe early 40s; broad in the shoulders but paunchy, a college athlete gone to seed. His shirt was wrinkled, his jeans worn away at the knee, and he looked exhausted - which she guessed made sense, if his journey had followed a similar trajectory to hers.

"You're American," she said.

"That surprise you?"

"I didn't see you on the flight out."

"I saw you. Kind of hard to miss the only other person on the plane without a uniform. I would've come over and said hi, but you looked like you were reading the whole way."

"Yeah. Probably a stupid thing to do, actually. They let us bring, what, 10 books? I shouldn't be burning through them like that, not this early on."

"I'd let you have mine, but I can't say I brought any. I'm not much of a reader."

"Then what are you planning on doing for the next six months?"

"Three months for me. And I figured I'd, you know... take a lot of walks. Immerse myself in the great outdoors. Go paddleboarding."

"They have paddleboards on the island?"

"Maybe. And if not... I can always build one. I've got time."

"Think I'll stick with the books."

He leaned forward to grip the rail, the top of his head dipping towards the cage.

"You read a lot?" he said.

"Comes with the territory. I own a bookstore."

"In Philly?"

"Oakland. They flew me out east before the plane ride yesterday."

14

"That's a lot of time in the air."

"Yeah. It really was."

"Tired?"

"Exhausted. Aren't you?"

"Dead on my feet. But I can go a little while longer. Plenty of time to sleep once we're there, right?"

"What about you?" she said, changing the subject. "What do you do?"

"Me? Custom carpentry. Used to be home remodelling, mostly. Now we do a lot of bookcase doors –the ones that open out into a panic room or a hidden passageway. Guess people are a little more fearful than they were 10 years ago."

"Hard to blame them for it," she said.

He pushed his face outward and over the rail, squinting through the tiny gaps in the mesh.

"See anything interesting out there?" she asked.

"I'm not sure. Land, maybe. Kind of hard to tell through... all this."

"It feels like we're slowing down. Maybe we're getting close."

The boat shuddered, unbalancing Robin and pitching Jack forward into the wire. With obvious effort, he pulled himself upright and rubbed a palm across his face and jaw. When he pulled back his hand, she saw blood on the palm.

"Not as soft as it looks," he said, grinning. "Maybe they'll give me a Band-Aid when we hit the shore."

"I think we just hit it," she said.

There was a protracted hiss and a thud, what sounded to Robin like water lapping angrily at the hull, and the boat jerked again, this time pulling to a stop.

"Guess you're right," said Jack.

They stood stock-still on the deck for a minute or more, shoulders pressed together. She heard something shifting in the cabins under their feet, but no voices, and nobody came up the stairs - not the captain, not the deckhand, not the Marshals.

When eventually there was movement, it came from the front of the boat, where they'd first been brought aboard. She turned at the sound, and saw the mesh behind them parting, the two new halves rolling upwards synchronistically to form a kind of doorway to a wooden jetty, and beyond it, a rocky stretch of beach.

A figure appeared in the doorway, the lines of it blurred and ill-defined in the newly-revealed sunlight. She shielded her eyes, and the parts of the whole came into focus: a sandy beard, a cable-knit sweater, a leather satchel stretched over an impressive gut.

"New arrivals!" he said, voice ringing out across the deck in an accent she couldn't place. "Welcome to Salt Rock."

The Induction Room was small, low-ceilinged and strip-lit, housed in a hut-like building a quarter-mile up from the jetty. The bearded man – a 6'2" Viking who'd introduced himself as Hampton, no first name - had driven them and their luggage across from the boat in an open trailer attached to the back of a modified ATV. It was one of only two wheeled vehicles on the island, he'd told them.

"Then how do you get anywhere?" Jack had shouted over the revving of the engine.

"You'll see," Hampton had shouted back.

The parts of the island they'd seen from the trailer had been uninspiring: more rocks, more sand, steep hills and steeper drops, and, far in the distance, what she thought might have been a woman on horseback, watching them move inland.

Suspended high over the land, maybe 80 feet above them, was another wire mesh, this one more dome than cage, sprouting upwards (or so it seemed from her limited perspective) from the sea itself - the jetty poking out from the side of it like a broken tongue. Looking at it made her claustrophobic; more so, somehow, than the cage over the boat.

Inside the Induction Room, they'd unstacked three plastic chairs and laid them out in a very rough triangle, Hampton straddling his backwards and Robin and Jack perched primly on the edge of their seats, legs crossed and hands folded in their laps.

"So," said Hampton. "You saw the wire."

"Does anyone miss it?" said Robin.

"Funny," he said, not smiling.

So you're *that* kind of warden, she thought. Okay. Straight faces only from here on out.

"We call it the bubble," he said. "Most of the other guests call it the cage. Doesn't matter what you call it, as long as you get yourself used to seeing it staring down at you every day. You both clear on what it is, and what it does?"

"Of course," said Robin.

"Not really," said Jack, meeker than she'd seen him previously.

"Really?" she said, surprised. "They didn't tell you about it at your sentencing?"

"I didn't get to go to mine," he said. "Everything happened... sort of fast."

Hampton sighed.

"It's like a Faraday Cage," he said. "A signal blocker. Not *exactly* like a Faraday Cage – but it works on the same principles."

"I don't know what that is," said Jack.

"It's for cellphones and WIFI," said Robin. "It blocks anything with an electromagnetic field. Stops the waves getting through."

"It stops *anything* getting through," said Hampton. "Or it should do, anyway. It's a shield, a barrier. Nothing gets in, nothing gets out."

"Why?" said Jack. "It's not like we're allowed cellphones."

"Think of it as a contingency measure," said Hampton. "You know the deal: no calls, no email, no contact with the mainland. But communication... it's not an easy thing to give up for a lot of our guests. So we've removed the temptation. Made sure it won't even present itself as a possibility. All you have to do is look up, and you see: nope, can't be done."

"Pretty brutal," said Jack quietly.

"You're not on vacation," said Hampton.

"Is it dangerous?" said Robin.

"Only if you dive face-first into it," Hampton laughed, staring pointedly at the cut on Jack's cheek. "But you mean, is it radioactive? Will it give you cancer? No. Hell, it scares off radio waves - it might even keep the cancer away. Believe me... if it were dangerous, the residents would have something to say about it."

"I thought we were guests," she said, more bitterness seeping into her voice than she'd have liked.

"I wasn't talking about you," said Hampton. "Believe it or not, there are other people here on the island. Locals."

"People are *from* here?" said Jack.

"More than a hundred of them, born and raised," said Hampton. "Been here generations. And the few rules we have here on Salt Rock? They're mostly about them. Or I should probably say: about how to keep out of their way. They're not big on outsiders. Or conversation."

He turned his chair back towards them, rearranging himself into a sitting position.

"What you have to understand about the residents," he said, leaning in, "is they don't mix. And they don't *want* to mix. You'll see them all around – unloading the boats, managing the supplies, keeping an eye on things. And don't get me wrong - they're great, really hard workers. We couldn't run this place without them. But you don't engage with them if you can help it. Don't talk to them, don't bother them or ask them questions. And for God's sake, don't try to get to know them. They really don't like that."

"Understood," said Robin.

"They live by themselves," he said. "In a village at the east end of the island, out past the caves. You do not - and let me repeat this more strenuously - *do not* go there, under any circumstances. You'll never *need* to go, and it's not like any of the residents are going to want you over for dinner. But should hell ever freeze over and someone someday asks you to go there, or says you should - you give them a clear, firm no. Got it?"

"Got it," said Jack, dipping his fingers to his temple in a half-salute. "No fraternizing."

"Good," said Hampton. "Now, none of this goes for the other guests. The ones who are just... staying here for a while."

"So these we *can* talk to," said Jack.

"These you *should* talk to," said Hampton. "Even if they're not exactly... like you."

"What does that mean?" said Robin.

"It means," said Hampton, "that they might be different than the kind of people you're used to being around. Different views, different politics, different backgrounds... different ways of looking at the world. I don't know what you did to bring you here, and I don't want to know. Let's be clear: I'm not interested in being your therapist. But I've worked here a year now, and since the beginning we've had guests fanning out into... I suppose you'd call them factions. Ingroups, whatever. Keeping to themselves, not integrating. And it's no good for anybody. We don't need gangs here. This isn't a prison."

"It isn't?" said Robin. "Then what would you call it?"

"A chance to reflect," said Hampton.

It was a short walk to the living quarters, across hard stone and thin patches of grass, the wire mesh cage bearing down on them from overhead.

Her apartment was a ground floor studio, really no more than a couch and a single mattress already made up with a threadbare quilt and pillow – one of several dozen other apartments that spilled out onto a college-style quad in which a handful of other men and women sat, and talked, and read. She'd thought, as she passed them, that she recognized one or two of them; considered it a definite possibility, given the setting.

"Is mine the same as this?" asked Jack as they stepped inside.

"All the rooms are identical," said Hampton. "Likewise the furnishings."

What furnishings there were, she thought. There was a cheap wooden desk and chair set opposite the couch in lieu of a television; a floating bookshelf fixed to an otherwise bare wall. The apartment as a whole felt starkly institutional, consciously curated to seem as unwelcoming and impersonal as possible to the casual observer.

"Is there a bathroom?" said Jack.

"Toilet and shower to your right," said Hampton, gesturing toward a squat door built into an alcove beside the bed.

"But no kitchen," said Robin.

"Cooking is communal, in the dining hall," said Hampton. "Breakfast 6 'til 9, lunch 12 'til 2, dinner 7 'til 9, just like any hotel restaurant. The guests divide up chores on a rota basis. Although if you've got a particular preference, I'm sure they'd be happy to take it into account."

"Is there somewhere to get coffee?" said Jack hopefully.

"No machine," said Hampton. "But you can get a cup in the dining hall, when we have it. Just be aware that it's distributed on a first-come, first-served basis. Same goes for snacks and biscuits, rolling paper and tobacco. The boat delivery drop is once every two weeks for non-essential items, so we have to be conservative."

"What about liquor?" said Robin. "Do people drink here?"

Jack eyed her curiously.

I didn't mean *can I drink?* she added silently, glowering back at him. So stop looking at me like that.

"There's no alcohol on the island," said Hampton. "We're dry. Keeps things more manageable."

"Of course it does," said Robin.

# CHAPTER 2

There was a tentative rap at the open door, and a pair of heads poked around it, one male and one female: his scruffy, sixty-something and bushy-eyebrowed, and hers younger and more neatly put-together, greying curls cropped tight to her scalp.

"Knock knock," said the man.

"We thought we'd come and introduce ourselves," said the woman.

"Robin and Jack, meet Bill and Carol," said Hampton.

The man and woman walked through the doorframe and into the studio. He was short, almost as short as Robin, his tubby teddy-bear frame tucked into a badly fitted jacket too long for his arms. She was better dressed, taller and more willowy, and she moved more gracefully than he did, navigating the room like a dancer or a catwalk model, chin up and shoulders back.

The addition of their bodies seemed to fill the space to bursting point, compounding Robin's claustrophobia; the presence in what was nominally her space of so many strangers - uninvited strangers - like a colony of ants under her skin. She was struck, momentarily, by the compulsion to run outside, out into the quad and away. Then remembered what *outside* really meant here: strange air and alien landscapes and a wire-mesh sky that penned them in on all sides.

TC PARKER

"We like to do this with new arrivals," said Bill, voice thickly New England.

"Help them get acclimatized," added Carol, hers recognizably British by comparison. Northern English, maybe, Robin thought. More kitchen-sink realism than period drama.

"Bill and Carol are old hands," said Hampton. "They've been here... what, four months now?"

"Five and a half," said Bill.

"They're practically natives," said Hampton.

Bill and Carol laughed, awkwardly.

"Would you like us to show you around?" said Carol, directly to Robin. "We can take you up to the canteen for something to drink, if you haven't been there already?"

Robin looked without thinking at Hampton, seeking approval, then cursed herself for it.

"Fine by me," said Hampton. "I think we're done here anyway. Let's go get you settled in," he added, guiding Jack outside.

Bill closed the door after them carefully, the latch making barely a click.

"You okay there?" he asked Robin, gently.

She reflected for a second on her circumstances.

"Not so much," she said.

"It's a lot to take in," said Carol, resting a thin hand on Robin's elbow. "But you adjust. I promise."

"We did," said Bill.

"You came here together?" said Robin.

"Lord, no!" said Carol.

"We met on the boat on the way over," said Bill. "Like you and... Jack, was it? Been thick as thieves since."

"So you're...?" started Robin, unsure even as she spoke how to end the question.

"A couple, yes," said Bill.

24

"Seeing each other," Carol corrected.

"That's nice," said Robin, uncomfortably.

"I think it's what's kept us both sane, actually," said Bill. "Having someone to talk to, someone to laugh with."

"Someone to rail at about surveillance societies and the manifold injustices of the prison-industrial complex," said Carol with a smile, casting an affectionate glance Bill's way.

"That too," he agreed.

There was a silence, long and suffocating.

"I'm sorry," said Robin eventually. "I don't really know what I'm supposed to say here."

"You don't have to say anything," said Carol. "And we won't stay long. I think we both have an idea of how tired you must be. But it's really important you know from the start that you're not on your own here. The island... I wouldn't call it a community as such, but some of us do try to... keep an eye on things. To look out for one another."

Robin closed her eyes, exhaustion and anxiety eroding what remained of her patience.

"I should get some rest," she said. "I don't mean to be rude, and I appreciate the welcome, but could we maybe do the grand tour tomorrow instead?"

Bill and Carol exchanged a loaded look that Robin didn't have the energy to interpret.

"Of course we can," said Carol. "Why don't we get breakfast together tomorrow and go from there? Bill's on frying duty."

"Freeze-dried steak and powdered eggs," said Bill. "You can't say no to that."

"Sure," said Robin.

"We'll leave you," said Carol, opening the door and ushering Bill into the courtyard.

"But we're just down the hall, okay?" he said, over his shoulder. "Apartment 12."

"Got it," said Robin, pulling the door shut and turning the lock.

In the comforting quiet she unpacked her cases, reassessing every shirt, every bar of soap for utility, versatility, longevity - regretting the things she'd brought, and already missing the things she hadn't. Mourning the things that might have reminded her of her own apartment, her own city, things that might easily had fitted into the cases if she'd only remembered: photographs and postcards, matchboxes and jewellery cases, notebooks and refrigerator magnets. Tiny, useless signifiers of home.

After a while her vision swam and her legs cramped, and she lay down on the narrow bed, fully clothed, arms crossed across her chest.

When she slept, she dreamed of tides, and rotten wood, and the slow salt-burn of water on metal.

# CHAPTER 3

Her first morning on the island - *the first of many*, she thought, before she could stop herself - she went to the beach.

She hadn't been to one since college, she'd realized the day before – and even then, had preferred forests and mountain-tops, hiking over swimming. Now she thought of it: she probably hadn't been in the water since college, either. And she hadn't been much of a swimmer, even back then.

That the cold, windy, stone-spiked beach of Salt Rock should look and feel the diametric opposite of any beach she'd ever known in Northern California wasn't, in itself, a surprise. Her expectations, in any case, had been low from the minute she'd tilted up her head and seen again - as she'd see every day of the next six months, she reminded herself - not clouds or weak dawn sunlight but a wire net, pulled tight across the sky.

What *was* surprising was the smell: an invasive, animal stink that called to mind salted pork and beef jerky, the curing barrels of old sea voyages. It clung to her skin and hair as she walked; darted in and out of her mouth and nostrils as she breathed.

That'll be the bubble, she thought. Filtering out the good air, the air you want to breathe, and curing us all in dead saltwater.

There was a woman on the beach.

She sat on the sand, directly in Robin's path; legs folded under her, dark hair blown in every direction and half-covering her face. Not *doing* anything, that Robin could see; just sitting, her angular face turned out to the sea.

Robin's natural inclination - what she was sure was the *right*, the ethical inclination - was to march by without acknowledging her; to leave her to her thoughts, or her morning meditations, or whatever it was she was doing.

And she would have done - would have left her be.

Except the woman turned, and looked at her. Looked her dead in the eye as she walked past.

So Robin changed course.

"Hello," she said, coming to a stop just in front of where the woman sat.

"Can I help you?" said the woman sharply. Another Brit, thought Robin. And a rude one, too.

"I thought I'd come say hi," she said.

"And now you've said it," said the woman.

"I guess I have," said Robin, faltering.

"Was there anything else?" said the woman.

"No. Just... that."

"Alright, then," said the woman, and turned her attention back to the sea and away from Robin.

Robin stood where she was for a beat too long, unsure of how to react to the dismissal, then straightened her spine and walked away, along the sand.

Conscious of her hunger, and that she hadn't eaten in almost 24 hours, she left the beach and trekked back to the quad, following the scent of toasting bread and fried mushrooms to an open-plan canteen area that had to be the dining hall.

Inside were rows of institutional furniture under fluorescent strip lights, long wooden benches and plastic chairs facing a cafeteria-style food dispensary, behind which stood Carol, ladling scrambled eggs onto the plates of the three or four men standing in line to receive it.

There was no coffee that she could see, though there was at least a water cooler tucked away in the far corner. She poured herself a cup and joined the queue.

"Hello again," said Carol, seeming genuinely pleased to see her. "Did you manage to get some rest?"

"Some," said Robin. "I woke up a little disoriented, but I seemed to shake if off once I walked around a while."

"That'll pass. The first week I was here, I forgot where I was one morning and tried to call room service. Took me a while to work out why I couldn't find the phone."

"I'm not sure the concierge would have been up to much anyway, if Hampton's any indication."

"Unfortunately I suspect that young man over there may be as good as it gets as far as service is concerned," said Carol, pointing with her ladle in the direction of a thin-faced boy in a black horsehair cap, no older than 18 or 19, watching them sullenly from one of the benches.

"He works for Hampton?" said Robin.

"In a way. He's one of the residents. Evidently today he's drawn mess hall duty."

"He doesn't look too happy about it."

"They never do. From what I can gather they view us as a terrible nuisance. Interlopers, invading their patch."

"What's the deal with the islanders? How do they fit in here? Hampton wasn't all that forthcoming on the specifics."

"It's complicated. I can explain, but... perhaps now's not the time. And," she added, "you seem to be holding up the queue."

Robin glanced back, and saw a girl barely older than the island boy standing close behind her, slivers of metal studding her nose and eyebrows, an intricate circuit board tattoo running from her forearm to her biceps and up the sleeve of her t-shirt.

"Sorry," she said to the girl. "Won't be a second."

"Take your time," the girl replied in a lazy West Coast drawl. "It's not like I've got anything else to do."

"Can I get some breakfast?" said Robin to Carol.

"What would you like?" said Carol. "Bill's at the griddle, so whatever you want, it'll have to be fried. I'm not sure that man believes in other methods of cooking."

"I'll take some eggs and orange juice," said Robin.

Carol handed her the food.

"There you go," she said, swinging the ladle back towards the tray of fluffy, artificially yellow eggs. "I'll come and find you later, shall I? Give you that tour we promised you?"

"Sure," said Robin, yesterday's irritation mellowing by the moment - though whether by Carol's geniality or the promise of answers to her growing stack of questions, she wasn't sure.

She took her eggs and juice to one of the empty tables and started to eat, hunching over the plate and shoveling forkful after forkful into her mouth like a wary con in a prison canteen. And it's only day one, she thought ruefully.

She was nearly finished with the eggs - and weighing up whether to try for a second helping - when Jack sat down next to her, chicory-scented steam rising from the cup in his hand. He'd exchanged the previous day's button-down for an uncreased summer sweater, but looked every bit as exhausted as he had on the boat over. The circles under his eyes were dark enough to be bruises, and the eyes themselves were bloodshot. She wondered if he'd been crying.

"Rough night?" she asked.

"I've had worse," he said. "Horses kept me up, though."

"Horses?"

"You didn't hear them? Sounded like the damn things were right by my window."

"Not so much as a hoofbeat. Must have been dead to the world."

"Think I should mention it to someone? That Hampton guy, maybe?"

"If you think he'll do something about it."

He stared down into his cup mournfully.

"Hey," he said, suddenly brightening, "you want to go check out the island? Take a walk, do a little exploring?"

"Already took one. There isn't a lot to see, unless you like rocks or copper netting. I don't think they chose this place for its overwhelming natural beauty."

His face fell.

"I wasn't out long, though," she added. "Maybe we could go out a little further. See if I missed anything."

"Only if you want to?" he said.

She looked back at the sullen islander boy, still watching them from his empty corner of the dining hall.

"Sure. Might be good to get out of here, anyway."

The beach smelled just as bad as it had earlier that morning, but was at least lighter, the sun pressing more effectively than before through the thin gaps in the wire.

It was also better populated. On the short walk from the quad to the water, they passed 4 more islanders - all female, all on horseback, the horses larger than any she'd seen in the flesh. None of them wore saddles.

"I guess that explains the hoofbeats," she said, as another rode past them.

"Why do you think that is?" said Jack. "I mean, why wouldn't you drive a car or one of those ATVs Hampton picked us up in?"

"Could be some sort of local tradition. Or could be practical. I don't see many roads here, do you?"

"Think they're wild?"

"The horses?"

"Yeah."

"I'm not really an expert."

"They look wild to me. It's the manes, you know? And the size of them. Domestic horses don't get that big."

"How do you know this? Aren't you from Philadelphia?"

"My uncle Albert owns a dude ranch in Wyoming. We used to go there on vacation, every summer 'til I was 16."

"Then I bow to your superior knowledge. We don't get a lot of wild horses in the East Bay."

Two more horses padded past them, carrying another pair of riders, these ones moving more slowly across the sand than the others. Robin caught snatches of their conversation, a rapid-fire interchange in a language she could neither understand nor identify.

"You hear that?" said Jack.

"Those women? Yeah. Couldn't tell you what they were saying, though."

"I used to work with a guy from Iceland. Get him loaded and he'd start speaking Icelandic to every girl who'd listen at the bar. Sounded sort of like that to me."

"We're pretty far from Iceland."

"Not really. Not geographically, anyway. It's maybe 800 miles from Scotland to Reykjavik."

"Something else I didn't know."

"I was really into Vikings for a while as a kid. Longboats and sacred trees and Valhalla, all that stuff."

"That's... nice?"

"They conquered Scotland. The Vikings. Not all of it, but some of the outlying parts, the islands. Islands like this one."

"You think this place used to be a Viking colony?"

"Maybe. A long time ago."

They followed the bend of the coastline, her toes stubbing every few feet against loose quartz pebbles. Both of them, she noticed, avoided looking up at the place where the sky should have been.

"So," said Jack, "what are you in for?"

"What do you mean?" she said.

"You know what I mean. What did you do? Why'd they send you here?"

She slowed her pace, startled by the question.

"I'd rather not talk about it," she said.

"Your call," he said, still friendly. "You want to know why *I'm* here?"

"Only if you want to tell me."

He bent down, picked up one of the pebbles and held it up to what light the wire allowed.

"Amethyst," he said by way of explanation. "You wouldn't expect it in a place like this, but here it is."

He paused; brushed the dirt off the pebble and slipped it into the pocket of his jeans.

"I drink," he said, more quietly. "Not, you know... sometimes. All the time. I'm a drinker."

He pulled the pebble back out of his pocket and held it, rubbing it between his finger and thumb as he spoke.

"You know that guy," he said, "the one you invite to your wedding, and he has a little too much whiskey and makes a scene? And then you see him at the next wedding, and he's still drinking and still making a scene, so you stop inviting him to things, and eventually everyone else does too? That's me. I'm that guy."

"Okay," she said.

"So one day," he said, "I'm on the subway, heading home. Nobody else in the carriage. And I've had some whiskey, and a couple beers, and some wine with dinner. I don't feel any more buzzed than usual, but I guess that probably doesn't say much. A few stops in, and this girl and her friend get on and sit down just across from me. They're laughing and taking pictures on their phones, so I figure they've been out at a bar too. Anyway, the train starts moving, and I start to feel sleepy - just real tired, like I can't keep my eyes open. I guess I must have dozed off a little, because when I open them again, the girls are standing right next to me, still laughing and taking pictures. Only now they're taking pictures of me, passed out in my seat."

"I'm sorry."

"Me too. Only I'm mostly sorry about what happened next. See, what I should have done is stand up and get off the train. Gone home, climbed into bed, slept it off and tried not to get into that situation again, at least in public. But I didn't do that."

"No?"

"No. I don't know what it was... the drink, or the tiredness, or just this sense that they shouldn't have done that, that it wasn't right. But I got mad. Really mad. I don't even remember what it was I was saying, but one minute I'm telling them to stop doing that, and the next I'm shouting at them, screaming, calling them mean little bitches and God knows what else. And they're filming it all. Getting their cameras right up in my face, which only makes me madder, so I keep screaming until the next station, when they get off."

"But that wasn't the end of it?"

"Not by a long way. Evidently they went home and the first thing they did was upload what they'd filmed online. I found out later it got something like 100,000 shares in the first 12 hours it was out there."

"Fuck."

"Yeah. And there are all these posts, and comments on it, and people after my blood, calling me a piece of shit and a misogynist bastard and everything else you can imagine. So I keep my head down, and try not to think about it. Until a week later, when I get a call from the cops telling me the algorithm's logged half a million separate units of outrage, and asking me to come down to the station to make a statement. You can probably guess what happened after that."

"And now you're here," she said.

"Yep. The evidence was pretty watertight. My lawyer didn't even try to contest it. Told me I should be grateful I got off as lightly as I did."

"Mine said the same thing. Sounds like we both need better lawyers."

"I get that it's my fault, you know? That I did this to myself. I just wish... Hey, wait. Is that Chuck Valentine?"

He pointed towards a stretch of beach not far from theirs, where a tall blond man in nothing but running shorts and sneakers was performing an elaborate hamstring stretch.

"The TV preacher?" she said. "That's him?"

"I think so. Sort of makes sense if you think about it, after what he did."

"He's the one they caught in the bathroom stall with the prostitute, right?"

"Two of them - two bathroom stalls, two hookers. Not sure either of those boys was much past 21, either."

"Someone sent me that clip, the one where he got arrested. I remember watching it."

"Me too. Come to think of it, I think I heard he'd ended up somewhere like this. I just didn't know it was *here*. Jesus. Makes you wonder how many units *that* video clocked..."

The shirtless man spotted them and waved, then jumped to his feet and ran towards them.

Up close, he was better looking than Robin remembered him from television, older but perfectly maintained, his jaw square and teeth artificially white. Sweat dripped from his neck and chest.

"You caught me!" he said. "I just finished up a run. You folks new here?"

"Yes," said Robin, her thought process temporarily suspended by the presence of someone she'd known exclusively through TV screens. Jack stayed silent, apparently similarly afflicted.

"I won't say it's good to have you here," said the man, "because I know not one of us wants to be in this godforsaken place. But it's very nice to meet you."

"I'm Robin," said Robin.

"You're Chuck Valentine!" said Jack, the words bursting out of him.

The man laughed, deep and hearty.

"You've heard of me, then," he said, amused.

"No," said Robin, flustered. "I mean, yes. Obviously yes. Sorry."

"Nothing to apologize for, sweetheart," said Chuck. "We're all celebrities here, aren't we? You can't swing a cat on this beach without hitting some tabloid sensation or other."

"We just got here yesterday," said Robin.

"Still finding your feet, huh? Takes a while."

"So I've heard," she said.

"You met Bill and Carol yet?" he asked. "They love to get the first bite out of the newcomers."

"Yesterday," she said. "And I guess this morning."

"They're good people, Bill and Carol," he said. "Can't say I approve of their politics, but they're good people. You stick with them and you'll be just fine."

"We'll try," she said.

"I'll let you get on with your day," he said. "But come by and say hi when you're settled in, okay? I wouldn't claim to have much to offer by way of refreshment, but I'll be happy to fix you up a pot of whatever's come in on the boat that day."

"Thank you," she said. "We'd love to."

"You take care, now," said Chuck, and sprinted away from them, towards the quad.

"We just met Chuck fucking Valentine," said Jack, when he was safely out of earshot.

"Yeah, we did," said Robin.

"Do you think he's right about the others? That they're all, you know... famous, somehow?"

"He's probably exaggerating. *We're* not, are we? I've never seen or heard of your video, and I have no idea who Bill and Carol are or why they're here. Or that Englishwoman from earlier."

"What Englishwoman?"

"Some woman on beach this morning. Not somebody I recognized. Although I may not be the best judge of who's who or what they've done."

"No? I figured you as somebody who, you know... knows stuff."

"Not me. I don't even watch the news anymore. Can't handle it."

"Kind of ironic that you ended up here then, right?"

"It really is," she said. "It really, really is."

# CHAPTER 4

Lunch on Salt Rock meant sandwiches: a choice of pink lunchmeat or orange cheese, held loosely in place between slices of stale-looking bread and laid out in trays buffet-style on the cafeteria counter.

"It's always sandwiches," said Carol from beside Robin on the bench. "I think they come in on the boat in batches. The island people bring them here after breakfast, great cling-film swathes of them, and leave them for us to pick at until tea-time."

"We don't get to make our own lunch?" said Jack, holding a slice of cheese up for scrutiny.

"There's nothing stopping you," said Carol. "But I wouldn't recommend it. We have barely enough supplies to cover our cooked meals half the time, and what's left over... it makes *these* look gourmet."

"Do you have to eat what they give you?" said Robin, examining her own sandwich. "Isn't there anything you could grow yourselves here?"

"You want to start a community garden?" said Jack, dropping the slice of cheese uneaten onto his plate.

"It's something to do," she said, shrugging. "And it's not that hard, especially in summer. I grew vegetables for a while back home."

"We've tried," said Carol. "Bill's very enthusiastic about his tomatoes. And his cannabis. He grows his own, from what he's told me, in his greenhouse back in Rhode Island. He managed to bring some seed packs over with him - though I'm not sure how, and quite honestly, I haven't wanted to ask."

"He wants to grow weed *here*?" said Jack.

"And radishes, and cucumbers, and potatoes," said Carol. "I think he thought they'd be easiest to cultivate in this kind of climate. But it's a pointless exercise. Nothing grows."

"Nothing at all?" said Robin.

"Almost nothing," said Carol. "It's that bloody chicken coop hanging over us - it stops the light getting in. Apparently most fruits and vegetables need at least a small amount of direct sunlight. And there's only so much watercress you can stomach."

"Mushrooms?" said Jack. "Don't mushrooms grow in the dark, or something?"

"Even they don't seem to like it here," said Carol. "We found a patch of them in the grassland near Hampton's office. But I'm not sure how wise it would be to try to eat them."

"Sandwiches it is, then," said Robin, biting into the bread and lunchmeat. The bread was dry, immediately disintegrating into crumbs in her mouth. The meat she chose not to think about at all.

"So, we just met Chuck Valentine at the beach," said Jack to Carol.

"Oh, yes?" said Carol. "On one of his topless runs, I assume?"

"He had shorts on, at least," said Robin.

"That's something," said Carol. "He likes to show off what he's got, does Chuck."

"He seemed nice," said Robin.

"He is," said Carol. "Once you get past the showbiz. And the religion, I suppose, though I'm not sure he means half of what he says there. Fire and brimstone don't mix so well with some of his other interests."

"Because he's gay?" said Robin.

"He's not gay," said Carol. "He'll swear blind to it. He's still married to his wife, who's very much a woman."

"But what about, you know...?" said Jack.

"The boys?" said Carol.

"Yeah," said Jack. "The evidence seemed pretty conclusive, from the videos I saw."

"He's 'struggling with same-sex attraction,'" said Carol. "I think that's how he put it. It's how he'll tell you he thinks of himself: as a straight man, trying to overcome an addiction."

"Guess that explains the crystal meth they found in his wallet, too," said Robin, drily.

"Sounds kind of sad," said Jack. "If he doesn't feel like he can come out, even after everything. Even though everyone knows already."

"I shouldn't feel too sorry for him," said Carol. "As I say, I'm not sure he believes half of what he's saying sometimes. And whatever 'struggle' he might be going through, it certainly hasn't held him back since he's been here. If they ever let the press out here, there'd be at least a couple of men on the island with stories to tell."

"Residents?" said Jack. "Or people like us?"

"'Guests,'" said Robin. "We're 'guests,' remember?"

"Islanders," said Carol. "You saw one of them earlier - the lad playing prison guard at breakfast."

"The boy in the cap? He seemed ... young."

"He's older than you think. He has a wife too, and a baby. We see the three of them sometimes, out walking."

"Wow," said Robin.

"I thought the residents didn't want anything to do with us?" said Jack.

"They don't, generally," said Carol. "But Chuck is... Chuck. He can be terribly charismatic when he wants to be."

"Evidently," said Robin.

"What's funny," said Carol, "is he wasn't always the way he is now. Bill knew him when he was a student - apparently he was very left-wing, very radical. I don't know if he was out then, but from what Bill says, it certainly wouldn't have been off the menu for him. Until he found God."

"He and Bill went to college together?" said Jack, confused. "I thought Bill was a little... older."

Carol laughed.

"I'll pass that along to him," she said, delighted. "As it happens, he *is* older, though probably not by as much as you'd think. He teaches at a university in Connecticut, a tiny liberal arts place. Has done for nearly 30 years. Chuck was one of his students, way back in the day."

"What does he teach?" said Robin.

"History and politics," said Carol. "It's what brought him here, actually."

"It did?" said Robin. "How?"

"I'll let him fill you in," said Carol. "Though it's not as if it's a secret. I tell you what: if you don't fancy a tour of the island, why don't the two of you come round to our place later? Well, I say "our place"... it's really Bill's place, but I spend so much time there I may as well have moved in."

"Sounds great," said Jack.

"Lovely," said Carol. "He's still in the kitchens cleaning up the mess from breakfast, but I'll let him know you're coming. There's no wine, and there's certainly nothing to smoke, but I think he's got a couple of tea bags tucked away in the cupboard that you're welcome to. You must both be missing the caffeine."

"Like you wouldn't believe," said Jack.

"Just... keep it to yourself, if you wouldn't mind?" said Carol. "We're a chicory economy here, mostly. Tea bags are like gold dust."

Jack disappeared straight after lunch, pleading nausea and exhaustion. His hands were shaking, and his forehead was slick with a sickly-looking grease that Robin hoped signaled alcohol withdrawal, not serious illness.

She went back to her apartment and read for a while, lingering over every word, her legs dangling over the armrest of her too-small couch. But she couldn't focus - her mind playing over the rotten-meat smell of the sea, the dying soil. A chapter in, she gave up altogether and threw the book down onto the floor; watched it bounce across the thin blue carpet.

It landed face-up, opening onto the title page. Even from three feet away she could see the inscription: a chirpy, years-old birthday message in green ink and her brother's sloppy, looping script; the handwriting of a child, not a grown man of 40. Something else she didn't want to think about.

She pulled on her jacket and stepped out into the quad, intending to take another walk but with no real destination in mind.

Virtually outside her door, perched stiffly on one of the concrete slabs that doubled here as outdoor seating and looking straight at Robin, was the woman from the beach - the Englishwoman with the sharp face and the horrible attitude, her mass of black hair no longer windswept but pulled back from her temples in a taut, angry bun.

And here, as before, there seemed to be no polite way of ignoring her.

This time, the woman spoke first.

"We met earlier," she said.

"Yes, we did," said Robin.

"I was rude," she said.

"A little," said Robin.

The woman looked down at her shoes - a pair of heavy-looking walking boots, laced up to the ankle and coated in sand.

"I owe you an apology," she said, not looking up.

"It's okay," said Robin.

"I was having a bad morning."

"You don't have to explain. It's fine, really."

"It's not fine. Especially not when you've only just arrived at this hellhole."

"News travels fast here, then."

"I saw you move in yesterday. You and the other man with Hampton, the one with the cut on his face."

"He had a run-in with some wire mesh."

"Something like that, you mean?" The woman pointed upwards, at the wire. "Perfectly understandable. There've been more than a few moments when I've wanted to take a headlong run at it myself."

"What stopped you?"

"Practicality. I have a surprisingly soft head."

Robin laughed, quick and jagged. For the first time in days, she realized later. Maybe weeks.

"Why was it a bad morning?" she asked.

"I had a letter," said the woman.

"And that was bad?"

"It was... a reminder. Of what I'm missing while I'm trapped here, away from everyone and everything. Wonderful to have it, but it took me to rather a dark place. If that makes any sense to you?"

"A lot of sense, actually. Though I don't know how many letters I'll be getting."

"I won't ask."

"It's not... I mean, I haven't been disowned or anything. I just don't really... have anyone. Not immediate family, anyway. And I told a lot of my friends to stay away. I wasn't sure if they screened the letters and parcels and whatever before they passed them on to us, and I don't want anyone to land in trouble if they write something stupid because they forget for a second who they're talking to. You know?"

"Very sensible. I'd always advocate caution, especially with Hampton sniffing around. Though it may make for a lonely few... how long are you here for?"

44

"Six months."

"Six months. Well, that's manageable. It could be far worse."

"I know. I'm not sure if I could handle any longer."

"No," said the woman, quietly. "I imagine that would be very difficult."

Robin flashed back to one of the very few articles about Salt Rock she'd been able to access before they shipped her out - one that suggested that some of the people there would be counting their sentences in years, not weeks or months - and kicked herself.

"Shit," she said. "I shouldn't have said that. It was insensitive."

"It's absolutely fine," said the woman, with patently false brightness. "In any case, three years really isn't so long, is it?"

"Three years?" said Robin, and kicked herself again.

"I expect you're wondering what terrible thing I must have done to have warranted that long a sentence? You don't seem as if you know who I am."

"I don't. But I don't think any of us here are so terrible. It's all just... bad luck, right? Situations beyond our control."

"Luck has nothing to do with it," said the woman, the words threaded with anger. "Bad or otherwise."

"Maybe," said Robin. "But the control part feels right. I've never felt more swallowed by circumstance."

"It's overwhelming, isn't it? And I'm afraid it doesn't get any easier to deal with. Occasionally I wonder whether it really is easier to be here than back in the world, with opprobrium sliding in from every quarter."

"Only occasionally?"

"I have a son, in London. However attractive it might seem, running away from the world is never really an option when you have children."

"Jesus," said Robin. "That's... I'm so sorry. It must be terrible, not being able to see him."

"It seems to get a little worse every day, actually. And occasionally the discomfort coalesces into something genuinely unbearable, which is what you saw this morning."

"He sent you the letter?"

"Part of it. He's six, so he tends to go off on a lot of tangents, mostly about things he's been doing at school. This week it was an ode to a koala bear he'd seen at the zoo, which segued into a soliloquy on the merits of the species."

"They're pretty cute, koala bears."

"They're riddled with chlamydia. But I assume his other mother is saving that revelation for secondary school."

"You're married?"

"Not any more, no. Not because of... my being here. Just because. And now, again, *I'm* sorry. I really have no idea why I'm telling you any of this."

"Probably good to get it off your chest. Besides, I asked."

"I think perhaps there's something in the air in this place that engenders strange intimacies. Accelerated intimacies. Like real prison. Or reality television."

"You might be right about that. This is the second heart-to-heart I've had today."

"In that case, I hope your other one was rather less one-sided."

"I can't say that I was, actually. But, you know... I like to listen."

"I'm not sure that I left you with a great deal of choice. But please do seek me out if you ever feel the need to unburden yourself while you're here. Though I must tell you, I'm an appalling listener."

"Thanks. I'll keep that in mind."

"I'm Julia, by the way. Julia Mitchell."

"Good to meet you," said Robin, and meant it.

"Who's Julia Mitchell?" asked Robin later, over loose black tea and gossip in Bill's apartment, the tea served mate-style in a copper pot with a metal drinking straw and passed awkwardly around the room like a joint at a dorm-room party.

("It's not a cultural thing," Bill had said, as he'd introduced her to the process. "And it sure as hell ain't Yerba in there. But it saves on tea leaves").

Carol, mid-way to topping up the pot with a thermos of hot water, paused.

"Met her too, did you?" she said, more chilly than Robin was used to from her.

"This afternoon," said Robin. "Out in the yard. She seemed nice."

"You think so?" said Carol, pouring in the water. A little too aggressively, Robin thought, watching a trickle of sodden leaves roll down the sides of the pot and onto the table between them.

"Carol's not a fan," said Bill. He took the pot from Carol's hand and passed it to Jack, who put it straight to his mouth and sucked greedily at the straw. Two long gulps later, he pulled back from the straw, wincing.

"It's like drinking a wet cigarette," he said.

"Give it time," said Bill. "It'll grow on you."

"Why not?" Robin asked Carol. "Julia Mitchell, what did she do?"

"To me, personally?" said Carol. "Nothing. I barely know the woman."

"You know what she means, Cai," said Bill.

"Alright," said Carol, shooting him a look that seemed to Robin more redolent of 20 years of marriage than two months of dating. "Alright."

Then to Robin, she said:

"She's a murderer. Julia Mitchell - she killed people. Three of them."

"For God's sake, Cai!" said Bill. "That's not fair, and you know it. Give the girl some context."

"Why?" said Carol. "It's true, isn't it? They may not have been able to prove it at the trial, but you know she did it."

Bill sighed.

"Listen," he said to Robin. "What Carol's saying - it's right, and it isn't.

Technically, yes, she killed people, inasmuch as she was probably responsible for what happened to them. But we're not talking Norman Bates here. She wasn't chasing after anyone with a butcher knife."

"That's not the point!" said Carol. "I remember when it happened, Bill. I interviewed some of the families. The damage she caused... it doesn't matter *how* she did it. She did it."

"I think I'm gonna need more detail," said Jack. "Because right now, you've lost me. This Julia woman... I never heard of her, let alone any people she murdered."

"Doesn't surprise me," said Bill. "I hadn't heard of her either 'til I rocked up here. What we're talking about - the deaths, the trial - it all happened in London. I'm not sure it got much of a mention outside of Europe. I only know what I know about it because Carol here covered the case for her paper. She's a reporter," he added.

"Journalist," said Carol absently.

"What was the case?" said Robin.

"You want to fill them in'?" Bill asked Carol. "It's more yours than mine to tell."

Carol nodded, and told them.

# CHAPTER 5

Four years earlier, Carol explained, Julia Mitchell had gone to her employers with an idea.

The idea, at that stage thinly-sketched, proposed a new-model neuroprosthetic for information recall: specifically a device, a chip, smaller than a penny, designed to be implanted directly into the left hippocampus of patients in pursuit of a shortcut to an eidetic memory.

Like existing devices on the market, the chip would come equipped with both electrodes (to record learning signals, stimulate the necessary neurons and 'burn' information permanently into the brain) and a microprocessor - a tiny computer to decode the information recorded and enable the implant to function.

Unlike existing devices, which relied on batteries needing to be changed on a semi-regular basis (and which therefore necessitated that the patient submit to extensive semi-regular surgical interventions following implantation), Mitchell's proposition imagined an entirely different and self-sufficient power source: a kind of clockwork engine, powered by the electrical energy of the brain itself, requiring neither charging nor updating. Once installed, she suggested, the engine - and the device it powered - would last more or less forever.

Her employers, the management team of a world-leading bioengineering firm with a reputation for innovative thinking, were delighted with the idea, and especially by its potential for market disruption (leading inevitably to market domination). They gave her free rein to pursue its development on the company's dime, and offered to furnish her with anything she might need to get the job done, and get it done quickly.

A dedicated team was assembled, led by Mitchell herself, and nine months later, a prototype was born.

Pre-clinical trials - first on mice, then chimpanzees - were very promising, her employers' delight compounding with every positive outcome. Finally, after much checking and re-checking of results, and with the support of a pair of pre-eminent British neurosurgeons, the device was approved for testing on human subjects.

And it was here that the real problems began.

The study cohort was small - five men and three women, carefully selected from a pool of volunteers lured to participate in some cases by the promise of total recall, and in others by a recruitment fee twice the size of those made available to clinical trial participants elsewhere. Six of the cohort were students, working towards degrees in law, medicine, architecture. One was a trainee solicitor, mid-way through his training contract; another was a software developer for a Tech City startup. None were over 25.

Implantation in all cases went off without a hitch, and recovery time for all subjects was shorter than average. Mitchell's employers deemed the trial a win, and directed their energies towards their projected release of the implant into the European market in the year ahead.

Until the first subject suffered a seizure.

The girl, a second year undergraduate at the London School of Economics, had collapsed one morning on her way to lectures. She was taken immediately by ambulance to the Royal Free Hospital, but, after suffering a second seizure en-route, was declared dead on arrival. An autopsy, performed the following day, noted the implant still lodged in her brain, but found insufficient evidence to label it a cause a death.

Mitchell's firm, who'd been in contact daily with the volunteers since their surgery, flew into a panic.

They immediately recalled the remaining subjects to their headquarters for closer monitoring. Once there, two other subjects - both medical students at University College - suffered similar seizures; both, like the first girl, died almost instantly.

The firm acted quickly and decisively, scheduling the removal of the implants from the remaining subjects for that same evening.

By then, however, the damage was done. Post-mortems of the two dead boys were less hesitant than the first in attributing their seizures to the implanted devices. Forensic examination of the devices themselves showed that all three - the girl's included - had malfunctioned, precipitating sudden, massive rushes of electrical activity across multiple areas of their brains.

A wider police investigation was mounted, and eventually, almost a year later, charges of corporate manslaughter were levelled at the firm.

At the trial, the firm was steadfast in rejecting all accusations of wrongdoing: they'd acted, they said, in good faith, basing the decisions they'd made on pre-clinical results that seemed, on the surface, to have been good. They couldn't, they said, have foreseen the outcome of the first human study. It was a horror and a tragedy, they agreed; but a horror and a tragedy for which they bore no legal responsibility.

All three managing partners gave evidence, the testimony of each corroborating the story told by the others. On the fifth day of the trial, another witness from the firm was called: a lab technician, working directly under Mitchell and her team for the duration of the study. A whistleblower.

Mitchell, he said, had been a difficult and mercurial boss, with a reputation for anger and impulsive decision-making that the wider team attributed, privately, to exhaustion brought on by recent motherhood. She had a child, they all knew; a toddler, prone to illness and disrupted sleep, whose crying and distress regularly kept her and her wife up all night.

At the outset of the project, he said, she'd seemed happy with their performance - convinced that the work was moving in the right direction, and that the developed prototype would meet both safety and performance standards, and the internal deadlines set by the firm.

As they progressed, though, he said, her behaviour altered. She become more forgetful, more erratic, committing basic processual errors and then working late to remedy them and cover her tracks. Two of her team, he claimed - both too afraid to come forward and put their statements on the record - had uncovered fundamental flaws in her modelling of the prototype, only to have their concerns dismissed out of hand when they raised them with Mitchell.

These colleagues, he said, had confided in him their shock at the early success of the prototype - which, they'd told him privately, *shouldn't* have worked. Not on mice, not on chimpanzees, and certainly not on humans.

Around the time of the animal studies, he said, Mitchell had become more secretive, more controlling; insisting on managing the trials - and even some of the implantations - herself, and occasionally demanding outright that members of the team leave her alone in the lab to handle the results.

A third colleague, he said - likewise afraid to speak out publicly - had speculated that Mitchell might have *done something* to the study results. At best, massaged the data to produce more favorable outcomes; at worst, concealed evidence of failure. There was a discrepancy, he'd told the lab tech, in the number of mice delivered to the lab versus the number accounted for at the end of the first study. Five were missing; nobody on the team could explain where they'd gone.

Of course, said the whistleblower, he couldn't *prove* anything. There was no official evidence of Mitchell having done anything wrong, no paper trail or smoking gun. But still, he said - he wouldn't have been able to live with himself, had he not spoken up.

A verdict of not guilty was delivered. In his summation, the judge agreed that the managing partners - as representatives of the firm as a whole - couldn't have known that the device would malfunction, much less that it would prove fatal in human subjects. He tacitly communicated his approval of the firm's pledge of a £250,000 goodwill gesture to the families of the dead students, while also noting somberly that no amount of money would bring back those whom they'd lost.

Finally, he urged the Crown Prosecution Service to further investigate some of the allegations made over the course of the trial - conveying his hope that, should new evidence be brought to light, the appropriate person might be brought to justice for their role in the debacle.

No charges were filed against Mitchell - the sworn testimony of the lab tech offering inadequate grounds for the building of a case likely to end in conviction. But it didn't matter. Now jobless (the firm having quietly let her go, albeit with a settlement, before the start of the trial) and newly single (her relationship with her wife, or so it was reported, having cracked under the strain of the preceding months), she became a tabloid hate-figure, excoriated weekly in the pages of the Mail and the Sun while the more vociferous talking heads bayed for her blood on mid-morning television.

Finally, perhaps on the advice of her lawyer or a well-meaning friend in crisis management, Mitchell issued a public response via a little-used social media account: a perlocutionary act, impeccably assembled, that nevertheless failed utterly in its attempt to cast its writer in a favorable or sympathetic light.

The tone was all wrong. Where she might have seemed fragile, inviting audience compassion for her vulnerability, she was cold and unyielding; instead of remorse for her actions or their consequences, she expressed only a non-specific regret that "things unfolded as they did." Though the form of the statement suggested an apology, the talking heads agreed, she wasn't actually sorry; there was no authentic regret to be detected there, only the last-ditch efforts of a criminally negligent, possibly sociopathic murderer to save her own sad skin.

The public's retribution was swift and virtually unanimous: the algorithm logged 5.2 million separate instances of outrage in the UK alone, which almost doubled as the statement was reposted (sometimes verbatim, sometimes in translation) by commentators across France, Spain and Germany.

Of this outrage, at least, there was evidence enough, and this time Mitchell *did* stand trial. Her lawyer fought as best she could, but the numbers were clear and damning, impossible to contest. After scarcely an hour of jury deliberations, Mitchell was found guilty, and duly sentenced - the length of her confinement setting a new precedent for the punishment of crimes inciting outrage and displeasure.

The following week, she was shipped out to the island.

"And she definitely did it?" said Jack.

"There's no doubt in my mind," said Carol. "I was sat in the public gallery for most of the first trial. I believe what that man said. You would have too, if you'd seen her. She was there as well, you know, watching from the back when the verdict came in. Didn't even flinch. You can't tell me that's normal behaviour."

Robin stayed quiet, sipping bitter tea from the little pot, reconciling what she'd heard with the woman she'd met earlier, the one who missed her son and made her laugh. The pieces didn't fit, but then, she thought, maybe they didn't have to. Passing down judgement probably wouldn't get her far, here and now.

"So what are you two in for?" she asked. It came out more abruptly than she'd hoped it would.

"Straight to the point!" said Bill. "I like that. I'll do the honors on this one, shall I?"

"Be my guest," said Carol.

Bill snatched the pot from Robin and took a long, melodramatic swig.

"I like to think I'm here for being myself," he said.

"Now who's being disingenuous?" said Carol.

"That's fair," said Bill. "Okay. I'll be clearer. Now, I know Cai's told you what I do. That I teach."

"History, right?" said Jack.

"Close. Twentieth century politics, with a focus on Cold War policy and culture. I read a lot of books, but I also get to watch a lot of B movies."

"Cool," said Jack.

"I think it is," said Bill.

"I'm begging you not to get him started on The Attack of the 50 Foot Woman," said Carol.

"A classic, by the way," said Bill. "But I see where you're going with that. I'll stay on track. Right now, I head up the Polisci department at Sheldon University in Connecticut."

"I don't think I know it," said Robin.

"You wouldn't," said Bill. "We're a small school. Though I hope we punch above our weight in some areas. And I *say* I head up the department... but the truth is, I don't know that I still do. I can certainly tell you that I *used* to. But whether they'll take me back once I'm out of here - that's anyone's guess."

"I hear that," said Jack.

"But for now," said Bill. "I'm choosing to think that they will. So let's keep that one in the present tense, shall we? I head up the department. I am *currently* heading up the department."

"You always make such a meal of this," said Carol.

"Just giving them some of that context we talked about," said Bill, grinning.

"Context for what?" said Robin. "What did you actually do?"

"What did I do?" said Bill. "Exactly what I'm paid to do. I gave a lecture."

"Must have been some lecture," said Robin.

"It was an overview of Eisenhower's response to the Taiwan Strait Crisis," said Bill.

"In which he compared the current US administration to The Blob," said Carol.

"It was an aside!" said Bill. "And hardly an original observation. It's not as if I was the first to have made it to a roomful of students. I doubt I'm even the first to have had the students film it on their goddamn phones."

"But he may have been the first to have those students put it up on Sense."

"What's Sense?" said Jack.

"It's a right-wing news site," said Carol.

"Which apparently a lot of kids subscribe to," said Bill. "Isn't that just about the most depressing thing you've ever heard? Enough of them that suddenly I'm public enemy number 1. A poster-child for the plague of liberal bias in the American academy."

"How many units did you clock?" said Jack.

"2 million," said Bill. "Or as I prefer to think of it: 12 months' worth. Could be more by now - who knew there were so many angry teenage fascists out there? But I'm happy to say that the law hasn't descended quite so far yet into full-blown insanity that I can be re-sentenced retroactively, so 12 months it is."

"Mine's the same, before you ask," said Carol. "12 months, do not pass Go, do not collect £200. Though my reasons for being here are slightly different from Bill's. And I suspect from both of yours."

"Different how?" said Robin.

"Different in that she hasn't actually done anything wrong," said Bill. "Not that any of us are exactly criminals, but at least we all know why they rounded us up for the gulag. Carol didn't actually break any law, not even any of the crazy ones. They put her here to shut her up."

"Who's 'they'?" said Jack.

"The Security Service," said Carol. "I assume on the orders of a more senior authority. They came for me in my flat one morning. The deal, as I understand it, is that I spend the year here thinking about what I've done and understanding why I shouldn't have done it, then return to Manchester vowing never to poke my head above the parapet again, lest I be more permanently disappeared."

"It's like something out of a movie," said Jack.

"Not a very interesting one," said Carol. "I haven't been tortured or locked away in a dungeon. This is... I suppose you could call it a warning. And I'm sad to say, I've learned my lesson."

"What lesson is that, exactly?" said Robin.

"Don't write about the island," said Bill.

"Salt Rock?" said Robin. "You were writing about Salt Rock?"

"In a way," said Carol. "It was part of a bigger piece I was pulling together - a kind of exposé, I suppose. Of Vanderhalden."

"Who's Vanderhalden?" said Jack.

"*What's* Vanderhalden," said Bill. "They're the company that run this place. They're based out of Bristol, England."

"And Austin," said Carol. "And Milwaukee. They're a very transatlantic venture."

"What were you writing about?" said Robin.

"I was documenting some of their acquisitions," said Carol. "Trying to make sense of them. I knew about the island - everybody knows about the island - but I hadn't realized that they owned it. When I first started digging, I assumed they were running it, that they'd won some sort of tender and were managing it like a prison. But it seems they actually bought the place from the Scottish government."

"So they *own* it?" said Robin.

"Outright," said Carol. "Which explains why they've got the islanders running around after us. They've set themselves up as the only employer on the island – the only game in town. I should think they've driven everything else out of business."

"Doesn't look good for Scotland," said Jack. "You can see why they'd send their people in after you."

Bill and Carol laughed.

"That wasn't exactly the story she was trying to bust open," said Bill.

"Then what was?" said Robin.

"The connections," said Carol, more seriously. "Vanderhalden own the island, in their own name - that's not been kept particularly under wraps. I was certainly able to find out easily enough. But what's interesting, and what a lot of people - my own government included - would rather *didn't* make it into the public domain, is that, in a very roundabout sort of way, Vanderhalden also own Medida."

"Medida?" said Robin.

"You haven't heard that name?" said Carol, surprised.

"It's the tech company that operates the algorithm," Bill explained. "The one that sent the rest of us here."

It took Robin a few seconds to process the information, what it meant.

"Fuck," she said, barely audible.

"That's about the size of it," said Bill. "Vanderhalden owns Medida – or I should say, Vanderhalden is the parent company. They own *another* company called Trip, and *that's* the one that owns Medida. And Medida runs the algorithm – which weighs us, and measures us, and passes the naughtier ones among us along to the cops and the prosecutors. Who send us out here, right back to the waiting arms of Vanderhalden."

"And who get paid God knows how much per head for their trouble," said Carol.

"It's a closed circuit," said Robin, slowly.

"A very lucrative one," said Bill.

"Fuck," said Robin again.

"Makes you wonder who's sponsoring those bills to get "outrage" turned into something you can prosecute, doesn't it?" said Bill. "Though maybe I'm being cynical. Or maybe I've fallen too deep down the rabbit hole of conspiracy theory."

"No, I think you're probably right on the money," said Robin. "Though I really wish I didn't."

The four of them fell into silence, Robin still working through the enormity of the revelation, the fundamental *wrongness* of it.

"How do you live with it?" she said. "Knowing what you know... how can you stay so calm, so upbeat?"

"What are my options?" said Carol. "There's no way off the island - you've seen as much yourself. I can't spend the best part of a year wailing and rending my garments."

"And you got me," said Bill, squeezing her hand.

Robin studied them, half-envying the ease of their intimacy.

"That I do," said Carol, squeezing back. "That I do."

# CHAPTER 6

The studio was draughty first thing in the morning, and for the second day running, Robin woke up before dawn, cold sweat leeching into the hooded top she'd worn for warmth in the night, soaking into the single, flat pillow that separated her head from the mattress.

She showered in a hurry, not trusting the hot water to last, and dressed just as quickly, intent on getting out of the still-suffocating room as quickly as possible.

In the half-light, at least, the wire was less conspicuous; for a half-hour or so, she thought, she could kid herself that she really was outside, breathing something fresh and vital into her lungs, not trapped like an insect under a whiskey glass.

She followed the path down from the quad and down towards the water, tracing roughly the route she'd taken with Jack the day before. Today the beach made for a strange sight: in the mid-distance the tide was high and angry, riven with waves, but narrowed to innumerable waist-high jets by the tight metal weaving a long way before it hit the sand. The effect was disconcerting, putting her in mind of an upturned sieve or a leaking dam ready to burst, and the sound of it equally alien - deafening but far removed, an airplane take-off heard from the next town over.

She pulled her eyes away; looked straight ahead, and kept walking.

Despite her best efforts to tamp it down, to deaden herself against it, she was angry, still. Or perhaps: cognizant again of how angry she'd been, on some level, for the last few weeks and months. The last year, even. What Carol had told them about Vanderhalden and the island and the vertically integrated punishment system that had landed her here - it had turned up the temperature. But the anger had been there the whole time, simmering on low along her nerve-endings, waiting to catalyze again into something so hot and corrosive that she'd have to acknowledge it.

It was the unfairness of it, she thought. The embarrassment, the inconvenience, even having to close up the bookstore... she could live with it, all of it. They were just... things to get past or wait out. The unfairness, though... it stung. Burned. Would burn through her, if she let it.

It hadn't always been that way, she knew. She used to experience anger in a normal, contained way; would feel it rage then fade away, resolved or diminished. Would have a hold of it, would have control. *Too much* control, her brother had told her - more than once, and then again the very last time she'd seen him. It might have been the last thing he'd said to her, though she thought it probably wasn't - that instead her mind had refashioned it that way, trying however it could to string the half-remembered tail-end of an argument into a narrative thread she could follow retroactively, that she could revisit and retell herself.

They'd been shouting; she remembered that much. Shouting, and crying. She remembered the tears falling down her chin and onto her chest; the dim worry, even as she screamed at him across the narrow kitchen of her apartment, that a scream like that might tear her throat, do some kind of damage to her vocal cords.

He'd come over for dinner, the way he always did on a Thursday; she'd cooked for him, spaghetti and meatballs and a store-bought peach cobbler, but he'd arrived late, and the food had gone cold, and she'd been pissed even before he'd walked in the door.

"You could have let me know," she'd said, slamming the plates down on the table.

"I got tied up," he'd replied, nothing like as apologetic as he should have been.

"Doing what?" she'd said.

"I was at a meeting. In the city."

"AA?" she'd asked. He'd been clean for a decade by then, but it had seemed like a possibility.

"No," he'd said, seeming shifty, evasive.

"What, then?"

"A planning meeting. For the march this Saturday."

Even with her self-imposed withdrawal from the news in place, she'd hearing about the protest for weeks: from friends, from customers, from the book groups who rented the basement of the store on weekends. It was the second like it in the Bay Area that winter. The first had drawn almost 50,000 people - mostly peaceful, a minority disruptive. The Governor, anticipating trouble, had called up the National Guard as well as the city PD. They'd used tear gas and rubber bullets to disperse the crowd. Next time, one of the customers had told her with certainty as he'd leafed through a Ray Bradbury collection, they'd use tazers and live rounds on the troublemakers - the Governor had authorized it.

"It's not safe," she'd said.

"What is?" he'd said, and she remembered thinking at the time that he'd rehearsed the answer, that he'd known in advance what she'd say, how she'd object. "That's the whole point. That's why I'm going. Nothing's safe anymore in this country. They keep changing the rules. I can't just sit around and wait for the cops to come and take me away in the middle of the night because I... I don't know, chewed gum in the street or told my boss to go fuck himself."

"When have you ever had a boss?"

"You know what I mean, Robin."

"And you know what I mean. Please, David. Please don't go."

"I have to. And you should think about it yourself. This stuff affects you too."

"Why? What difference does it make if you're there or not? It's not like it's going to change anything. How many of these protests have there been, for Christ's sake? In how many cities? And how many of them have actually achieved anything? Nobody's listening, nobody who matters. Best case scenario, all it's gonna do is antagonize people. Worst case... people will get hurt."

"So we should stop trying? Just roll over and let them do whatever they want to us?"

"There are other ways to fight. Smarter ways."

"Like those petitions you used to sign? The flyers you'd leave out by the cash register? And you're not even doing that anymore, right? Just staying home, not watching the news, pretending everything's fine when it's going to shit all around you. Jesus, Robin. When did you get so fucking spineless?"

"At least staying home at nights won't get me shot."

"You don't know that. You don't know what they're gonna come down on next. You know they're taking registers at treatment centers now? Not just current patients, either. They've gone way back in the files, for anyone using in the last 10 years. That's me, Robin. I'm on a fucking register."

"No."

"Yes. So I wouldn't get complacent if I were you. You're the reader in the family, so come on, you tell me: who else was it they used to put on registers, again?"

"What the fuck does that mean?"

"You know what it means. You're no more safe than I am, so stop giving me shit for wanting things to be better."

"Whatever I do or don't do, it's safer than standing in front of the National Guard with a target on my chest!"

She'd been shouting by then, screeching, her voice an entirely different register than she was used to.

He'd shouted back, louder and worse; she couldn't say how long they'd stood there, trading anger and insults across the table, until finally he'd cracked, picked up his battered messenger bag and walked out of the apartment, the door slamming shut behind him.

And by the Saturday night, he was gone.

Out at sea, birds were circling: she couldn't see them through the cage, but she could hear them, cawing and squawking just outside of it. She wondered how many of them had damaged themselves on it, had broken wings or worse hurling their bodies against the metal. Evidently none had ever got through: she'd seen no birds at all on the inside.

No plants, no birds, no direct sunlight. The place was a wasteland.

She'd already walked further, she realized, than she'd gone the previous day. The landscape was changing, very slightly - the rocks sharper, the dry sloping grass leading up to the sand denser and more wild. She wondered if she was edging closer to the Residents' village; if she should turn around and go back.

Up ahead, she saw something that looked like a cave: a jut of rock, low and jagged, set between the beach and the slightly higher ground of the grassland. A pile of something, dark and shapeless in the half-light, lay just outside of what she assumed must be the entrance. Canvas, maybe? Tarp?

She jogged toward it.

The pile of... whatever it was moved, just a little. Flapped back and forth - once, twice - in the almost-breeze.

She slowed her pace, but kept walking, her curiosity piqued. Then, a few feet from the mouth of the cave, she stopped altogether.

It wasn't a canvas, or a tarp, or the fox she thought it might have been.

It was a man. A half-naked man, pale-white and face-down on the ground, bleeding heavily from what seemed like everywhere at once. Blood soaked his legs and feet; matted his hair, ran down onto his neck and stomach and into the fabric of his shorts. He was breathing, or he seemed to be.

She ran towards him, then sank to her knees on the sand to get closer. She grabbed the bleeding skin of his shoulders and pulled, hard, rolling him over and onto his back.

The body - the man - was Chuck Valentine.

His face was broken: one eye fused shut with dried blood, cheekbones black with bruising. His jaw was swollen; when he opened his mouth, she saw that several of his teeth were cracked, and others missing. His bare chest was shredded with cuts and yet more bruises, a large half-moon contusion darkening the skin across his ribs.

"Help me," he said, breath leaving his body in a ruptured wheeze as he spoke. "Please God, help me."

She tried to hold it together, to suppress the flares of panic, her nausea at the sight and smell of blood. Tried to weigh her options; to see what was possible.

"I'm going to turn you onto your side, okay?" she said, as calmly as she could. "It'll keep you from choking."

"Okay," he said.

She gripped his biceps again - ignoring the liquid slickness she felt there, the blood pouring down onto her hands - and moved him into what she hoped was a recovery position. He groaned as he was maneuvered, holding broken fingers against the meat of his waist.

"I need to get you some help," she said. "But it means I'm going to need to leave you for a couple minutes. You don't have to speak, but nod if it's okay, okay?"

He nodded.

"I'll be back," she said, and took off down the beach at a sprint, back towards the quad. She hadn't run - hadn't taken any kind of exercise at all - in a month or more, but her muscles seemed to remember what to do, and she picked up speed quickly, barely conscious of the stones tearing into her feet as she ran.

She'd been running maybe five minutes when she saw the horse, and on it, with no saddle holding him in place, the rider: another skinny teenage boy in another horsehair cap, his expression blank as he stared out at the water.

Both he and the horse turned as she approached them, the boy's expression shifting from disinterest to unease as he took in her appearance, the blood smeared all over her, coating her hands and clothes.

"There's a man," she said. "Something's happened to him. He's hurt."

The boy stared blankly back at her.

"He needs help!" she said. "Now! You need to help him!"

"Where is he?" said the boy, the words sounding foreign in his mouth. She wondered, behind her panic, how used he was to speaking English, or to speaking much at all.

"That way," she said, pointing behind her. "Outside the cave. Please, you have to go quickly."

"Hampton," said the boy. "I'll get Hampton."

"Then get him now!" she said. "The man, Chuck... he's in really bad shape. It can't wait."

"Hampton will ken wha tae dae," said the boy. He kicked the horse's flank with the side of his boot, and the two of them sped away, onto the grass and away from the beach.

She watched him until he faded out of view, then turned back, first jogging then running back to the cave, to Chuck.

The light was better when she reached him. Not perfect, not *sunlight*, but enough that she could see his body from a distance, see that it *was* a body, something human not inanimate.

See that he wasn't moving - that the body was still.

She knelt back down beside him, digging her knees into the sand. It was darker than it should have been; stained purple with his blood.

He didn't speak; didn't stir.

She put her palms against his shoulders and *pulled*, the gesture beginning to feel familiar. He fell against her, his bare back against the rough material of her jeans. He wasn't breathing.

She felt for a pulse at his wrist, then on his neck, digging the pads of her fingers into the skin and deeper, down into the tissue, but there was nothing. He was dead.

Still holding the body against her, she sat down on her heels and waited. Eventually, she thought, someone would come.

# CHAPTER 7

S he was still holding the body when Hampton arrived.

He came with backup: the teenage boy she'd asked for help and two island men, older and stern, all on horseback, their animals a stark old-world contrast to Hampton's ATV.

"You're too late," she said.

Hampton walked over to them slowly, cautiously, his eyes on her rather than the body.

"How did this happen?" he said, crouching down beside it.

"I don't know," she said.

He reached out a hand to the body; felt for a pulse at the wrist, then at the neck, almost exactly the way that Robin had an hour earlier - and then, with unexpected gentleness, shifted it - him - away from her and onto the sand.

"We need to get you out of here," he said, pulling her to her feet.

"What are you going to do with him?" she asked. She was freezing cold, suddenly, and shivering. She wrapped her arms around herself for warmth; felt her sweatshirt, stiff with drying blood, chafe against her forearms.

"We'll take him to my office for now," said Hampton. "Then send him back to the mainland on the next boat out. We need to know what did this. How he got like this."

"He was like this when I found him," she said.

"I believe you."

"Are you calling the cops?" she asked.

"We'll have to," he said. "But there's not a lot we can do for now, until the boat comes in."

"Will they want to talk to me?"

"That isn't something for you to worry about right now."

He gestured to the teenager, who climbed down from his horse and walked across to him. The horse stayed exactly where it was, still as a statue.

"Take her back to the Guest area," he said. The boy dipped his head deferentially.

"I'll walk," she said.

"You can't walk there like this," said Hampton. "Look at you."

"Please," she said. "I have to think. Clear my head. I'll go straight back to my apartment, I swear. I just need to walk."

Hampton looked skeptical.

"The other guests can't know about this," he said. "Not until we're clear on what actually happened. The last thing we need is hysteria."

"I'm not going to tell anyone anything," she said. "I don't want to *see* anyone. I just need to walk. Please, let me."

He started to speak, then hesitated. Unzipped his jacket, took it off and draped it over her shoulders.

"Wear this," he said, "It'll stop you shaking."

"Thank you," she said.

"And do it up, all the way to the collar."

She slipped the sleeves over her arms; zipped the jacket up to the throat.

"You go straight back to your apartment," he said. Telling, not asking.

"I will."

"You don't stop anywhere, and you don't talk to anyone. Just go home, lock your door and wait. I'll be over to check on you as soon as I can."

"Okay."

"I mean it."

"I know. And I won't."

"Go, then. Quickly."

He turned, deliberately, to the body, his back to her.

She took the cue, pivoting on her heels and moving away from the cave - still shaking, the imprint of the body still clinging to her hands.

She felt the eyes of the island men on her the whole walk back.

There was no one on the beach, no prisoners and no islanders, and she made it to the living area without seeing a soul. The quad was empty, too; given the time of day, she assumed that everyone was at breakfast, or sleeping in.

She was almost at her apartment, just a few steps from the door, when she saw Julia Mitchell walk out of the dining hall and into the courtyard.

She spotted Robin and immediately changed course, heading towards her.

Robin thought fast: pulled the sleeves of Hampton's jacket down over her hands, covering the dried blood as best she could, and tried to regulate her breathing.

Julia came closer, stopping maybe half a foot away from Robin. Close enough, thought Robin, to read the horror on her face; to smell the blood, if she leaned in.

"Been out for a walk?" She asked.

"Yes," said Robin. Her voice sounded weak but not distressed to her ears; strained in a way that she thought could be attributed to tiredness rather than anything more serious.

"I go out early myself - early, or very late at night. I find it's easier to pretend the bars aren't there when I can't actually see them."

Robin nodded.

"How are you finding things?" said Julia.

"Okay," said Robin.

"That's good. I can't say I coped well, initially. I thought I was going to lose my mind my first week here. There were fewer people then, of course, which I think perhaps was a blessing. All I wanted to do was scream into that bloody sea."

"I can understand that."

Julia studied her.

"Are you quite sure you're holding up?" she asked.

"I'm sure," said Robin uneasily. She was warmer now; too hot, sweating under the weight of the jacket, moistening the dried blood along her arms. She hoped it didn't show.

"Because I meant what I said yesterday. If you want to talk."

"I'm fine," said Robin. "Really."

Automatically she reached up to push a damp strand of hair behind her ear, a nervous tic from childhood she'd never quite shed - realizing a beat too late that, in doing so, she'd pulled back the jacket sleeve, exposing the red stains on her hands and wrists.

"That's blood," said Julia, staring down at them.

Robin scrambled for the sleeve; pulled the material back down over her fingers.

"Is it yours?" said Julia, stepping forward into Robin's space. "Did something happen to you?"

"No," said Robin quickly. "I'm fine. Everything's fine. But I have to go. I'm sorry."

She took a step forward, towards her apartment. Julia followed her, blocking her path.

"Tell me what happened," she said, lowering her voice. "Please."

"I can't," said Robin, quieter still. "I can't talk about this."

"Did you see something?" said Julia urgently. "Find something?"

Robin bit her lip.

"I can't tell you," she said. "Hampton... he was very clear."

"This is something to do with Hampton?"

"Please, just let me into my apartment."

Julia moved aside.

"Did he do something to you?" she said, as Robin brushed past her, making a beeline for the door. "Hurt you?"

"I have to go," said Robin again.

She opened the door and crept inside, leaving Julia staring after her from the courtyard.

The jacket went first. She left it, carefully folded, on the desk, before stripping off the rest of her clothes: jeans, sweatshirt, vest, tank top, underwear. The blood, she saw, had soaked through every layer of fabric, right down to her skin. She bundled it all into a laundry bag, tied the string into a double knot, and placed the bag on the desk by the jacket. Something else she'd have to deal with later.

The water was cold, but she showered anyway, scrubbing and rinsing until she was sore; brushed the taste of blood out of her teeth; clipped her nails down almost to the cuticles.

She was barely dressed, her hair dripping wet, when Hampton let himself in.

At least he knocked first, she told herself.

"You washed the blood off," he said, looking her up and down. "That's good."

"Your jacket's over there," she said, indicating the chair.

He picked it up, still folded, and slid it into his satchel.

"You didn't see anybody?" he said casually, sitting down on the end of the bed. "Tell anyone what you saw?"

"I came straight back here," she said. "I didn't tell anybody anything."

It wasn't a lie, she thought; not really. It had the shape of the truth, if not the substance.

"I'm going to need you to keep on keeping it to yourself," he said. "Can you do that?"

"I guess."

"The boat came in a few minutes ago. One of the island boys is speaking to the captain now. He's taking the body with him when he leaves. I've already talked to the police on the mainland. They'll be waiting at the docks with a forensics team. We'll know more about what happened once they've finished their examinations and whatever else it is that they do."

"How?" she said.

"How what? How do they do it? Couldn't tell you."

"How did you speak to the police? I thought the cage blocked phone signals."

"Until we get the results back," he said, ignoring the question, "we won't have any answers for you, or for anyone. I know it must have been traumatic, seeing him like that. And I promise you, once we have those answers, we'll share them with you. But for now... please, help us keep this under wraps. Panic isn't going to help anyone."

"What makes you think there'd be panic?"

"You think there wouldn't be? A guest - a very well-known, high-profile guest - washes up dead on the beach, injuries all over his body, we have no way of working out who or what killed him... and you think they'd just, what? Keep calm and carry on? *I'm* a little worried, and I have a weapon."

She'd assumed, on some half-conscious level, that he was armed; that he

74

kept a pistol in his satchel, a rifle stowed away in his office. But hearing it confirmed was no consolation at all.

"You don't think they deserve to know what's going on?" she said.

"I think it's my job to work out how to manage the guests on this island," he said. "To decide what they do and don't need to know."

"And if your decisions put people in danger? You saw his body. Somebody beat him to death."

"We can't be sure of that yet."

"His jaw was broken. Half his teeth were missing. It's the one thing I'm absolutely sure of."

He stood up from the bed and walked towards her, backing her up against the wall.

"Let me put it to you another way," he said. "You're not a doctor, I'm not a doctor, and the real doctor on the mainland hasn't gotten so much as a look at him yet... but let's say you're right. The guy was beaten, and left out there to die. Well, then... what kind of evidence am I looking at? What is it I'll need to be telling the police? That a woman who's been with us all of three days, who's still frankly kind of a mystery to all of us but who we know must have done *something*, because she's here... she comes up to one of my boys one morning, covered in blood, and tells him to get help. And then when the cavalry comes, they find her cradling a body on an empty beach - a body that by her own admission literally just gave it up, that second - and nobody else around for miles. How do you think they'd take that?"

The anger was back: sharp and scalding, crackling along her joints, through her fingertips. It tore through her common sense, her self-preservation.

"That's crazy," she said. "All the things you're suggesting, they're crazy."

"They sound pretty plausible to me. Especially when I've got three of my boys there to back up every word I'm saying. And when I can point the police to that canvas bag on the table over there, that I'd bet you even money is full of bloody clothes."

He grabbed the bag before she could stop him, fastening it around his neck and over his chest like a gunslinger's belt.

"You're a piece of shit," she said.

"I'm a pragmatist," he said lightly. "Now: are we both on the same page? Are you going to help me keep this whole thing quiet, until we know what's what?"

"Do I have a choice?"

"There are always choices. But also, consequences."

"Why do you care so much? What does it matter to you if I do or don't tell anyone? They'll all know soon enough anyway. People are going to notice that he's gone."

"That's true. And I'd like to manage how and when that happens."

"So nobody panics?"

"So things stay orderly. Somewhere like this, you need order. Order, and predictability."

He opened the door. There were people in the courtyard now, a half dozen or more. They turned to look at the two of them: Robin speechless and disheveled, Hampton - the satchel and the laundry bag at his hips - a movie cowboy figure in the half-lit doorway.

"We'll talk again soon," he said, and closed the door behind him.

# CHAPTER 8

For the next 3 days, Robin was a ghost: skipping breakfast, taking meals out of the cafeteria and eating them alone in her studio, avoiding all but the most essential human contact. She slept, and read, and wrote: impossible bucket lists, and letters to her brother, and rage-filled diary entries, only semi-coherent, that she crossed out in thick black pen then left to soak under a running faucet until the paper disintegrated.

Every day, Jack called for her. On the first, she pled sickness, an upset stomach, her sallow skin and the red rings around her eyes lending credence to the argument. He'd come back later that afternoon with a blanket and a cup of chicory, so sincere in his concern that she'd cried after he left.

The second day, he woke her up around midday with a plate of dry lunchmeat sandwiches and a plastic beaker of apple juice. He didn't stay long - just passed along hellos from Bill and Carol, repeated a sliver of gossip he'd heard about a woman sent to the island for trapping a cat in a garbage can, and wrapped her up in a hug awkward enough to leave her wondering how long it had been since either of them had held another person.

The third day, he was less eager to leave.

"You sure you don't want to take a walk?" he said, hovering in the doorway, the same way Hampton had a few days earlier. The thought of it tied a knot in her stomach; brought bile to the back of her throat.

"I think I'm just going to stay here," she said. "Curl up with a book, get some rest."

"Might do you good to get outside."

"And take in some of that fresh sea air?"

He shuffled uncomfortably on the spot.

"I'm worried about you," he said. "I know we haven't known each other long, but that look you're wearing - I recognize it. I've worn it myself. I don't know, maybe you *are* sick... but it seems like there's something else going on with you, too. Something that's eating you up. And if there is... I'm not so sure how healthy it is to be shutting yourself away."

"I'm fine," she said, and how many other times had she said that in the last week?

"I'm pretty sure that's a lie," he said.

"Look, Jack... I appreciate what you're trying to do here. I really do. But can you just let me be for a little bit?"

"I'm worried about you," he said again.

"I know. And... that means a lot, it really does. I just need some time."

He held up his hands, conciliatory, and took a deliberate step back into the courtyard.

"I'm gonna go," he said. "But you'll come find me? If you need me?"

"I promise," she said.

By the fourth day, she was beginning to unravel - feeling the magnolia walls of the tiny apartment closing in on her, leaving her headachy and struggling for breath and desperate to get out.

The quad held little appeal, the cafeteria even less so. For all Carol's friendliness, she thought, she and Bill and their over-familiarity were the last things she needed.

The thought of the beach sickened her, took her back to places she didn't want to go - to blood-soaked sand and the weight of a cooling body on her forearms.

Which left the rest of the island.

She set out from the quad in a new direction than the one she'd gotten used to, turning right instead of left where the apartment block ended and letting the rough path there guide her along another, unfamiliar stretch of stone and parched grassland.

There were rocks here too, tall ones, some of them as high as her and higher, poking out of the dry earth like stalagmites but *arranged*, somehow - more akin to standing stones than natural formations. Time and erosion had left them with peculiar markings, ridges and indentations that, with a low light and an active imagination, might easily look like eyes and mouths, noses and cheekbones.

She sped up, passing them quickly, and pressed on, through more acres of open grass and desiccated soil, walking fast and long enough to tug at the muscles in her calves and ankles. Eventually she came to another set of rocks, these ones very deliberately assembled into a crumbling dry stack wall, running at least a quarter mile into the distance and ending at what looked, if she focused, like a dense cluster of low-rise buildings.

"I wouldn't go any further, if I were you," said a familiar voice behind her.

"Were you following me?" she said, turning around.

"Only for the last few minutes," said Julia.

She looked neater than she had previously, better put-together: hair loose but styled, green silk shirt tucked into a tailored blazer. Robin had no trouble, suddenly, picturing her in a corporate environment.

"Why?" said Robin.

"Why was I following you?"

"Why shouldn't I go any further?"

Julia came closer.

"You see those cottages over there?" she said.

"If that's what they are, sure."

"That's the Residents village. Where the islanders live. Where their children live. I would strongly advise against dropping in for a visit."

"Because they hate us."

"They're wary. It's understandable."

"They don't like strangers?"

"They don't like that their ancestral home has been turned into a set of stocks for humiliating foolish Americans."

"It's not just Americans. You English guys are here too."

"And I would think they regard us with equal contempt."

The two of them stood in silence for a moment, looking out at the village.

"Why were you following me?" said Robin.

"Civic responsibility," said Julia wryly. "I was on my way home, but when I saw where you were heading, I thought I ought to intervene."

"Thank you, then. I'm not really in the mood to be run out of town with pitchforks and burning torches."

"I also wanted to see how you were. After the last time we saw each other."

"I'm fine."

"Of course you are," she said sardonically. "I mean, you look just wonderful."

"I'm tired," said Robin, conscious of her red eyes, the new lines etched around her mouth. "That's all."

"I'm not trying to harass you. You don't have to tell me what happened to you the other day, or what any of it has to do with Hampton. I know what he's like. But whatever it is... he's put the thumbscrews on you somehow, hasn't he?"

"I can't talk about it."

"Then don't. And I won't ask again. But how about I walk with you back to your flat? Get you out of range of those pitchforks?"

"I don't think I want to go back inside again yet."

"Why not come back to my place, then? I have coffee."

"Seriously?"

"Hand on heart."

"Isn't it, like, contraband here?"

"Just impossibly hard to get hold of."

"But you have some?"

"A little, squirrelled away. I'm very unlikeable, thankfully, so I rarely have to share it with anyone."

"Have you heard any more from your son?" asked Robin, weaving in between the standing stones. The almost-faces were less sinister with another person nearby, though no less strange.

"Not this week. The letters usually come once a fortnight, but it really depends on how well the sorting office is handling the island post on the mainland. The whole setup here is very new, so they're still working out the kinks. As things stand, a geriatric homing pigeon would be more efficient."

"If only it could squeeze through wire mesh. Does he know you're here, your son?"

"God, no. He thinks I'm working away, somewhere out of the country. How do you explain *this* to a six year old?"

"I don't even know how to explain it to myself, half the time."

"He'll find out eventually. I've resigned myself to that. One of the kids at school will say something, or one of the parents, or he'll see something he shouldn't see on the news. And there'll be fallout. But we'll have to deal with it when it happens. Hopefully by then he'll be old enough to have some appreciation of context."

"I've heard that word a few times this last week."

"I'm sure you have. It's one of the few things that godforsaken algorithm can't measure. Although I can't say that our respective judiciaries have much appreciation for it either."

"I'd say that's a reasonable assessment."

"It's such a strange thing, isn't it? When you take a step back."

"What?"

"Our situation. That a few lines of code and some bits of machinery are enough to have us all hung, drawn and quartered."

"I don't know," said Robin, thinking of Vanderhalden, of what Carol and Bill had told her. "I think maybe people played their part, too. I'd be reluctant to put all the blame on the technology."

"That's true, of course. And I daresay someone, somewhere is benefitting from these absurd outrage laws. It's not as if there are victims to be placated or social reparations to be made. In no sense is *justice* being served by our being here."

Vanderhalden, thought Robin. Vanderhalden are benefitting.

# CHAPTER 9

Two weeks ago," she said, "I'd have called you paranoid."

"I doubt you would have," said Julia. "To my face, anyway. You seem far too polite. Though I'm sure you'd have thought it, furiously."

"I don't feel very polite lately. Just beat down and angry."

"Then it's clearly something deep-seated. For example: we've been speaking for nearly an hour, and not once have you asked me what I did to land myself here. You aren't even tiptoeing around it. Which suggests that either you know already, and are too polite to ask, or you genuinely believe - very commendably - that it's none of your business. In either case, your manners are impeccable."

"Or I'm really not interested in knowing. Did you think about that?"

"Don't be ridiculous. Prurient curiosity is one of the few real pleasures we have left on this island. Of course you're interested."

Embarrassed, and feeling - completely illogically - *caught out*, somehow, Robin quickened her pace, looking everywhere but at Julia.

"If I were to guess," said Julia, lengthening her stride to keep up, "I'd say that you *do* know."

"Are you always this confrontational?" said Robin.

"I think I am, actually. But even if I weren't... there's something about being here that begets directness. It's a heterotopic sort of space, isn't it? The normal behavioural rules don't really apply."

"I know why you're here, okay? But I don't want to talk about it, because it really *isn't* any of my business."

"Then you're in a very small minority. Everyone seems to have something to say about it, back in the real world."

"I'm not everyone."

They didn't speak the rest of the way back to the quad - Robin keeping up a brisk pace, and Julia walking faster still to outdo her, the one-upmanship leaving both of them pink-cheeked and short of breath.

Inside, Julia's studio was every bit as spartan as Robin's, more a cell than an apartment. Except for the books. There were dozens of them: fiction and theory, hardback and soft cover, lined up like dominos along the walls, dollar-store sci-fi jostling for space with Marvin Minsky and *The Feynman Lectures*.

"How did you get these?" said Robin, incredulous. "I was told I could bring 10 books, maximum."

"My ex-wife sends them," said Julia. "Two or three with every letter."

"Can we do that? Have them sent in?"

"If you're willing to pay. Though Hampton puts his own tax on everything that comes in. It's more than the price of the book, sometimes. And while I'm sure she still hates me in many ways, Grace at least understands that I need them, that I'd go mad without them."

Robin scanned them all, title after title.

"Can I borrow one?" she asked, unexpectedly greedy, covetous.

"Be my guest," said Julia.

There was a desk in the corner of the room, identical to Robin's but for the drawers in the bottom. She opened one of them; retrieved two cups, a very small portable kettle and a smaller jar of instant coffee crystals, already one-third empty.

"There's no milk or sugar," she said apologetically.

"Black's fine," said Robin, cautiously extracting a collection of short stories from line-up.

She watched as Julia filled up the kettle at the sink in the bathroom.

"Does that work here?" she asked, pointing to the kettle. "I thought we were off the grid."

"It has a battery," said Julia. "It won't last forever, but then, I'd prefer to keep thinking it won't need to."

The kettle boiled, pouring odorless clouds of vapor out into the room. The coffee itself was cheap, somehow bland as well as astringent, but it was warm and familiar, which was enough.

"It's disgusting, I know," said Julia, sipping at hers with distaste.

"It's the best cup of coffee I've had all week," said Robin, smiling.

Julia smiled back, and clinked her cup against Robin's.

"So," she said. "You don't want to talk about me. Do you want to talk about you?"

"What about me?" said Robin, wary again. "What are you asking?"

"I suppose in the first instance, I'm asking what brought you here. What egregious sin it was that sent you catapulting into purgatory."

"And if I don't want to tell you?"

"Then I suppose I'll have to sate my curiosity elsewhere, won't I?"

"I hear there's a lady around here somewhere who stuck a cat in a garbage can, if it's gossip you're after."

"Even my curiosity has limits. But thank you."

Robin drained her cup.

"Someone took a picture of me," she said eventually.

"Doing what, exactly?"

"It's not what you think. I was at a march. A demonstration."

"A protest."

"Yeah."

"Against what?"

"The Governor, mainly. And the police. They've been getting heavy-handed with protestors. We've had a couple people die at rallies. Kids - college students. And there've been... disappearances, I guess you'd call them. I don't know much of this has been talked about in England, or even outside of California, but we've had people going missing for a while: a couple hundred of them, at least. Students, and activists, and union organizers - people like that, people speaking out against the Governor, against the President. Nobody knows where they've gone - I mean, they could be someplace like here, for all I know. But the point is, they've gone. And nobody official is looking for them."

"And you knew them, these people?"

"Most of them? No. Just my brother."

Just Davey, she thought. And he's probably dead. Probably they all are. And if they aren't... well, none of them have been let out to tell the tale, have they?

Julia leaned in towards her; touched her, very lightly, on the shoulder. She didn't say anything, and Robin was grateful for it.

"So I went to this march to the Governor's Mansion, up in Sacramento. The first one I've ever been to, actually. There's this group that organizes the protests - the brothers and sisters and moms and dads and grandmas of the people who've disappeared. They model themselves on the Mothers of the Plaza de Mayo in Argentina – the old ladies with the white headscarves, you know? They got in touch with me after David, my brother... after he went missing. Chartered a bus to take us all out there."

They'd been so nice, she remembered – so *normal*. Sweet middle-aged women in pantsuits, women who'd reminded her of her mom; grandmothers in pearls and summer dresses and Sunday wigs; college kids with innocuous banners. Half of them looking like they could have been on their way to church.

"What's funny," she said, "is the march mostly wasn't that eventful. The first few hours, it was just us and a few hundred others, walking through the streets with signs and placards. Then when we got near the Mansion... something changed. There were more people, suddenly, and they had weapons, sticks and batons. It looked like one man was carrying a machete, although I remember thinking it couldn't have been, not with that many people around. Then the police showed up, and the National Guard, and they really *were* armed. They started firing into the crowd. Rubber bullets, I think, but still - people were hurt, falling down, getting trampled."

She hadn't known what to do, where to go. There'd been bodies pressing in on her on all sides: some deliberately, some – like the very old lady in the turban who'd looked up at her, called out for help as she was mown down – completely involuntarily. She hadn't known, then, that the bullets were rubber: had only seen the Guardsmen firing, the people falling.

"Some of us ran," she said, "but some of the others - I guess they stayed and fought. I read afterwards that five protestors were reported missing, and three others died in the crush. But that wasn't all of it. Three Guardsmen died too; two of them beaten, one of them shot. So when that makes the news, it's not the protestors they're talking about, it's the Guardsmen - and the monsters who killed them, these out-of-control dissidents who can't be trusted to protest peacefully.

They never caught the guys with the weapons, as far as I know - or if they did, it didn't get reported. But someone must have been taking pictures, because when the story broke, there was one photograph that made it into every article, and it was my face in close-up, under some kind of anti-government banner, with a guy holding a two-by-four with a nail in it in the background. And I must have been running when it was taken - but it had been cut to look like I was running *toward* the Guard, not away from them. Like I was trying to attack them.

And it got everywhere, that photo - you couldn't get away from it. I'm kind of a Luddite, and I don't do very much online, so it took the police nearly a week to work out who I was. But once they had - well, by then, a lot of people had a lot of opinions about what ought to happen to me. And unfortunately they'd expressed those opinions in the public sphere."

Traitor, they'd called her; cop-killer. Groups of them had shown up at her trial, flag-waving men and women, shouting and picketing the courtroom like pro-lifers outside an abortion clinic. One of them, thick-necked man with a rage-reddened face and a veteran's pin, had spat at her on her way up the steps – two thick globules of saliva that had missed her by inches, coming to rest instead on the lapel of her lawyer's jacket.

Cunt, he'd shouted at her back as she'd walked through the doors. I hope they fucking *bury* you.

"So here I am," she said.

She swallowed, her throat dry from talking for so long uninterrupted.

"I'm so very sorry," said Julia, her hand still on Robin's shoulder.

"Me too," said Robin, letting it rest there.

She felt lighter afterwards, unexpectedly flooded with relief - at having shared a quasi-secret, and at managing to forget, temporarily, about Hampton and the body.

Leaving Julia's studio, a second cup of the terrible coffee in her belly and the paperback tucked under her arm, she thought she might even be happy - happier, certainly, than she'd been earlier that morning.

Jack was waiting for her outside her apartment. He looked anxious; edgy and jittery.

"Something's happened," he said, a twinge of panic taking his voice up an octave. "I don't know what, but Hampton's called an emergency meeting for everyone in the cafeteria, and Bill said..."

"What?" said Robin. "What did Bill say?"

"That this type of thing... it's not usual. That Hampton wouldn't do it unless something really serious was going on. Or something really bad had happened."

Around them, she noticed, the courtyard was beginning to swell with people - all of them prisoners, all of them heading towards the dining hall.

"When?" she said, trying to keep the fear out of her own voice. "When is the meeting?"

"Now," he said urgently. "That's why I came to get you. It's starting right now."

# CHAPTER 10

The cafeteria had been reorganized: the dining tables pushed to the sides of the room, the long wooden benches arranged in rows facing a single, shorter bench on which Hampton stood, surveying his audience, looking every inch a pastor preparing for a tent revival. Two of the islanders, middle-aged woman in heavy winter coats, flanked him on each side.

For the first time, she realized, she was seeing all the prisoners together in one place, dozens of them, all turned to Hampton and his dais. This time she was sure she recognized a couple: a boyband singer caught in a racist rant at a birthday party; a young British actor who'd left an underage fan to overdose in the back of a taxi cab; a property CEO notorious for his wandering hands. People named and shamed in gossip columns, across the celebrity news sites she'd taken to reading in lieu of proper news.

Bill and Carol, she saw, had positioned themselves at the front, close to Hampton and the islanders. Julia was nowhere at all that, she could see.

She moved to the very back of the room, Jack following behind her, and took a seat in the middle of the last but one row - a dozen or more heads obscuring her view of Hampton and, she hoped, his view of her.

"I think he's getting ready to start," said Jack, sitting down next to her.

"Looks that way," she said, eyes straight ahead.

She felt the bench shift under extra weight and, turning, saw that someone else had joined the two of them on the bench to her right: the girl she remembered speaking to in the queue for breakfast days before, her circuit board tattoo half-covered now by the rolled-up sleeve of a lumberjack shirt. Today there was a silver spike though her lip, and a second tattoo - a string of source code Robin couldn't decipher - looped around her wrist.

"You mind if I sit here?" she asked, seeing Robin stare.

"Not at all," said Robin quietly.

"Hello, everyone," said Hampton, projecting across the room. "There's no easy way to say this, so I'm just going to say it... Earlier today, we lost one of our guests, someone all of you know."

"Bill was right," whispered Jack. "It's bad."

Earlier today? thought Robin.

The double doors to the cafeteria swung inwards, and Julia stepped inside, her boot heels loud as gunshots in the silence. She didn't sit down.

Hampton cleared his throat.

"At around 7am this morning, one of our Residents, Mary Hoy, was riding her horse along the beach just up from the landing, and she found something - a body on the sand. A man. It was Chuck Valentine."

Low murmurs of surprise rippled across the room.

"Evidently he'd been out for a run sometime last night, because he had on his running shorts and sneakers. We think he must have lost his balance in the dark, tripped and hit his head on one of the rocks in the sand."

"That's not right," said Robin, half to herself. "That's not what happened."

Beside her, the girl shifted in her seat, pivoting in towards Robin.

"What did you say?" said Jack. "I can't hear you."

"Mary did everything that she could," said Hampton from the dais, "but by the time she found him, Chuck was already gone."

92

"This is bullshit," said Robin, the words lost in the louder expressions of shock ricocheting through the benches.

"Stop talking," said the girl next to her, directly into her ear. "Like, right now."

"What?" said Robin.

"We've alerted police on the mainland," said Hampton, "and they'll be sending a small team of their officers across later today to investigate the scene and collect the body. We've been told that the east side of the beach will be sealed off for the course of their investigation, so we'd ask you all not to venture out too far from your living quarters during this time."

"What? No!" said Robin.

Jack, interpreting the outburst as grief, took her hand in his and held it, sympathetically.

"I'm not kidding," said the girl in her ear. "You need to be quiet."

"We hope to have more information to share with you over the coming days," said Hampton. Then, leaning in towards the audience, added: "I know this will have been a shock to a lot of you. We all knew Chuck, we all liked him. I really am sorry."

He stepped down from the dais and walked quickly out through the double doors, not looking back. The island women stayed behind, staring out into the crowd, expressionless.

"I can't believe it," said Jack.

"I know," said Robin, distracted. Beside her, the girl cracked her knuckles, giving every impression of disinterest in the two of them and whatever they might be saying.

With Hampton gone, the prisoners began to leave their seats - some making a move toward the exit, others locked in animated conversation. Julia stood alone by the furthest wall, apparently deep in thought.

"I should go speak to Bill and Carol," said Jack. "They knew the guy."

"Of course," said Robin.

"You'll wait here? I'll be 5 minutes, tops."

"Sure," she said.

He released her hand and slid free of the bench, walking over to the front of the room where Bill and Carol were talking between themselves - her head bowed, his arm around her.

The girl leaned back in toward Robin.

"Come with me," she said. "Now."

"What?" said Robin, alarmed.

"Sorry. That was dramatic. You should still come with me, though."

"What? Why?"

"Because."

"That's not a reason."

"Okay. How about: because I know some stuff, and judging from the way you reacted to him talking just now, you're gonna want to know it too. About Hampton."

"What about Hampton? Who are you?"

"Just somebody who knows stuff."

"That really doesn't tell me anything."

"I'm gonna sound dramatic again, but I think maybe it's unavoidable right now, so... Come with me, and I'll tell you everything."

"You're a total stranger. And my friend is over there."

"Then tell him you'll see him later."

"I'm not going to do that."

"What if I gave you my apartment number, and you came by in, like, 15 minutes, after you got rid of him?"

"Why? Why would that be something I would do?"

"Look... I'm sorry, what's your name?"

"Robin. And you are?"

"Sat."

"Just Sat?"

"Just Sat. Sat who knows some stuff, and who wants to tell you the stuff that she knows. So come with me, or tell me you'll come see me, and we'll talk about it."

"And you won't give me any more detail than that? Just 'I know stuff'?"

"It's not something we should talk about out here. Just like you shouldn't go around telling anyone that what Hampton just said up there was, like, a pile of horseshit. You've gotta be smart."

"Alright. Fine. I'll do it, I'll come to your apartment."

"See? That's smart. Apartment 35."

"Where is that?"

"You'll know it when you see it. I'll be waiting."

She stood up and wandered away, leaving Robin alone on the bench.

\*\*\*

By the time Jack came back to get her, the room was clearing, prisoners spilling out of the cafeteria and into the courtyard.

"Carol's upset," he said. "I don't think they were close, but it's hit her hard. I guess it's not something you expect to happen in a place like this."

"I guess not," said Robin.

"I thought the one benefit of being literally trapped in a cage was that nothing bad could happen to you once you were inside it. The worst thing that could happen had already happened. Because, you know... you're in a cage."

"What are they doing now, Bill and Carol?"

"Going back to Bill's place, I think. There's not a lot of other places to go, if the beach is closed off."

"Are you going with them?"

"I think so. There's not a lot else for me to be doing, either. And I kind of want a drink right now, so it's probably good for me to be around other people, at least for a little while."

"Don't let them make you any more of that tea."

"You're not coming with me?"

"I might want to be alone, I think. If that's okay."

"I'm still worried about you, you know."

"I know. Maybe we can take a walk tomorrow? Somewhere other than the beach?"

He pulled her into another hug, and she let herself relax into it; it felt more natural the second time, less stiff and alien.

"I'd really like that," he said.

She looked up, her arms still around his waist, and scanned the room. Julia, she noticed, had gone already. It took her a moment to recognize what she was feeling as disappointment.

"You looking for someone?" said Jack.

"No," she said. "Nobody."

Apartment 35 was set back from the other blocks, a standalone building the size and shape of a single storage unit that made Robin wonder if it was space the designers had run out of when they were putting together the living quarters, or just imagination.

She walked past the door twice before approaching it, still only partway sure she should be approaching it at all. It opened before she could knock.

"I heard you outside," said Sat, widening the crack just enough for Robin to enter. "You have really loud footsteps, for a little person."

"I'm 5'3," said Robin, already defensive.

"That's little," said Sat, ushering her inside.

The studio was less sparse than Robin's, than Julia's or Bill's. There were Japanese landscape prints on the walls; a photo of a fiftysomething Indian couple at a funfair, a man and woman, clutching cotton candy to their chests from a picture frame on the desk; rugs on the uncarpeted floor, threadbare Afghans that reminded Robin of her first apartment.

Sat slid down, cross-legged, onto one of them, and invited Robin to do the same.

"Why am I here?" said Robin, still standing.

"Wow. No pleasantries at all, huh?"

"My patience for other people's nonsense is wearing pretty thin. So tell me why I'm here, or I'm leaving."

"Hampton's a liar," said Sat, her tone harder, the valley girl drawl slipping a little. "And Chuck Valentine's death wasn't an accident. He didn't fall, and he didn't hit his head. Everything that Hampton said back there was garbage. Made up."

"How do you know that?" said Robin.

"Because Chuck wasn't the first. It's happened before."

Robin flashed back to that morning on the beach: Chuck's face, the state of his body, the air whistling through his broken teeth as he begged her for help. She felt sick again; dizzy.

"You should really sit down," said Sat.

This time she did, leaning back against the wall for support, then letting herself slide down onto the floor.

"There've been others?" she said. "Other people who died?"

"Three of them, that I know of anyway."

"You saw them? The ones who died?"

"Saw them? What do you mean, *saw* them?"

"Found them. Their bodies. The way I found Chuck."

"No! God, no. Wait... you found the body? Chuck Valentine's body?"

"Early this week. On the beach. Not this morning, like Hampton said. And not... it wasn't a fall. The way his body looked - somebody *did* that to him."

"Woah. Okay. Well, listen - the people I'm talking about... I wasn't even here when the first one went missing. I only found out about her later. The second one - I barely knew she'd gone, until it was already, like, out there in

97

the public domain. The third one, though... I knew him. He was my friend. So I noticed when he, you know, disappeared."

Robin's stomach clenched involuntarily at the word.

"And these three people who went missing," she said. "*When* they went missing... Hampton did what he did just now? He covered it up?"

"Not the whole, like, press conference thing he did today. But did he lie about what happened to them? Totally."

"Tell me," said Robin slowly, nausea spreading up through her gut and into her chest. "All of it. From the start."

# CHAPTER 11

Here's the thing, said Sat. I've been on Salt Rock, like, 6 months now, since just before Christmas last year. So by any regular standard I'm - what do they call it in prison movies? New fish? Fresh fish?

But here... here I'm practically a veteran. This place - this *iteration* of this place - was barely 3 months old when I arrived. Even Hampton was shiny and new.

My first month, I think I spoke to maybe one person, other than Hampton, and that was the friend I just told you about. Tony. It's a crazy coincidence, if you think about it, but I actually knew him a little bit before I came here. He lived in my building, and I used to see him with his dog when I went to pick up the mail. A really sweet guy. Too sweet to ever deserve to be somewhere like this.

We start hanging out, eating dinner together and going for walks on the beach - which sounds romantic, but really, what else are you supposed to do here? And one day he tells me about this friend *he* made, the first month *he* was here. Who was that first woman I mentioned. Let's call her Sylvia, because honestly, I never actually knew her name.

She was literally the first person on the island, other than Hampton and the Residents and whichever construction company Vanderhalden brought over to build these beautiful apartments. She came over on the boat with the first load of prisoners - I'm sorry, *guests*.

I felt kind of sorry for her, from what he told me. She was English, from way out in the countryside somewhere. Wiltshire, maybe? Somewhere with a lot of green space. She had a little farm with a feed store attached to it that her nephew helped her run - this, like, high-school kid who, I've got to say, does not sound like the sort of person you want running your store. But still.

So, I guess she's out one day on her farm, chopping wheat or whatever, and she finds something, some sort of animal habitat in the ground that shouldn't be there. For badgers, I think. And these animals, they carry a bunch of diseases that you really *don't* want on your farm. So she decides to get rid of them, and she brings this kid, her nephew, in to help her.

He shows up with his shotguns - did you know they're allowed to have them in England? - and they blast the shit out of these badgers. They drag their dead badger bodies out of the ground to stop them rotting in there - and then the kid, who again I stress is *not* the smartest, takes a picture of the two of them, right next to this pile of animal carcasses.

Only he edits it somehow, crops himself out of the frame. So when he sends it to his friends, it's just his aunt in there, looking like she's just committed some sort of badger genocide. And you know the rest - of course you do, you're *here*. His friends send it to *their* friends, who send it to *their* friends... and then all of sudden, PETA's on the case and this farmer lady, who doesn't even own a computer, is seeing herself on the BBC News as the new face of animal cruelty.

Anyway. She's on the island, doing her thing, sharing stories about her dog with my friend over cups of hot water, when all of a sudden... she's gone. Nobody knows where. My friend Tony is frantic, just totally torn up with worry, so he breaks into her apartment in case something's happened to her and she's just lying there, sick or worse. And she's not there - but all of her stuff is. Even this photograph of her dog as a puppy, which she takes with her, like, everywhere.

Two days go by like this, with Tony giving himself a stomach ulcer. He asks everyone he sees where Sylvia went, but nobody knows. He goes looking for Hampton, to ask *him* where she went – but Hampton is nowhere. And when he tries to ask the island dudes, they don't even answer him. Just look at him like he's dirt on their shoes.

Then, one morning, Hampton shows up, at Tony's door. He says sorry for not letting him know sooner, but he has good news: the farm lady, his friend, she qualified for an early release, so she's been sent back to the mainland. He hasn't announced to the others yet, because he doesn't want to make anyone jealous or upset - but he knows the two of them were close, so thought my friend deserved an explanation.

And my friend Tony doesn't say anything - because he's I think a little afraid of Hampton, even when he's being nice - but he's thinking, there's no way she'd leave without that picture. Something's wrong here.

He keeps his suspicions to himself at first. I think actually the only reason he told me was because I was around right after the second woman disappeared, and he needed somebody to listen and tell him he wasn't crazy.

Now this second woman – let's call *her* Letitia – I saw her around, but I never, you know, spoke to her. So I don't actually know what she was like at all. I don't even know why she was here. To be totally honest, the first time I ever really thought about her was when Tony told me she was dead.

This time he's *really* fucked up about it - like, crying. And paranoid. Saying she was murdered, and that Hampton was going to try to pin it on him if he'd didn't stay quiet.

Oh my God, your face right now! That's what happened to you, isn't it?

Okay, alright. I'm talking.

He wouldn't tell me a lot, because he was so, like, scared, but what I got from him was that he'd been on the beach doing yoga - he was a real yoga guy - and he'd seen something at the edge of the sand, with the water sort of washing over it. And the water looked kind of strange - like, darker than it should be. So he goes over to check it out.

And it's this woman, Letitia, and she's dead - *really* dead, cold and turning sort of blue. And her body - it's messed up. I mean *seriously* messed up - like, half her head is gone, and there are these really deep scratches all over her arms and stomach. And she's naked.

I guess he freaks out and goes to get Hampton or something. I don't know what happened after that, because he wouldn't tell me the rest, and then he just kind of runs off, back to his room. But I'm getting kind of scared, because obviously there's some kind of psycho murderer on the island and we're all stuck here with him, and I'm like, is this going to turn into an Agatha Christie novel? Are we all going to get, like, plucked off one by one?

What? I'm not allowed to read?

I'm thinking, if there *is* some kind of serial killer on the loose, probably the best thing I can do is stay in my apartment, right? Just stay right here. So I don't hear until later - like, over a week later - that Hampton's told the others that this second lady, *she* got an early release, just like the first lady, Sylvia. Nobody questioned what he was saying, but I don't know - maybe it was more believable then. I mean, the whole place was maybe 5 months old - none of us knew *what* was supposed to happen.

And now, my friend Tony is missing too.

This time Hampton deals with it straight away: gets everyone together, the whole dozen or so of us, and says that there's been a medical emergency, and that he had to send Tony back to the mainland on the morning boat so they could get him to a hospital. He doesn't know exactly what's wrong, he says, but it doesn't look like Tony will be coming back to the island any time soon - or ever, even. He actually takes me aside afterwards: says he knows we were close, and that I'm probably really worried, but that I shouldn't be, because my friend is going to be fine. Then he puts his arm over my shoulder, and it's sort of paternal and sort of skeevy uncle, and tells me that if I ever need anything, or I ever get lonely, I should come find him.

So now I'm creeped out as well as, like, scared to death. Because not only are people disappearing *in general* - the people who *notice* that people are disappearing are also themselves disappearing.

I figure there are 2 things I need to do: A. Not tell anyone anything, and B. find out for myself what's going on.

The first thing is actually easy enough. You might not get this from me, because I've been basically talking at you for the last hour, but I'm not really a sharer, so it's really not that difficult for me to just stay away from everybody. Plus, a lot of the people here are sort of terrible.

The second thing is harder, and takes a little more... specialist equipment. But I do it. Don't ask me how, because I'm not going to tell you yet, if I decide I want to tell you at all, but I find a way to get in touch with a guy I know back in San Jose, a guy I used to work with.

Me? Software engineering.

Oh, please... I *look* it? How can you *look* like a software engineer? I could have been, like, a florist for all you knew.

Okay, okay. Jesus. I can't tell *my* story at my own pace?

Okay.

Now *this* guy, this guy from work - I really trust him. We've been through a lot together. He had my back all the way through, you know... all through the crap that got me put away out here. He's a good guy.

Again, do *not* ask me how, but I tell him what's going on - or at least, like, the outline of it. I don't name any names or give away the kind of detail that might land me in trouble if it got out. But I give him the highlights. And I ask him to check, just to make totally sure that I'm not *actually* going crazy, whether my friend Tony – Tony the Dog Dude - was ever checked in to any of the hospitals on the mainland.

He goes away and I guess spends an afternoon on the phone rolling out some lame cover story to, like, every hospital in Scotland, then he comes back and tells me - you guessed it. Nobody - no American - matching Tony's description has showed up anywhere in any of the hospitals he's called.

He's a careful guy, and he likes to think things through logically and cover all the bases, so he tells me not to assume the worst, necessarily. Because Tony could be somewhere else than a regular hospital. Maybe he's in a different kind of treatment center – a military hospital, or a prison clinic. Maybe they even sent him back to the US for treatment.

But I think back to what he told me, about that body on the beach and the way it looked, and I remember all the shit that Hampton's covered up already, and I think: no. Tony, he's gone.

He doesn't say it out loud, but I know my friend back home is scared for me. *I'm* scared for me. But there's not, you know, a lot he can do from over there - not without letting on that I've talked to him, and maybe landing me in something worse than I'm in already.

So we figure: all I can is wait it out. Keep my head down, not draw any attention - especially not, you know, from Hampton or his band of weird-ass horse people. And hope that nothing, like, really bad happens until I've finished up my time and can get out of here.

Only... I guess now it has, hasn't it?

"How did you do it?" said Robin. "How did you make contact?"

Sat sighed.

"I *literally* just told you not to ask me that," she said.

"I need to know. If there's a way... you have to tell me.'

"You know, I really don't."

"Please. You can trust me."

"Even though you're, and I'm quoting you directly here, a total stranger?"

"You know what I've seen. And I know what you know. What's the harm in telling me more? I'm sure as hell not going to say anything."

"Mutually assured destruction," said Sat. "Right."

She uncrossed her legs and stood up, stretching her arms above her head, then moved quickly across the room, towards the bed.

With one hand she lifted a corner of the mattress and, legs bending under the weight, slipped her other hand underneath. A few seconds later, she pulled out an old-fashioned cellphone: a lightweight thing, handheld, barely three inches long.

She threw it across to Robin who, failing to catch it, let it land in her lap.

"You have a cellphone," she said, hypnotized by the device.

"Don't get too excited," said Sat. "It stopped working a couple weeks ago."

Robin was suddenly, irrationally crushed.

"Can it be fixed?" she said.

"I doubt it. There's nothing wrong with it, exactly. The battery just kind of... gave up. I think it must be the, like, proximity to the materials in the cage."

"Wait," said Robin. "How did you get to use it in the first place, if the cage blocks signals in and out? I can't even get an alarm clock to work here."

"Ah," said Sat, sitting back down. "See, that's the part where I'm old-school. Watch."

She pulled back the rug, exposing the bare floorboard underneath.

"Can you pass me that picture?" she said, gesturing to the framed photo of the older couple on the desk. "And that pen just next to it?"

Robin picked it up and handed it across wordlessly.

"Thanks," said Sat.

She uncapped the top of the pen, revealing the head of a makeshift screwdriver that she pressed, gently, against the back of the picture frame. She turned the handle, twice, and a screw loosened, falling into the outstretched palm of her hand.

"Are they your parents?" asked Robin, indicating the photo.

"These people?" said Sat, concentrating. "No. They came with the frame."

She separated the back of the frame from the front and shook it, dislodging a slim, flat strip of metal. She pulled the ends, and the metal extended.

"You brought a slim jim," said Robin.

"I thought it might, you know, come in handy," said Sat. "Guess I was right."

Squatting closer to the floor, she lowered the metal strip down into one of the cracks beside the floorboard and pressed, releasing the board upward. She reached down and grabbed something - something Robin couldn't quite see.

"Got 'em," she said.

She stood up, a very long, very sharp pair of hedge shears dangling from one hand.

Robin took a step back in response, alarmed.

"Relax," said Sat. "They're purely functional. I'm not gonna, like, Freddy Krueger you with them."

"There's no way you brought them in with you," said Robin.

"Well... no. It's possible I might have, you know... found them."

"You found them?"

"Found, stole... it's such a thin line, isn't it?"

"Where were they? Who do they belong to?"

"Okay. So, I admit this *sounds* bad... They're Hampton's."

"Oh my God."

"It's fine! He's got, like, 5 pairs."

"Why? Where?"

"He keeps them in his office. They're his backup."

"For what?"

"There's a sort of door in the cage, by the landing. You must have seen it when you arrived. It's where the boat gets in. It's meant to open and close once a day, at these set times, so the boat can pass through. But occasionally it, you know, *sticks*. So then he has to go out there with these," she shook the shears for effect, "and, like, *slice* into the wire before it'll lift. Sort of reminding it that it needs to open."

"Why?" said Robin. "Why do you have them?"

"Isn't it obvious?"

"Spell it out for me."

"They're cutters. What do you think I did? I used them to cut a hole in the wire."

It was evening when she eventually left the apartment, a weak red sunset seeping in from above her through the gaps in the mesh.

Directly outside in the courtyard, looking out to the beach from one of the stone benches, was Julia.

"Now I know you're following me," said Robin.

Julia spun around on the seat. Her makeup, immaculate that morning, was smudged and uneven; there was sand on her boots again, salting the leather up to the ankle, and her forehead shone with sweat.

"Purely coincidental this time, I'm afraid," she said. She sounded tired, Robin thought; drained.

"Have you been out again?" said Robin, gesturing down at the sand.

"What? Oh. No. I think they may just need a clean. Possibly more urgently than I thought."

"Right," said Robin skeptically.

Julia stood up to face her.

"Terrible news earlier," she said.

She looked directly at Robin; measuring her, watching for a reaction.

"Sure was," said Robin, trying for impassive.

"It was you who found him, wasn't it? Four days ago, not this morning?"

*You shouldn't go around telling anyone*, thought Robin, Sat's voice in her head. *You've gotta be smart.*

*People are disappearing.*

"I found him," she said, not meaning to say anything at all. Then she was crying - the fear and shock and outright horror of the last week coalescing into thick shaking bawls that stole her breath and caught in her throat.

And Julia's arms were around her, pulling her closer, steadying her as she cried.

They stayed like that for a while: Robin's face buried in Julia's neck, her slumping body half-held up by Julia's. When the crying stopped, finally, it was later and darker, the low, striated sun casting strange shadows across the courtyard.

"Do you feel better?" said Julia, rubbing light circles across the small of her back.

Robin nodded.

"Good," said Julia. She leaned in closer, bringing her head to rest on Robin's shoulder, her mouth to Robin's ear.

"Listen to me," she said, in a whisper so low Robin strained to hear it. "You cannot mention again what you saw that day. Not to anyone else on this island. Do you understand me? It's not safe."

Robin jerked backwards. Julia dropped her hands, letting her go.

"Is this some sort of game?" said Robin. "Push the new girl? See how long you can make her cry on your shoulder before you go back to scaring the shit out of her?"

"It's not a game," said Julia, keeping her voice low, neutral. "I meant what I said, that first day we met. I want you to talk to me. I'm glad you feel you *can* talk to me. God knows, you've had enough on your mind. But if you've seen what I think you've seen, then you've tangled yourself up in something I can't begin to explain. And it will put you in tremendous danger if you aren't very, very careful."

Robin watched, listened; tried to see something other than concern in her expression, hear something other than concern in her voice.

"I have to go," she said.

And she ran, across the courtyard and back to her apartment.

# CHAPTER 12

She's running on the beach.

The sand is sharp, and her bare feet are bleeding, but it's only the pain that lets her know it, because the sand is red and wet, saturated with blood as far out into the distance as she can see.

There's something behind her, catching up to her on the bloody sand. She can't see it - can't bear the thought of turning around to look - but she knows it's there. It sounds like hoofbeats; smells like spoiled meat and dry earth.

The mesh is still there, above her, but there's something wrong with it. It's aged somehow, wilted and tarnished, the copper turned to rust.

The water is wrong, too: still and shallow inside the cage, but high and wild outside, waves pounding down hard enough to strain the wire. In their way, the waves - and the sound they make as they hit the metal - leave her as frightened as the hoofbeats.

She blinks away the salt and the water dripping down from her hairline, and when she opens her eyes, sees the cave in front of her, so close that she wonders how she didn't see it before.

She stops running, and the hoofbeats slow too, following the pace she sets. The mouth of the cave is dark, but she can see into it, just. There's someone inside - a shape, huddled into itself against the back wall. It shifts as she enters the cave; solidifies into something almost human, a woman's figure, tall and bandaged in shadow.

As she steps further inside and her vision adjusts to the darkness, she realizes that she recognizes the shape. It's Julia, or at least a version of Julia, but older, much older, her posture stooped and hair turned to brittle white, the skin of her face loose and lined. She's looking straight ahead, fixing on Robin, but her eyes are different too - the brown of her pupils clouded blue and white with cataracts.

The hoofbeats are louder suddenly, the quality of the sound changing from soft to hard, thudding to clipped - the difference, Robin thinks, between hitting sand and hitting the stone floor of a cave.

If this Julia sees whatever it is the hoofbeats belong to, she doesn't flinch - just moves closer to Robin, towards the light.

She reaches out to her; grasps Robin's wrist with preternatural speed and grips, tight.

Robin screams.

She was still screaming as she came to, on her back on the floor of her studio.

It took a second to reacclimate herself, to remember where she was, and why - that she'd barely slept at all the night before, trace memories of Sat and Julia taking turns to torment her, to remind her that things were bad, that she was in danger. That finally, frustrated and exhausted, the morning half-light seeping in through her window, she'd rolled off the uncomfortable mattress and onto the carpet where, to her surprise, she'd fallen immediately asleep.

That for the first time, lying there in the dark with nothing to focus on but the ebb and flow of her own heartbeat, she'd heard the hoofbeats Jack had talked about, the ones that had kept him awake their first night on the island. They'd been alternately quiet and resonant, distant and close by; sometimes right in front of her apartment, other times far enough away that she'd wondered if the horse (and, she'd guessed, the rider) were circling the courtyard then doubling back.

She opened her eyes, lifted her head; lifted up her socks to check her feet, and found them smooth and clean, uncut.

Someone was knocking at the door.

She stumbled up from the carpet, reached for jeans and a sweater and threw them on over her sleep-shirt.

Jack was on the doorstep.

He looked, she thought, as bad as she'd ever seen him: unkempt, bloodshot and greasy, his clothes rumpled, patchy salt-and-pepper beard growth springing up from his cheeks.

"I'm not okay," he said, before she could speak.

"What time is it?" she said.

"Past 3. Were you sleeping?"

"A little. What's wrong?"

He didn't answer. She ushered him inside and onto the couch. He was shivering; clenching his jaw, grinding his teeth together.

She filled a glass with tepid water and passed it over to him - though his hand, she noticed, was shaking so violently that some of it spilled over the rim and onto the stained cotton of his t-shirt.

"I saw something," he said, less to her than to himself. "Last night. In my room, out of the window."

"Okay. What was it? What did you see?"

"You don't understand. I couldn't have seen it. What it was... something like that isn't *possible*. It isn't possible, but I saw it, and oh Jesus... I can't get it out of my head."

She'd been here before, she realized. Years ago, with David, before he got sober: sitting with him the same way, on the couch at her old apartment, her then-girlfriend shut away in the bedroom while he shivered and sweated and told her, over and over, that she had to do something about the spiders in the walls, that they were *everywhere*.

He'd been 4 days into withdrawal when it kicked in, she remembered. It must have been longer for Jack.

"When did you last have a drink?" she said.

"You think I've been hallucinating?" he said, more hopeful than affronted.

"I think it's a possibility. What did you see?"

He took another slug of the water, seeming to steady himself against the glass.

"I don't smoke," he said. "I mean, not anymore. Not for years."

She stayed quiet; waited for him to go on.

"I'm not sleeping," he said. "It's been a weird few days, right? And last night was bad, really bad. It got to maybe 4am, and I was still lying there, trying to stop myself from thinking about anything. So I got up and... this is going to sound crazy, okay? I got up and I pretended to smoke a cigarette. Opened the curtains, cracked the window, leaned my head out and just... blew air up at the sky."

She thought again of David: how she'd given up drinking for months when he'd first got into the program, clogging her kitchen sink with vodka and whiskey and Malbec in a show of solidarity he'd barely registered at the time. How for months after, when nobody was watching, she'd served her soda in a tumbler and her grape juice in a champagne flute.

"I get it," she said. "It's the ritual. It's comforting."

"Comforting," he said dully. "Yeah. Guess that's what I was going for."

She waited again; let him gather himself and his thoughts before she spoke.

"You leaned out of the window," she said, prompting him. "What happened then?"

"Then?" he said. "Then I saw it."

"Saw what?"

"This... thing. Like a horse, only not. Not really like a horse at all, you know?"

"Honestly, not really. In what way *like* a horse?"

"Like... the shape of a horse. Four legs, a head and a tail. But bigger than a horse, any kind of horse - way, way bigger. And someone on top, a rider. Only... I don't think he was a rider. Riders just sort of sit there, don't they? They ride, it's what they do. This guy... it's like he was fused to the horse, somehow. Like it wasn't a horse and a man I was looking at, it was some sort of combination of the two of them. A hybrid, you know? Something terrible, something out of a nightmare. And it didn't... it didn't have any skin, Robin. None at all. Even in the dark, you could see it - all the stuff underneath, the tendons, and the gristle, and this black blood just sort of pumping through the veins. But no skin, nothing keeping any of the blood or the muscle inside of it. I mean, what is that? What the hell kind of thing can walk around without any skin? It isn't real. It can't be."

He broke down; threw a hand across his face and cried, shoulders quaking, knuckles pressed against the ridge of his brows.

"It *wasn't* real," said Robin calmly. "You need to know that. Whatever you saw, it wasn't real. Your mind was messing with you. Making you see things that weren't there."

"How do you know that?" he said, hand still covering his nose and mouth.

"I know what withdrawal looks like. The kind of tricks it plays on you."

"You think it's just in my head?"

"In your head, in your bloodstream... wherever it is, it isn't out in the world. It isn't outside your window. And it isn't going to last. It's awful, I know. But it's temporary."

"You promise?" he said, sounding utterly lost, a five year old boy in middle-aged drag.

"I promise," she said.

They sat quietly together on the sofa while he gathered himself, legs pressed together at the knee.

"I'm sorry," he said after a while.

"You don't need to be," she said. "It's nothing you've done. It's just... bodies. Bodies break down sometimes, especially when you take away something that they're used to. And sometimes they drag the rest of you with them when they do. It's not something to feel bad about."

"How long am I gonna feel like this?"

"I think probably it's different for everybody. Not too long, I think."

"What am I supposed to do in the meantime? That *thing* out in the yard... even if it's not real, even if it's 20 years of bourbon leaking out of my system and into my brain... I can still *see* it. Every time I close my eyes. Every time I *stop*."

"I know."

"Then what? What do I do?"

"Keep moving," she said, before she'd really thought about it - before she'd had time to work out for herself whether or not it was good advice.

"Keep moving," he said, chewing it over. "Okay. Makes sense. Guess if I can't make it go away, I can at least try to outrun it until it loses interest, right? It's got to be better than sitting here wetting my pants while I think about it."

"I'm not a doctor," she said, backtracking. "I only know what I've seen. I can't say exactly what's going to work for you."

"Other than drugs, which I'm pretty sure I couldn't get even if I asked, what's a doctor gonna give me? We're all we've got here. And what you just said... it makes a lot of sense. I have to keep moving."

He stood up suddenly, violently, dragging the couch an inch or so forward with him.

"Come with me," he said.

"What? Where?"

"Somewhere. Anywhere. Just... outside."

"Hampton said they closed off the beach."

"Not the beach, then. Somewhere else. There's gotta be more to this island than sand anyway."

"I'm not sure we should be outside right now, with everything that's going on."

It's not safe, she thought. Not for me. Maybe not for you either.

"Please," he said. "Please, Robin."

She looked at him and saw David: David younger, and markedly worse off, but the same kind of desperate as he begged her to help him, to get him straight. It was another cheap trick, she thought; the memory of him just another chemical flooding her cells and overriding her better judgement.

"Alright," she said. "I think I know a place we can go."

The standing stones - if that's what they were - were every bit as eerie as they'd been the first time Robin had seen them: the shadows they cast longer, the grooves between the maybe-mouths and could-be noses more pronounced in the late afternoon half-light.

"Well, this is creepy as hell," said Jack, stopping to catch his breath. "Have to hand it to you, though - it's taking my mind off of the other stuff."

"That's something, then," said Robin distantly, eyes fixed to the stones. No matter what angle she looked at them from, or how many times she looked away then looked back again, she couldn't shake the sense that they'd *moved* since the day before, rearranged themselves into new configurations while her back was turned.

"Where now?"

She looked around, surveying the rolling acres of barren land closing in on them from all sides, the crumbling rock wall in the distance that she knew led down and into the Residents village.

"This way," she said, leading them away from the wall.

"You know where you're going?"

"Not really."

He shrugged and followed her anyway, still breathing hard.

"So who was it?" he said.

"Who was who?"

"Whoever it was you saw going through... the thing I am. The drinker in your life."

"What makes you think it was someone else? How do you know it wasn't me?"

"It wasn't you. I might not be the smartest guy in the room - or on the island, I guess - but other drinkers... I can smell 'em. Spot 'em from a mile off. They get this *look,* sometimes. Like hunger, or something. Starvation. Like they'll tear out their own eyeballs if they don't get a drink in them, and soon. And that look - you don't have it. I'm sure you've got your own stuff going on – I know you do – but you're not a drinker. Not the way I am."

"My brother," she said eventually. "But don't ask me about him. Not now. Please."

He reached into his pocket; pulled out the little pink stone she'd seen him find on the beach days earlier and held it tightly between his fingers.

"You're a hard woman to get to know, you know that?" he said, smiling but obviously hurt by the deflection.

"So I've been told," she said, hating herself for how flippant she sounded, how detached. Then, as a peace offering: "Ask me something else."

"Like what?"

"Something else. Something else personal."

"Suddenly feel like sharing, huh?"

"I want to try."

He struck an exaggerated pose of thoughtfulness, cradling his elbow and stroking his chin as he walked.

"How did you get to own a bookstore?" he asked, finally.

She laughed.

"That's a lot less personal than I was expecting," she said.

"It's a valid thing to ask," he said, mock-defensively.

"If you say so."

"So, are you gonna answer it?"

"I was given it."

"You were given it."

"Yes. By a friend."

"Must have been some friend."

"She was."

He was dying to know more; she could feel it.

"We were... involved," she said, throwing him a bone. "A long time ago. When I was still in grad school. She was older than me, more settled. More solvent. It didn't last, but we stayed close after."

"It's true, then," he said - satisfied, as if he'd finally heard the answer to a question he hadn't quite known how to articulate. "You guys, lesbians... you really *are* better at staying friends after. Better than me at least. I'm pretty sure my ex-wife would take a claw hammer to my skull if she ever saw me again."

"Why, what did you do?"

"Nope. You're the one sharing here, not me. So keep talking."

"What else do you want to know?"

"This friend... why'd she give you her store?"

He stopped walking unexpectedly.

"Fuck," he said. "I'm such a fucking idiot. Did she... did something happen to her? When you said she gave it to you... did she, you know, leave it to you? In her will?"

"Oh my God!" she laughed. "No! Why would you think that?"

She pushed him lightly, reproachingly on the shoulder, and he made a show of toppling backwards - reminding her again of David in a way that made her stomach twist even as it made her smile.

"So she didn't die?" he said.

"No, she didn't die! She moved to Santa Fe with her pilates instructor."

"And she just *gave* you her store?"

"She's a sentimentalist. She didn't want to sell up, and I think she thought I'd... I don't know, look after it. That I'd be a good custodian."

"She didn't want the money?"

"She doesn't *need* the money. She was in tech before she bought the bookstore. Put in her seven years at a startup that went public, waited for her stocks to vest and then got the hell out."

"So, do you own it now? The store?"

"Technically, yes. But since it was given to me on the understanding that I'd never actually sell it... I'm not sure how much you could say that it's really mine, you know?"

"It's worth a lot of money?"

"It's 500 square feet of real estate in the middle of the East Bay. What do you think?"

"I think I don't really know California, but from the sound of your voice, I'm gonna say yes."

He whistled through his teeth, then grinned at her widely.

"What?" she said.

"I just never would have thought that about you," he said.

"Thought what? What about me?"

"That you'd be the type to have a sugar mama."

She pushed him again, harder. He kept grinning.

"I had a job before the store, thank you," she said. "A real one. Not for long, but I had one."

"Doing what?"

"I taught high school. English and government."

"Now I feel bad. That *is* a real job. Why'd you give it up?"

"A lot of reasons. The money was a big one: bookstores may not be goldmines, but at least this way I'm not pulling shifts at Taco Bell over summer vacation."

"A high school teacher with a sugar mama. I think I read about you once in Penthouse."

"You're an asshole, you know that?"

He laughed; pressed his shoulder into hers affectionately. *But I'm your asshole*, Davey would have said.

They walked on, over the dry grassland. There was another strip of sand, another stretch of dark water in the far distance; another side of the island, one she'd never been to, the landscape here interrupted by the outline of a squat, crumbling grey-brick building that even from a distance looked derelict. Around them, afternoon was turning to evening, half-light to fuller dark. At some point soon, she realized, they'd have to head back to the quad.

*To the compound*, she thought, and shuddered.

Jack, evidently, was thinking something similar.

"I don't think I can handle going back yet," he said.

"We probably should, though," she said, half-heartedly.

"Or what? Hampton's gonna ground us for breaking curfew?"

"Or send one of the island kids after us."

She thought, briefly, of the islanders, their hard faces and strange horses - and then of Jack's monster, bloody and skinless, its hooves beating down on the cobblestones outside their windows. She shuddered again; hoped he wouldn't notice.

"Let's go down to the beach," he said. "It won't take long."

"Then back?"

"Then back. Scout's honor."

She picked up her pace, striding out towards the strip of sand at what was basically a speed-walk. He struggled to keep up, huffing and puffing beside her. As they neared the little grey building, he stopped altogether; bent double at the waist, hands on his thighs, and gasped for air.

"You gotta slow down," he said, wiping the sweat from his forehead.

"Or you could speed up."

"Do I look like I can speed up? You're killing me here. This is the most exercise I've had in a decade."

He glanced around; took in their surroundings.

"What do you suppose that is?" he said, indicating the building.

"No clue," she said, though that wasn't entirely true. In fact, it looked to her like a little church; the rounded grey-stone walls and crucifix-style design to the roof reminding her of some of the ruined medieval chapels she'd seen in the travel guides they stocked in the store but never sold.

"You want to take a look inside?" he said.

No, she thought. Not at all, actually.

"Come on," he said. "Just for a second."

There was a door; a wide oak barrier the thickness of the bricks around it, layered with dark green moss. She prayed for it to be locked, bolted somehow from the inside - for there to be a legitimate reason that they should keep out, move on - but it swung open as he pushed it, inviting them in.

It really *was* a chapel, she saw, and a living one, not a ruin, lit up at every corner with votive candles, some burned nearly down to the wick. A chapel that people used - people who prayed in the makeshift stone pews that were still half-rock, who got down on their hands and knees and prostrated themselves in front of the raised altar along the far wall.

"Did not expect *this*," said Jack.

She walked up the aisle, Jack trailing after her. As they got closer, she saw the statues - wood carvings, all of them. One of them, the largest of the three, placed right on top of the altar: a woman's head and neck, the hair long and tangled and the face contorted, rising up from what looked like a body of water. Then two more: thick-set horses reared up on their hind

122

legs, each one a foot high, painted and polished and arranged on either side of the altar like effigies of the Virgin Mary. Closer still, she saw the detail: that they weren't horses at all, at least not in the sense that she understood them, but something monstrous, something for which she had no real frame of reference. Something like *centaurs*, she thought, reaching for the word - but really not centaurs at all, not the sculpted, essentially human half-horse men she'd pictured from Greek myths and The Chronicles of Narnia. Each one had four legs and a winding, snake-like tail; a sharp equine snout, lips pulled back behind pointed teeth; the cloven hooves of a goat or a camel. From its wide mid-section grew the upper body of a man, bald and skeletal, his arms thin as elastic and unnaturally long. It was hard to know for sure, in the flickering light of the candles, but it seemed to her that its skin was missing; that its flesh was nothing but veins and tendons stretched taut over bone.

"Do you see them?" said Jack, his voice shaking. "Robin, do you see them?"

"Yes," she said. "Yes, I see them."

# CHAPTER 13

It was pitch black outside when they left the chapel, so dark Robin struggled to see the hand in front of her face. They walked slowly, cautiously over the grassland, Jack's arm wrapped tight in hers, the two of them negotiating the rocks underfoot more by feel and sense memory than by sight.

There were lights in the distance, clusters of them, so far away it was as if she was seeing them from overhead. By unspoken consensus, they headed in that direction; both of them hoping, or so she assumed, that following the specks of brightness would eventually lead them back to the quad, or at the very least somewhere safer than their current location.

In the absence of any sound but the dry crunch of their feet on the grass, there was only the sea - equally far but thunderous, crashing in on itself and, she supposed, against the wire mesh that held it at bay. A fine saltwater mist of something that could have been rain but probably wasn't sprayed intermittently against their faces.

"It was real," said Jack. "What I saw. It was real."

"We don't know that," said Robin, sounding unconvinced even to herself. "There are other explanations."

"Like what?"

"I don't know. But there have to be."

"Those statues - that was him. *It*. The thing I saw. And if someone else saw it too - more than one someone else, maybe - then it isn't just in my head. It can't be. It's *here*."

"Let's talk about it later, okay?"

He stopped dead, pulling her with him.

"You just saw what I saw!" he said, half-shouting. "What's *wrong* with you? Why are you so calm? There's a goddamn monster out here!"

Hold it together, she thought. Just for now, hold it together. Until you're somewhere else, somewhere away from here. Somewhere with lights, and other people, and doors that lock.

"Keep your voice down," she said. "You want Hampton to hear you? Or one of the island people?"

He yanked his arm away from hers - but didn't, she noticed, move away from her, even an inch.

"We need to get back to the quad," she said, injecting as much calm as she could into each word. "Whatever's going on... we shouldn't talk about it out here. Please."

She slipped her arm back into his. He let her.

They walked on towards the lights, steadying each other whenever the ground threatened to slip away from them.

Eventually they passed the standing stones. The darkness, she saw, had done peculiar things to the shape of them - twisting and stretching their outlines into bulbous, elongated stumps that made her think of banyan trees in winter.

"Guess we're on the right track, then," he said, more subdued than before.

Later - she couldn't say how much - there were hoofbeats, coming from somewhere to the left of them, each one louder than bullets in the silence.

She heard his breath catch in his throat; felt the muscles in his arm tense and tighten, his legs seizing up under him.

"It's okay," she said, pulling him back into motion, pushing past the thought of what might happen if they stopped, if the hoofbeats caught up to them - though of course it would be *nothing, nothing at all because they were horses, just horses, nothing but animals riding fast on hard ground.*

She relaxed, though only a little, as they approached the quad - seeing to her relief that the lights *had* drawn them there, and not to some other forbidden part of the island. She was relieved, too, to find some of the other guests awake and outside, talking and reading under the halogen lamps beaming yellow light down from the outer walls of the apartment blocks.

Bill and Carol were there, she saw, hunched in apparent concentration over a paper-and-ink checkerboard with sandstone pebbles for pieces.

Jack was running towards them before she could stop him.

"... a church on the other side of the island," she heard him say as she caught up to him, "with these statues inside. And they looked like..."

"Like horses," she said, pressing a hand to his arm to keep him from going any further.

"Horses?" said Carol, quizzically.

"Not horses," said Jack frantically, ignoring Robin's hand. "*Things*. Like... like what you'd get if you took a horse and a guy with no legs and stuck them together and ripped the skin off. You know?"

Bill and Carol stared up at them, perplexed.

"Can I talk to you for a second?" said Robin, tugging at Jack's arm and smiling apologetically at Bill and Carol.

He let himself be led to another bench a few feet away from them.

"You can't tell them what you saw," she said, as quietly as she knew how.

"Why not?" he said. "If that thing I saw is out there, people need to know about it, don't they?"

"No. Not right now. Not until we know what's actually going on."

"They deserve to know. So they can protect themselves if they need to."

"Know what, exactly? That you *think* you saw something that by any objective standard would make you sound like a crazy person?"

"I'm not crazy. You know I'm not crazy."

"I do. But they won't."

"They're my friends. Yours too. I trust them."

"And you've known them all of, what? A week?"

"That's how long I've known you."

"Just listen to me, okay? You can't tell them. You can't. Not yet. Let's just... figure out what we're looking at first."

"I *want* to tell them, Robin."

"And do you want to put them in danger? Because that's what you'll be doing if you tell them."

She hated herself for saying it; for playing to the guilt she knew instinctively would be his weak spot.

"What kind of danger?" he said.

"I don't know. That's the whole point. We don't know anything about the people on this island, or what they do here, or what the hell it is they're worshipping out in that church. And until we do... we need to be careful. Not let other people in on it. It's not just about protecting ourselves - it's about protecting them, too. Do you understand what I'm saying?"

"Yes, I understand. But I don't like it."

"Please," she said, consciously echoing the way he'd pleaded with her earlier. "Please, Jack."

He shrugged, once, like a dog shaking water off its fur. Then he nodded.

Something caught her attention across the courtyard: a flash of fabric, a click of heeled boots on cobblestones. She looked closer; saw Julia crossing the quad to her apartment, a pen and notebook tucked into her side. Felt, then immediately suppressed an echo of the anger - the sense of betrayal - she'd experienced the day before. Pushed down the memory of crying in the courtyard, inches from where she and Jack were standing now, with Julia's arms around her.

"Robin?" said Jack. "Are you listening?"

"Yes," she said, looking away. "Let's go."

They walked back over to Bill and Carol.

"You kids work out whatever you needed to work out?" asked Bill, bemused.

"Sorry," said Robin. "Had to... get a couple of things straight."

Jack stared down at the ground, hands pushed deep into the pockets of his chinos. Even by omission, she thought, he was a terrible liar.

Carol looked back and forth between them, curiosity writ large on her face. Eventually she seemed to settle on a conclusion and smiled back at the two of them approvingly - a dowager aunt watching an unlikely romance blossom between her favorite charges.

Let her believe it, thought Robin. God knows it's easier that way.

She stepped closer to Jack, setting her shoulder against his chest.

"Those statues you were talking about before," said Bill thoughtfully. "The ones you saw in the chapel while you were.... out for your walk. You said they were like horses?"

"A little like horses, yeah," said Robin warily.

"But skinless, right?" he said. "And a human chest and head on there too? Like a centaur kind of thing, but just that little bit more unpleasant?"

"It was dark," she said. "We couldn't see much."

"That was it," said Jack. "That was what it looked like."

"*They*," said Robin. "What *they* looked like."

"I think I know what they were," said Bill, seeming not to hear Jack's slip-up or her correction. "I mean, I'd like to check for myself, maybe go out there tomorrow and take a look... but I'm pretty sure. Skinless horse-men... it's a pretty vivid image, am I right?"

"What?" said Robin, breath catching in her chest. "What do you think we saw?"

Beside her, Jack was perfectly still, his body rigid.

"Nuckelavee," said Bill, with the kind of deliberate finality that begged them to ask what he meant. An old bit from the wily professor handbook, thought Robin - though probably one that played better in a lecture hall or a college auditorium.

"Alright, darling," said Carol. "I'll bite. Tell us, what's a Nuckelavee?"

"It's not *a* Nuckelavee," he said. "Just Nuckelavee. *The* Nuckelavee, possibly. Something like that probably deserves the definite article."

"And what kind of something *is* that, exactly?" said Carol. "We're not your students, Bill. You don't need to keep us in suspense."

"You really have no feel for delivery at all, do you?" he said, sighing. "Alright, you got it. Straight to the point. Nuckelavee - *the* Nuckelavee - is an ancient legend. A mythological beast. Orcadian, no less."

"Orcadian?" said Jack.

"From the Orkneys," said Carol. "A group of islands not far from here. Although how *you'd* know that," she added, directly at Bill, "I have no idea."

"I travel," said Bill, holding up his hands in mock-protest. "And I'll have you know, I enjoyed a very pleasant vacation in Scotland in the late 90s."

"And fell into a few distilleries in the process, I don't doubt," said Carol.

"Well, that's a given, of course," said Bill.

"And the Nuckelavee?" said Robin impatiently.

"Is a horse demon," said Bill. "Very old, and very like the thing you described. Vast, and skinless - half-man, half-horse, but not in a cute Harry Potter way. We're talking Creature From The Black Lagoon territory here. Literally, actually, since it's supposed to live at the bottom of the sea."

"You seem to know an awful lot about it," said Carol skeptically.

"There was a very informative ghost-walk on the island tour," said Bill. "And it helps that I saw it, obviously."

"You saw it?" said Jack. "Where? Where did you see it?"

Robin squeezed his arm, hard, to keep him from saying more.

"Maybe I misspoke," said Bill, sending another bemused look Jack's way. "Obviously I didn't actually *see* this beast of legend. But there was a very detailed sculpture on one of the Northern Isles. We actually jumped on a boat out there just to take a look, once we'd done the ghost-walk. Hideous thing - really, ugly as hell - but so intricate. You wouldn't think you'd get that much nuance out of a block of stone, but there it is."

"Where did it come from?" said Robin. Then: "I mean, where was it *supposed* to come from, the Nuckelavee?"

"'The bottom of the sea' is as good as I got geographically," said Bill. "But if you mean conceptually... well, you know what folklore's like. It's all bricolage and borrowing. I know the *word* Nuckelavee is something to do with the devil - probably some oblique reference to Old Nick - but the *idea* of it... I'd guess it's a composite. Part water horse, part mer-man, part sea dragon. Bits and pieces taken from a constellation of Norse and Celtic myth systems and pounded together into an unspeakable Orcadian whole."

"What does it want?" said Jack.

"*Want*?" said Bill. "I'm not sure it *wants* anything. It's a demon. An... I don't know exactly what you'd call it. An agent of chaos?"

"What he means," said Robin, thinking on her feet, "is: what does it *do*? I mean, all these old myths served a cultural purpose, right? They all *did* something, or represented something, or regulated something."

"Got it," said Bill. "Okay. Well, from what I remember, the Nuckelavee was all tied up with regulating seasons. Sunshine and crop cycles, that kind of thing."

"Like Persephone," said Carol.

"Exactly like Persephone, actually." said Bill. "But in reverse. She brings springtime, right? Vegetation and fecundity and all that good stuff. Well, the Nuckelavee brings winter. Darkness, decay, famine. And a case of acid breath so bad it makes everything around it wither and die."

"Sounds delightful," said Carol.

("But it's July," said Jack, too quiet for the others to hear him).

"What I don't understand," said Jack, "is why you'd find Nuckelavee icons in a church. We're talking about a monster - a harbinger of death, if you're an old Orcadian. It isn't something you want to come visit, and it definitely isn't something you worship. It'd be like praying to Grendel."

"They were there," said Robin, affecting indifference.

"It makes sense to me," said Carol to Bill. "People worship all sorts of things, and most of them aren't so cuddly. Or haven't you read the Old Testament?"

"I'm more of a Bhagavad Gita kind of guy," said Bill to Jack and Robin. "But that isn't the point. The Nuckelavee - it's like Godzilla. It comes, it destroys, it rides back into the sea. And you don't see people building temples to Godzilla."

"Yet," said Carol.

"I have to get out of here," whispered Robin to Jack as the older pair bickered.

"And go where?" whispered Jack. "I thought it wasn't safe?"

"I need to think. Or... work out *what* I think."

"Didn't you hear him just then? About what it is that's running around here at night?"

"We still don't know if that's true."

"You shouldn't be on your own."

"I *need* to be on my own. Just for a little while."

"I'm not leaving you."

"I'll be in my apartment. You'll know exactly where I am. You can see the door from right here."

"What about me? I don't think I can go back to mine, not after last night. And I can't stay out here."

"Stay with them," she said quietly, nodding towards Bill and Carol. "I can't see them objecting to you sleeping on their couch."

"What if they ask me why?"

"Tell them you don't want to be alone. It's not like it's a lie, is it?"

"I don't feel good about this."

"I know. But it's only for tonight. I'll come find you first thing tomorrow and we can... make a plan, I guess."

"I'm scared," he said, so softly she could barely hear.

She reached for his hand; linked her fingers through his in the only gesture of comfort she knew how to give him.

You should be, she thought. Both of us should be.

On her own in her apartment, with the door locked and the lights low, a stale sandwich and a handful of crackers in her empty stomach, she took stock of her position.

Usually, for her, the quiet was a panacea: a cool cloth to the temples, quelling the heat of the social world just enough for her to pull out, examine - and finally, *understand* - every rogue feeling, every spaghetti-strand of thought before the mass of them overwhelmed her.

Here and now, though, the quiet was an enemy: it held monsters. *Literal* monsters, she thought - almost (but not quite) laughing aloud at the absurdity of the idea.

She found herself wishing she'd waited with Jack after all - or had him come back with her (not *home*, never *home*), laid out her one spare blanket and pillow for him on the floor and talked to him about everything and nothing until the darkness outside lifted and they were safe again, or as safe as they'd ever be on the island.

It was late enough for the signs of life outside to have scattered; the voices and footsteps she'd heard in the courtyard just an hour before swept away into their own apartments, their own beds. She strained her ears listening for hoofbeats - then, when she finally heard them (so distant they could have been footsteps, or heeled boots on cobblestones), backed away from the window and closed the curtains, refusing to see what might be out there.

After a while, another sound overtook the hoofbeats - this one closer, seeming to originate from right outside the apartment. This time, she thought, it actually *was* footsteps, a rhythmic one-two she imagined echoing out across the empty quad. Not *just* footsteps, then: pacing. Someone pacing up and down outside her door.

This time, she was ready. She didn't wait for the knock, or the door handle to turn. Instead, she slipped on her sneakers, picked up the heaviest book she had from the desk and raised it, high and weaponized, above her head as she flung open the door.

She was more relieved than she cared to admit to find Julia on the other side.

To her credit, Robin conceded, she didn't flinch at the book, or the suddenness of Robin's appearance - just took a single, polite step backwards, away from the doorway.

"May I come in?" she said. "I think perhaps we should talk."

# CHAPTER 14

S he didn't sit down, and Robin didn't offer.

"I shouldn't have said what I did," she said.

"No," said Robin. "You shouldn't have."

"I'm sorry if I frightened you."

"Yeah. Cryptic threats will do that."

"I wanted you to stay safe."

"From the Nuckelavee?"

Julia looked confused, momentarily.

"I'm sorry, the what?" she asked.

So not *that*, thought Robin. Whatever has her so nervous, it isn't Celtic sea-monsters.

"Doesn't matter," she said. "Safe from what, then? What is it you think I need protecting from?"

"Are you absolutely sure you want to know?" said Julia.

And the anger was there again, hot and acidic, uncontainable.

"Enough!" she shouted. "Tell me or don't tell me, but don't behave as if you're looking out for me by withholding information. I'm not a fucking child. I don't *need* your protection."

"Someone is killing people," said Julia. "Here, on the island."

"Oh," said Robin, deflated.

"You're not surprised?"

"You're not telling me something I didn't already know, if that's what you're asking."

Julia sat down on the couch.

"You know about the others?" she said.

"Not a lot," said Robin. "I know they disappeared. Or turned up dead on the beach, like Chuck. And I know Hampton is mixed up in it, somehow."

"Then apparently you know exactly as much as I do," said Julia, although Robin wasn't sure she believed her.

"I don't know for sure," said Robin. "About Hampton. He came here before, after Chuck... after I found the body. Threatened me. And I know I'm not the first he's done that to. But it doesn't mean he's a murderer. He really *could* just be a guy who hates loose ends."

"Possibly. But whatever else he may be, he's an exceptionally nasty piece of work. And since you're now one of those loose ends - you really do need to be careful."

"I know," said Robin, suddenly exhausted. She rubbed her eyes; pinched the bridge of her nose to keep herself alert.

"You ought to sit down," said Julia, edging across the couch to make room. "You look absolutely spent."

"Would you believe me if I told you," said Robin, sliding in next to her, "that Hampton's been the least of my worries these last 24 hours?"

"I'd have no reason to doubt you. What else has happened?"

"You know what? Ignore that last question. You *wouldn't* believe me if I told you."

"Three years ago I had a family, a career and the kind of salary that would make a lot of people's eyes pop out of their sockets. Now I live in a cage on an island prison in the middle of the ocean that may very well also house a serial murderer. Disbelief is the single perennial condition of my existence. So please, try me."

"Is that a challenge?"

"It's a promise. Very little could shock me at this point."

"If you say so," said Robin, and told her: about Jack and his maybe-hallucination, about the chapel and the idols, about Bill and the Nuckelavee.

Julia said nothing while she talked; just sat and listened impassively, her mouth tight, eyes focused but unreadable.

"Have you or Jack shared this with anyone?" she said, when it was clear that Robin had finished.

"And have them think we've lost our minds? No."

"Do *you* think you've lost your minds?"

"I honestly don't know. A part of me thinks it could be some *folie à deux* thing - that I'm letting myself get sucked into Jack's fantasy because of where we are and everything else that's been going on. That living in a pressure cooker even for a week has made us both a little... untethered."

"But that's not what you actually believe, is it?"

"I don't know what I believe. And I don't know what Jack saw out of his window last night. But I know what *I* saw. And those statues... they *were* the things he told me about. Down to the last detail."

"And from this you infer that this creature - this Nuckelavee - is a thing that exists in the world?"

She didn't sound judgmental, Robin noted, nor even obviously skeptical. Just curious - appraising what she heard with the same objective interest Robin could imagine her applying to an unusual species of butterfly or a new strain of bacteria captured under a microscope.

"What do you think?" asked Robin. "Am I crazy?"

"I think I'm a scientist. I don't believe in monsters."

"So you *do* think I'm crazy."

"I didn't say that. You seem anxious, certainly. Perhaps a little paranoid, though I'm bound to say that you probably have good cause. But I wouldn't say you were... ill. And monstrous horses aside, your grip on reality seems reasonably secure."

"You've seen a lot of crazy?"

"Some, yes," said Julia.

Robin waited for a punchline, a modifier, but nothing came.

"You don't believe in monsters, and you don't think I'm crazy," she said, to break the silence as much as to hear the answer. "So how do you account for what we saw? What Jack saw?"

"All you saw," said Julia, "were two statues. Two very disturbing statues, admittedly - but no worse, by the sounds of it, than anything you'd find in an Egyptian temple or a shrine to Kali, or even some of the more hardcore Caravaggios. Devotional art is hardly known for shying away from the graphic."

"You don't think it's weird to find something like that out here?"

"Unusual, perhaps, but not unheard of. These weren't always Christian islands. And other people's gods tend to seem more monstrous than the ones we're used to."

"Bill didn't think it was a god, though. Just a monster."

"I feel like there's probably a joke in there somewhere. 'What's the difference between a god and a monster? Two and a half miles of water and a thousand years of Christian hegemony.'"

"It's not a great joke," said Robin.

"Perhaps not. Jokes aren't really my area. But regardless, I don't think religious iconography should be keeping you awake at night."

She didn't add, *when there are so, so many other things you ought to be worried about*, but Robin heard it anyway, loud and clear.

"And what Jack saw?" she said. "What's your explanation for that?"

"I don't have one," said Julia. "Although I can certainly think of a few hypotheses that might fit the bill."

"Such as?"

"That your first instinct was the right one - that it *was* a hallucination, or a waking dream. That he'd seen something that day, or even earlier, something that didn't register with him as significant at the time - a picture, or a photograph, or another carving, even - and that whatever it was lodged in his unconscious and reactivated itself when the alcohol withdrawal kicked in."

"And what are the odds that he'd remember whatever it was he saw *exactly* the way it looked on the statues?"

"Significantly higher, I would have thought, than the odds of an ancient Orcadian horse god roaming around the island at night. And in any case, I have other hypotheses. He actually *may* have seen something: a strange-looking horse that looked even stranger in the dark, say. Or something less prosaic: someone in costume on horseback, got up in fancy dress or... I don't know, performing some religious ritual or other. There are a lot of possibilities, all of them more plausible than the alternative."

*She's right*, thought Robin. *None of it holds up to scrutiny. It's all in my head.*

She felt suddenly, unexpectedly torn, between relief (that none of it was real, that there really were no monsters) and another kind of fear - that she could be carried away so completely, *frightened* so completely by an idea without a scrap of evidence or whisper of substance. Both sensations compounded by embarrassment, for reasons she preferred not to analyse, at all of it having played out in front of Julia.

"What's your conclusion, then?" she said. "I shouldn't worry about the Nuckelavee?"

"I think there are other monsters more deserving of your concern," said Julia. "Flesh and blood ones."

"You really know how to put a girl at ease, don't you?" said Robin.

"It's a talent," said Julia.

She smiled, and Robin found herself watching her closely: the set of her jaw, the line of her wrists. If Julia noticed, she didn't react.

"Did you manage to read the book?" she asked.

"The book?" said Robin. "*That* book?"

She pointed to the leather hardcover she'd planned to use as a ballistic - now back on the desktop, entirely benign.

"The one you borrowed," said Julia. "The Shirley Jackson stories."

"Oh, no," said Robin. "Not yet. Too busy finding bodies and hiding from mythical sea creatures. You know how it is."

"Sure do," said Julia.

Something broke in the atmosphere between them, and they were laughing; dark, cathartic laughter that spilled out of Robin like a toxin leaving her body. Then she was crying.

Julia closed the distance between them on the couch; put a hand on Robin's leg, sympathetic but undemanding.

"I'm sorry," said Robin after a while. "I can't seem to stop crying on you lately."

"It's normal," said Julia. "Or perhaps 'normal' isn't the right word; I'm not sure that there's anything normal about the situation in which we've found ourselves. But crying is certainly a reasonable response to the things you've been exposed to lately. Considering our circumstances, I'm surprised any of us ever stop."

"You don't seem like the crying type," said Robin.

"Well there, you see, you're absolutely wrong. I cry constantly. But I tend to be far away from other people when I do, so it's as if it never happened."

"I wouldn't have guessed that about you. That you cry," she clarified. "Not that you hate people. You're pretty upfront about that."

"This misanthropy is actually a relatively recent phenomenon. I used to be far more sociable."

"Before the court case?" said Robin, then realized what she'd done - what she'd given away.

"Ah," said Julia. "Of course. I forgot for a moment that you knew about that."

She stood up from the couch; walked to the center of the room, her head turned away from Robin.

"I really don't know much," said Robin, quickly, getting up after her. "Almost nothing, really."

"I didn't do it," said Julia, still not looking at Robin. Robin stepped around her, positioning herself in Julia's line of sight.

"It doesn't matter," she said. "You don't owe me anything."

"I realize that. Nevertheless, I'd like you to know. Whatever you may have heard about me - it isn't true. I'm many things, some of them undoubtedly terrible, but I'm not a killer. I wasn't responsible for what happened to those children."

"Who was?" said Robin, stepping closer, into Julia's space.

"I wish I could tell you," said Julia. "Or at least, I wish I'd known at the time. I'm not sure how much good the knowing would do me now. If you've heard about the trial, then you know that *someone* had an interest in making it seem that I was guilty. But whether it was my manager, or the CEO, or just a renegade lab technician with a chip on his shoulder... It could have come straight from the top, for all I know."

"From the top?"

"From Vanderhalden. The great and powerful."

Robin took a step back.

"Vanderhalden?" she said. "What does Vanderhalden have to do with this?"

"Oh, didn't you hear that part? They bought my company. About a month before... before those kids started dying."

"So, wait," said Robin. "Let me get this straight in my head. The people who run this island are the same people who own the company that - in a roundabout sort of way - are the reason you also ended up here, on this island?"

It was another... *something*, she thought. Another piece of a puzzle. One that would probably make more sense in hindsight, once the other pieces had landed and slotted together.

"The same people, yes," said Julia.

"And that doesn't seem at all suspicious to you?"

"Of course it does. And I've certainly considered what I imagine you're suggesting - that all of it was choreographed from on high, that I was *put* here for some reason."

"But you don't think so?"

"No, I don't think so. I think that a lot of the time, things just happen. That enormous multinational corporations with a thousand moving parts often chug along without each part ever really understanding what the other parts are doing. That the truth of it is probably a lot more prosaic than a conspiracy theory. And that a pissed off lab tech or an executive board trying to cover its own arse is a lot more likely than an omniscient corporate conglomerate locking a middle-aged, middle-management engineer in a dungeon and throwing away the key."

"So, what, it's all a coincidence?"

"A *series* of coincidences, I'd say," she said, obliquely. "And why not? The other option makes about as much sense as your water-horse."

"I don't believe that," said Robin.

"That's your prerogative. But as I say, it's hardly important now. I'm already ruined - the damage is done."

"You're not ruined."

"I'll never work again, not in research. I'm not sure, given my new reputation, that I'd be able to get a job anywhere at all. I have an enormous mortgage left to pay on a house I can't afford, friends who wouldn't answer my calls even if I were able to *make* calls, and a son who in all likelihood won't remember what I look like when I'm finally able to see him again. I appreciate you saying so, but really - I'm ruined."

"No, you're not," said Robin, stepping back towards her, pulling on her hands for emphasis. "Look, I'm not denying this is a hell of a setback, but people have come back from worse. And of course your son isn't going to forget you. You're his mother. And, if you don't mind me saying, you're not exactly a pushover. *You* can come back from this."

Julia smiled at her. And there was sadness in there, Robin thought, but something else too - hope, or something like it.

"That's a lot of faith to invest in a woman you've known for a week," she said, her eyes locked on Robin's.

"In all fairness," said Robin, looking back at her, still holding her hands, "I'm a lousy judge of character. And, if this last day is anything to go on, possibly also a little crazy."

"I'd say the jury's still out on that one," said Julia.

Robin laughed, and kissed her.

Later, much later, she'd wonder why she did it - why she'd thought it was a good idea, the right or the appropriate thing to do. Whether she'd given any thought to it at all before she acted.

In the moment, she wondered whether Julia would pull back, push her away, run out of the apartment altogether. And then, when none of that happened, the only thing she thought to think was: *this. This is good.*

Finally, it was her who pulled back, not Julia - back but not away, one hand still cupped around Julia's neck, the other caught up in her hair.

"Is this that thing you were talking about before?" she said. "Accelerated intimacy?"

"Could be," said Julia, her own hand bunched in the collar of Robin's shirt. "Is that a problem?"

"No. Just didn't want to go into this blind," said Robin, and kissed her again.

# CHAPTER 15

The bed was too small. It hadn't seemed so to Robin before, the handful of nights she'd slept on it, but the addition of another body brought it home. Too narrow, too short, too uncomfortable - pocked with dips and slopes, gnarled knots of old foam and hard springs poking up through the thin mattress.

If Julia noticed or cared, it didn't show. Instead she lay unselfconsciously on her side beside Robin: legs pressed into Robin's legs, hair lightly curled with sweat and fanned out across the pillow, fingers loosely interlocked with Robin's.

She seemed relaxed, Robin thought. Unguarded.

She shivered, the skin of her exposed arm turning to gooseflesh in the draught of the room.

"Are you cold?" Robin asked, pulling the blanket over them.

"I'm fine," said Julia. "Better than fine, actually. This may be the most human I've felt in months."

"Me too. Though you should know, I didn't intend for this to happen."

"No."

"I'm glad it did, though. I'd forgotten what this felt like."

"Which part of 'this'?"

"All of it. I haven't… it's been a long time."

"Would it be inappropriate to ask how long?"

"Completely. Lucky for you, we left propriety behind a while back."

"How long, then?"

"A year. Maybe longer."

"That's not so long."

"By what standard?"

"Mine, for starters."

"You haven't…?"

"Not since my divorce."

"Which was…?"

"Longer than a year ago, put it that way."

"I wouldn't have guessed. You seem… confident."

"If that's a euphemism for promiscuous, I'm going to be terribly offended."

Robin took a long, exaggerated look down at her, at the two of them, at Julia's body still pressed to hers.

"I wouldn't dare cast aspersions on your honor," she said, smiling.

Julia laughed, a rich throaty sound that Robin hadn't heard before, and turned around to kiss her, drawing Robin's hips away from the edge of the mattress.

"You taste like salt," she said.

"Are you surprised?" said Robin. "Even the air in this place is salted. It's like living on the Dead Sea."

"It's the water - the salinity. It's far higher than you'd expect, for the climate."

"That's a strange thing for you to know."

"I did some digging, when I… when I began to suspect that I might be sent here. Some reading."

"About salinity."

"About the island. The history, the geography of the place. The water around it is one of its better-known features: it's nearly 40% salt. Hence the name."

"That *is* a lot of salt. Though I have to tell you, your pillow talk needs work."

"Perhaps so. My aura of easy virtue notwithstanding, I'm a little out of practice."

Robin pulled her closer; pressed her lips against her knuckle.

"You're not doing so badly," she said.

They relaxed back into each other: Robin's arm around Julia's shoulders, Julia's palm splayed flat against Robin's stomach.

"What else did you read?" Robin asked after a while.

"About Salt Rock?"

"Yeah. I tried to look, too, before they came for me. Before the trial. But there wasn't anything - nothing I could find, anyway. At least not digitally. I thought maybe Vanderhalden had wiped away the traces before they set up shop here."

"Maybe they did," said Julia. "I went analogue. To a library, no less."

"There are books?"

"Several, according to the catalogue. Though I only managed to track down the one."

"What did it say? Other than the stuff about salt levels."

"Many things. Is there something particular you wanted to know?"

"What was it, before it was... this?"

"Before Vanderhalden? Just another island - another small, sparsely-populated Scottish island. Lighter on fishing than its neighbors, likely because there aren't any fish - barely anything can survive in an environment that high in salt. But essentially no different than any other of the Northern Isles."

"And people have always lived here? Hampton, when we first arrived... he said the islanders had been here for generations."

"He's right. There are records of families living here since the 16th century."

"Nothing before then?"

"I'm sure there were. But nothing was formally recorded. Salt Rock didn't exist before then, not as a settlement. It wasn't discovered until the 1760s."

"By who?"

"A naturalist - the Darwin of his day, a man named Jacob Edsell. He came out here looking for puffins to study."

"And didn't find any, I'm guessing."

"None. Just horses. Horses and people."

"Horses?"

"Wild horses. Dozens of them, grazing all over the island."

"Is that unusual?"

"He seemed to think so. He couldn't work out how they came to be there in those numbers, in the absence of any other wildlife. Neither could his colleagues, when he brought them over. And none of the island people spoke a word of English."

"And the islanders here now – they're their descendants?"

"I'm sure some are, although there was some mixing after Edsell and his colleague dropped in on the other islands in the archipelago and word spread about the animals. Then there was a bit of a wave of... it seems strange to call it immigration when we're talking about people from a couple of islands along, but I suppose that was what it was. Farmers and their families, mainly - people who saw a lot of strong, unclaimed horses as a windfall rather than a peculiarity. That's what the islanders did until recently, you know - they traded horses. Bred them here and sold them on to the mainland."

"That explains a few things, anyway. Jack said they didn't look like regular horses."

"I suppose they wouldn't be, if they're descended from wild animals."

Robin shifted onto her side, so she and Julia were face to face.

"These horses," she said. "Do you think they have anything to do with what we saw in the church?"

"In what way?" said Julia.

"I don't know exactly. But it feels like more than an accident that there'd be a bunch of statues of a horse demon on an island that's, by any definition, pretty horse-centric."

"I see. No, then: I doubt it's an accident. People make their gods in the images of things they see, things they know. The frame of reference dictates the form. If you see elephants all day, every day across the plains, it makes sense that you'd eventually start to conceive of a god that looked a bit like an elephant. If you're forever seeing coyotes howling and scavenging for food in the desert, eventually you might begin to imagine some kind of celestial trickster with fur and a tail that laughs its head off and wants to steal a piece of your soul. And if you live on a cold, wet island in the middle of nowhere with nothing but horses for company... I can see why you might eventually get around to thinking of god - or the devil for that matter - as a four legged equine thing that rises out of the sea."

"There's that logic again," said Robin, reaching out to touch her face.

"You'd prefer magical thinking?"

"God, no. I like the logic. I think you might have talked me down from the ledge earlier."

"If only it worked so well on everybody."

"It doesn't?"

"Not in my experience."

"Not mine, now I think of it. I used to date a woman who read tarot cards. Thought she was psychic. Drove me nuts."

"I'm afraid I can go one up on that. My mother was a paranoid schizophrenic. Utterly superstitious. Horseshoes over the doors, basins of freshwater by the windows, dark cloth over the mirrors. Terrified of absolutely everything."

"Wow. I... I'm sorry, I really don't know what to say. That must have been awful for you growing up."

"It certainly isn't something I'd wish for my son. She was only a little younger than I am now when she was diagnosed, and she had me in her 20s, so there was a fair amount of oddness in my childhood. A lot of deadbolts on the gates and hiding under the bed from the *pawbi*."

"What is that?"

"You know, I was never really sure. Some kind of malign wintertime spirit. The best my father and I could gather was that it came in the autumn, spread disease and was gone again by the spring. And that we ought to be desperately afraid of it."

"Sounds like the Nuckelavee."

"Possibly the stories derive from some common root. She was born on Skerry Head."

"Skerry Head?"

"Another island, not 20 miles west of here. It's one of those hilarious coincidences I mentioned."

"Your mom was from around here? That's a pretty big coincidence."

"On the surface, yes. But then, she left when she was a teenager, and it's not a part of the world I've ever visited. Or even given much thought to, before I landed here myself."

"She didn't talk about it?"

"Rarely. And what she did say wasn't always coherent, though I can't say I was always listening that intently. I was conscious even when I was very young that some of the things she came out with were... unreliable."

"My brother was like that for a while."

"He had mental health problems?"

"He drank. Put away a lot of other things, too, but it was the drink that was the real problem. And when he quit, he started seeing things that weren't there. Scared me half to death."

"You looked after him, while he was...?"

"The whole way through. He moved in with me for six months while he detoxed. Didn't do wonders for my relationship, I can tell you."

"This would be the woman you referred to earlier?"

"It was eight years ago. Three or four girlfriends back."

"You were close to him?"

"Very. He's nine years older, but I was all he had, really. He was certainly all I had. Our parents died my sophomore year of college."

It had been early in the morning, she remembered. She'd been eating breakfast; fending off a hangover with a bowl of cereal and a glass of juice she could barely keep down. They'd knocked at the door of her tiny off-campus apartment: patrol officers, a guy and a girl, barely older than she was. She'd seen the uniforms, the black shirts and polished badges, and immediately thought the worst.

She'd assumed, in the seconds before they spoke, that they were there about David: that he'd shot his mouth off at another guy in a bar, picked another fight that had ended in something more serious than a bloody nose and a night in the drunk tank. She'd wondered, in those seconds, why they'd come to her first; why they hadn't gone straight to her parents.

And then the girl had started to speak.

A home invasion, she'd said. And both of them dead, her mom and her dad. Shot.

Both of them? Robin had asked.

I'm sorry, ma'am, the boy had said. I'm afraid so.

Was there anyone they could call for her? the girl had said. A relative? A friend?

No, Robin had said, thinking of David, of how she'd tell him.

And she'd wondered *how* she'd tell him; how she'd *find* him to tell him. Which friend's couch he was staying on that week. Whether he'd even turned his cell on that morning.

They were so sorry to ask, the boy had said, but they'd need somebody to come down to the morgue to formally identify the bodies. Was that something she felt like she was able to do?

No, she'd said, but had gone anyway, riding down to the hospital in the back of the patrol car, the girl at the wheel and the boy sat awkwardly beside her, both of them silent.

They'd shown her the two of them, her mom and her dad, via a video link, their unmoving faces filling the screen one after the other: her mom's not so different than when she was taking a nap or out sunbathing in the yard on weekends; her dad's more beat up, a purple and red sunset of bruises playing out on the yellowing brown of his cheekbones, at the corner of both lips.

He tried to fight them off, she'd thought. Ran at one of them, maybe. And got pistol-whipped in the mouth for his trouble.

That's them, she'd said, her own voice sounding wrong, unfamiliar – someone else's words in someone else's mouth. Those are my parents.

She'd taken a cab back to her apartment, smoked a thick half-joint left over from a Christmas party; left a long voice recording to David's switched-off cell, gone to bed and slept for 14 hours, the covers pulled over her head.

And when finally she'd woken up, she'd seen the missed calls, the text messages from David – asking where she was, what the hell had happened, and why she wasn't answering her phone.

Julia laid her forehead against Robin's.

"That can't have been easy," she said.

"No. But Davey took care of me, mostly. He was a good guy, when he wasn't drinking. A good brother."

She stopped; cut herself off before she could say more.

"Sorry," she said. "Guess my pillow talk isn't so great either."

"My father died last year," said Julia quietly. "Throat cancer initially, though it got everywhere towards the end. I know rationally that my... situation wasn't the reason for it - the man smoked 40 a day for 40 years. But I do wonder if it accelerated things. He deteriorated more rapidly than anyone was expecting after the court case."

"Is your mom still alive?"

"As far as I know. I haven't heard from her in months, for obvious reasons. But when I left, she seemed to be in good hands."

"She has someone with her?"

"She's in a residential facility. A care home. So yes."

"You see her a lot? Before, I mean."

"Once a week, for an hour or two. Sometimes she even remembers who I am."

"Alzheimer's?"

"We're still trying to work that one out. It's hard to tell, with all of her other symptoms. But the memory loss is new. And she never used to be aggressive, even when she was having an episode, so it's safe to assume it's some kind of early-onset dementia."

"Jesus."

"It sounds horrific to say it, I know, but at the moment I'm more concerned about the cost of her care than I am about her condition. She's stable where she is; she's happy, as far as I'm able to tell. But as long as I'm here, the bills aren't getting paid, and I dread to think what would happen if she had to leave."

"There's nobody else to help out?"

"No. Just me."

And then she was crying, too, her face buried in the crook of Robin's neck.

"It's okay," said Robin, for want of something better.

They lay like that for a while, Julia's breathing warm and quick on Robin's skin.

"Sorry," said Julia, after enough time had passed that Robin was starting to wonder if she'd fallen asleep.

"Why are you apologizing, now?"

"That doesn't normally happen around other people."

Robin readjusted the blanket around them.

"It can happen some more," she said. "If you need it to."

Julia settled back against her chest. It was only when she smelled the salt and felt the moisture trickle down between her breasts that Robin realized she was crying again.

They must have slept, because the next thing Robin knew, it was morning, the grey semi-light she'd come to associate with dawn pouring in through a crack in the drapes, and someone was knocking at the door, fast and urgent.

"You should go and see who it is," said Julia, her face half-buried in the mattress.

"I don't think I've ever been this popular in my life," said Robin, easing herself upright and into the cleanest set of clothes she had to hand.

"Should I get up?"

"No. Stay, please."

The knocking continued. Julia smiled at her, more relaxed than Robin had ever seen her; slid lower on the bed and tugged the blanket higher, high enough that it covered her up to the neck. Robin threw her a t-shirt; she caught it, cat-like, as it flew through the air towards her, but made no move to put it on.

Robin moved across to the door; pulled it open a couple of inches, fully expecting to find Jack - or maybe Jack, Bill and Carol - outside in the courtyard.

Instead, she found Sat, swaddled in a thick down jacket, a hiker's backpack slung over one arm. Something was poking out from the top of it, Robin saw; some sort of green metallic tube. A handle, maybe.

Under the coat, her jeans were wet, all the way up past the knee.

"I'm in trouble," she said. "Will you help me?"

The valley girl accent was gone now; her tone harder, business-like.

"What do you need?" said Robin.

"You could let me in. That'd be a good start."

Robin acquiesced, widening the opening in the door enough for her to fit through. Sat cast a look backwards, the kind of furtive over-the-shoulder glance Robin associated with adulterers and movie espionage, and followed her inside, shutting and then locking the door behind her.

She started when she saw Julia, now sitting bolt upright in bed, the t-shirt clutched to her chest.

"Why are you here?" she said.

"I'm fairly sure it isn't me who should be answering that question," said Julia, more imperiously than Robin could have mustered in her shoes.

"She's a friend," said Robin.

She didn't look over at Julia, but she could imagine her expression: the raised eyebrow, the amused half-smile at her use of *friend*.

"Pretty good friend, if she sleeps in your bed," said Sat.

"Are you going to tell me what's going on?" said Robin.

"With *her* here?" said Sat, pointing at Julia.

"*She* can leave, if you'd prefer," said Julia to Robin. She stood up from the bed, the blanket draped around her like a toga.

"No," said Robin. "I want you here."

"I need to tell you some stuff," said Sat, pointedly.

"Then say it," said Robin.

"With Dr Death over there sitting in with us?"

"You of all people should know better than to believe everything you read in the papers," said Julia.

"I guess you two know each other, then?" said Robin.

"No," said Sat.

"Though apparently we know *of* each other," said Julia. "I supported you,

you know," she added to Sat. "All through your court case. I thought it was desperately unfair, what happened to you."

"What happened to you?" said Robin.

"We don't have time for that," said Sat. "*I* don't have time for that."

"Why not?" said Robin.

"Can I trust you?" said Sat, looking right at Julia.

"That really depends on what you're asking," said Julia carefully. "Though I know how to keep my mouth shut, if it's discretion you're after. I'm certainly not going to go running to Hampton about whatever it is you're failing to hide in that rucksack."

Sat seemed to consider her options for a moment.

"Good enough," she said.

She reached backwards, into the backpack, and drew out the stolen hedge cutters from under her floorboards. They were longer, sharper and altogether more dangerous-looking than Robin remembered.

You could do some real damage with those, she thought. If you wanted to.

"I need you to look after these," said Sat to Robin, handing over the cutters with both hands, leaving Robin no choice but to take them. They were heavier even than they looked; the weight of a set of encyclopedias.

"I can't...," said Robin. "You can't just give them to me."

"I have to. They're too big to take with me. They'll slow me down. And I don't wanna just... throw them into the sea. Besides... I thought maybe you could find a use for them."

She looked meaningfully at Robin, silently communicating something that Robin couldn't parse.

"Take them with you where?" said Julia. "Where are you going?"

"They saw me, late last night," said Sat to Robin. "Two of the island guys, out with their horses. They saw me."

"Doing what?" said Robin, fairly sure she already knew the answer.

"Going out. Or under, I guess. Through the hole I made in the cage."

"There's a hole in the cage?" said Julia.

"I took the cellphone," said Sat, ignoring Julia's interruption. "I figured maybe if I took it out far enough away from the wire, I could get *something*, you know? And I stayed where the water's shallow. Where it's *usually* shallow. But today... not so much. It was crazy out there. Waves as high as a house, solid as rock. The kind of high that makes you think of landslides and tsunamis. And there was electricity in the waves, threaded through them - like lightning bolts or something. I thought I was gonna drown out there. Or fry, maybe. Scared the crap out of me, even before I saw the horses."

"You have a *cellphone*?" said Julia.

"Doesn't work," said Sat. "Not anymore."

"Is it the battery?" said Julia.

"I think maybe."

"You should have kept it switched off. It must have worn itself down searching for a signal."

Robin wondered if she was imagining the trace of frustration she heard in Julia's voice; the effort it was taking her to keep that frustration from spilling out in words.

*She could have used it*, she thought. *Could have called her son.*

"The islanders," she asked Sat, "do you think they've told Hampton?"

"Yeah. I mean, I guess so. They rode off when they saw me seeing them."

"If Hampton knows you have these," said Julia, gesturing at the cutters, "then you're not safe here. You have to go, hide yourself somewhere."

"I know," said Sat. "I'm taking off. Like, right now."

"Where?" said Robin.

"I don't know yet. But this is a big place for, you know, a little place. There are a lot of hiding spaces. A lot of grottos out by the beach."

"Not there," said Robin, remembering her dream, seeing Chuck's body broken and bleeding by the mouth of the cave. "Somewhere else."

"Okay," said Sat, not understanding. "Not a grotto. Somewhere else, then."

"There's an empty crofter's cottage, out to the east," said Julia. "It's not far from the jetty. The ship's crew used to use it as a storeroom, before the island people took over the unloading. I've never seen anyone go in or out of it. You should be safe in there until you work out what you're going to do next."

"How do you know that?" said Robin.

"I know this island," said Julia. "I've walked just about every square inch of it, these last few months."

"Thanks," said Sat, hauling the backpack onto her shoulders.

Julia nodded.

"Good luck," she said.

"You're leaving now?" said Robin.

"Have to," said Sat. "It's not gonna look good for you if they find me in here, right? For *either* of you."

"She's right," said Julia, resting a hand in the small of Robin's back.

"Take care of yourselves, alright?" said Sat, unlocking the door. "Murder aside - there's some weird shit going on in this place. Some *seriously* weird shit."

# CHAPTER 16

These feel like they might be more of a curse than a blessing," said Robin once Sat had gone, gesturing down at the cutters.

"Do you know where you'll put them?" said Julia. She was fully dressed now, hair smoothed and pulled back and shirt buttoned; as neat and put-together as she'd been when she'd arrived on Robin's doorstep the night before.

Ready for the boardroom, Robin thought again. Or the courtroom, maybe.

"Long term?" she said. "No. Bury them in the sand, maybe? But for now..."

She walked across to the closet and pulled out an open suitcase, half-filled with shirts and underwear; the closest thing she had to a clothes basket, since Hampton had taken away her laundry bag. She dropped the cutters inside, arranging the shirts around them as padding; zipped up the case, dragged it back into the closet and closed the door.

"Do you think she'll be alright out there?" she said, collapsing onto the couch.

"If Hampton finds her?" said Julia, sitting down next to her. "I really don't know. As you said: he isn't a man who likes loose ends. And communicating with the mainland... that's a pretty substantial loose end. But she's a resourceful girl. If there's a way off the island that isn't stowing away on a cargo boat or diving headlong into the sea, then I'm sure she'll find it."

"Why do you think that? That she's resourceful?"

"Beyond the mobile phone and the concealed weapon?"

"Yeah. You said you knew her - knew *of* her. What do you know?"

"Only what everyone else does. No more than you do, I should think."

"I only met her this week. I really don't know anything about her."

Julia shifted position on the couch; turned to look at Robin, incredulous.

"You hadn't heard of her before now?" she said. "I find that very difficult to believe."

"I've been actively avoiding any real news these last couple of... years, I guess. So let's assume I'm not up on my current affairs. Who is she? What did she do?"

"You really don't know, do you?"

"No, I don't know! Are you going to tell me?"

"Yes. Of course. It's just so strange to think you don't know her."

"Spit it out, Julia. Who is she?"

"She's... well, I suppose you'd call her a programmer. A software designer. For Medida."

"The ones who came up with the algorithm?"

"Yes. She created their sentiment analysis engine. I'm sure she wouldn't see it this way, but... she's the reason we're here, on the island. All of us."

Sat was a clever child, Julia told her - graduating high school at 14, and Stanford at 18 with a BS in Symbolic Systems, Summa Cum Laude.

She was headhunted straight out of college by a mid-size startup called Pharmakon - the brainchild of a cognitive psychologist, Ellis Yu, and Malcolm Trieste, an applied mathematician with an interest in appraisal theory. Within 6 months, she'd been placed into their product development team; 18 months on, she was leading it.

Three years into working there, the partners tasked her with a side-project: producing a software concept, a next-generation opinion mining tool able to detect and catalogue specific emotions as expressed in not just digital spaces but physical spaces too, harvesting data from conversations across public and private spheres – plucking conversation threads out of everywhere from security cameras and telephones to home entertainment devices and restaurant payment systems, as well as the social media and online message board channels more traditionally used by sentiment-analysis tech.

The potential corpus was enormous, the reach of the tool unprecedented, and she found herself excited by the challenge: of doing it, and doing it right.

She had ethical concerns, even in the early days - about surveillance and panopticonism, about invasion of privacy. But they were easily dealt with: even if the program worked, she told herself (and she wasn't sure then that even she could pull it off), a truly dystopian application, one that saw the program used to log and interpret every word spoken, every keystroke logged - it would rely on a necessary interoperability, a willingness to co-operate on the part of different systems, to share access, share data. Valuable data. And no-one - no payment provider, no smart-home maker, no cellphone network - would go for it. Not out of fear of breaching data protection laws - she wasn't a political animal back then, but even she knew that they were meaningless. No: because nobody, anywhere - no provider, no manufacturer, no network - would ever willingly share sensitive information on its customers with competitors. There was no profit in it; it would make no business sense.

In real world terms, its full application was unworkable.

She raised this latter point with the partners.

Don't worry, they told her: we're not expecting anyone to buy it or use it. Not yet; not in this iteration. We just want to show its capabilities - *our* capabilities. Then, once we've done that, we can set to work on adapting the software into something marketable.

It's an exercise, they told her. This is our concept car. We're not offering something pragmatic - we're showing what's possible. Testing the limits of the technology.

Why would we do that? she said.

So everyone knows we're the best, they told her. You want people to know we're the best, right?

She agreed that she did. And then she set to work.

(Later, in the witness box at her trial, she would castigate herself for her naivety, her stupidity; would quote Robert Oppenheimer and Hannah Arendt on the banality of evil; would advocate for a new ethics of tech design while admitting her own culpability, the pleasure she took at the time in making something new, making it work).

She was uncharacteristically vague, afterwards, about how she got it done so quickly - how she'd taken the project, apparently single-handed, from nebulous idea to functional code in less than a year. She was fast as well as smart - that much was public knowledge. But even by the standards she'd set for herself, it was a remarkable achievement.

The code was previewed to more senior members of the Pharmakon team, to widespread enthusiasm and much enthusiastic high-fiving. Ellis and Malcolm were ecstatic. She was pretty happy herself.

And then one day, not long after, Ellis and Malcolm gathered all of Pharmakon together, and announced that they were selling the company.

Nobody saw it coming. There been no reason to suggest it might be: no structural changes, no budget cuts, no water cooler gossip.

They were selling, they said, to Trip – a social networking and software development behemoth up in Mountain View, one with a reputation for corporate malfeasance, a propensity to sell its customers' data to the highest bidder and (there were whispers) access to a regular stream of dark

162

money from an unknown backer with deeper pockets and more extensive connections even than Trip itself.

Several of the team handed in their resignations on the spot at the latter disclosure; others left later and more discreetly, scattering to machine learning labs and biotech accelerators across the West Coast.

As one of her colleagues put it as he packed up his desk: they signed up for the Rebel Alliance, and they got the Empire. They weren't going to stick around to help build the Death Star.

She *did* stick around, though. Partly through inertia, partly through curiosity about how the whole thing would play out - and partly through naked greed, unvarnished self-interest.

(Immediately after their announcement - while the others were loudly voicing their protests or quietly devising their exit strategies - Ellis and Malcolm had pulled her away into a meeting room and closed the door.

I'm out, Ellis said. I'm retiring.

And I don't *know* what I'm going to do next, said Malcolm. But I'm out, too.

Okay, she said, not sure where they were heading. Why are you telling me this, here?

They looked at each other.

Because someone will need to run this place, they said. And we can't think of anyone better).

The new job came with a 70% pay raise and the opportunity to turn the side-project into her main responsibility - refining the code, weeding out the bugs.

As Chief Product Officer, she reported in to Trip's Head of Special Projects - an older, kind-eyed white man named John Holland who reminded her a little of her grandfather and a little of Colonel Sanders, and who alternated unconditional support for her ideas with a rigorous critique that kept her sharp and pushed her thinking in a hundred new directions.

Around her, Pharmakon began to change shape, as she'd expected it would: ditching its name and rebranding as Medida, updating contracts, refurbishing the office, replacing the guys who'd left with transfers from across the wider Trip group. Few of the changes affected her directly; those that did (the switch to open-plan workspaces, the relative inflexibility around working hours) were resolved painlessly with minor concessions on both sides. By and large, she got what she wanted. She was happy.

Her first inkling that something might be wrong came during a catch-up session with Holland. The program, by then nicknamed A-FECT, was close to finished; as good, she thought, as she was going to get it. From her perspective, it was ready to launch.

Are you sure? he asked her, kind eyes uncharacteristically threaded with anxiety.

Totally, she said. It's, like, good to go.

We have to be sure, he said. It's a government contract. We can't just package it up and leave it to the marketing men to fix the problems. It has to be perfect.

A government contract? she said. What government contract?

He was surprised she didn't know already; had assumed that Ellis and Malcolm had filled her in before they left.

No, she said, doing her best to keep a lid on her unease. They didn't tell me.

So Holland filled her in instead.

A-FECT, he said, was the sole motivation for Trip's acquisition of the company. From the moment they'd heard of it, they knew that they wanted it - had understood its potential, its reach. How easy it would be, with their existing government connections, to sell it on to law enforcement, to the intelligence services. Their own, and other countries'.

(Government connections? she'd asked. What government connections? He hadn't answered).

With the Pharmakon purchase completed, selling on A-FECT – the *promise* of A-FECT – was exactly what they'd done. And the buyers - all the acronyms agencies she'd ever heard of, and a few foreign ones besides - were eager to start playing with their new toy.

For surveillance, she said. It wasn't a question.

What else? he said, grandfather-brows furrowing.

She bit her tongue for the rest of the meeting: smiling when she needed to, laughing at his jokes. Inside, she was screaming.

(I just kept thinking, she said on the stand: how can I stop this? What can I do, to make this not be happening?

I wish now I'd just done something to the program, you know? Just taken out a chunk of code. Rewritten it. Made it *not work*, somehow.

But it didn't even occur to me.

I guess on some level, I couldn't bring myself to do it. To even think about breaking something that beautiful.

It was my *baby*, right? I'd, like, created it. Grown it out of nothing.

And even though I knew what it was, knew what it could do - what it was going to do - I didn't want it *gone*.

Locked up, totally - it needed to be put away, somewhere safe, somewhere it couldn't hurt anyone.

But it was my baby. I wasn't gonna send it to the chair).

She was up all night that night, trying to figure out what to do, how to stop the thing she'd set in motion.

A-FECT couldn't go to the government, she knew that. In the wrong hands - and she couldn't imagine hands *more* wrong - it was the stuff of science fiction, way beyond any of the dystopian scenarios she'd imagined at the outset; a fast track to a police state. A *world* of police states.

The sale was already done and dusted; no chance of stopping *that*.

But maybe there was something she could do. Some other way out of the woods.

She went into the Medida building early the next morning; earlier than she ever had, even in the early days, when she and Malcolm and Ellis were working to launch dates so insane she thought she'd stroke out at her desk, when she'd smoke through packs of cigarettes just so the coughing would keep her awake.

There was nobody around but the night guard, who waved at her as she passed through the security checkpoint. Upstairs, the office was empty.

Since the Trip buyout, the rule was: you don't take anything home. Whatever you're working on - it stays in the office, under lock and key.

The station she wanted - the one she knew held the one finished copy of the A-FECT code - was under the tightest security Medida could provide: in a safe room, past an EEG scanner, behind a Faraday shield.

(Only much, much later would she appreciate the irony of the last measure).

There were three people in the building, that she knew of, with access to the safe room. She was one of them.

She wouldn't talk about how exactly she did it, afterwards: how she managed to transfer the code from the station to the Medida cloud, and from the cloud to her personal devices. But by 9am that morning, all trace of it had been wiped from the Medida systems, and a portion of code - one she figured, she said later, probably couldn't do a lot of harm on its own - had been delivered, with an anonymous explanatory note, to the desks of four privacy campaigners, three non-profits and the technology editors of six coastal newspapers.

Vanderhalden owns Trip, thought Robin, flashing back to her first conversation with Bill and Carol. Trip owns Medida. And Medida owns the algorithm.

It's a closed circuit.

"She's a whistleblower?" she said.

"*The* whistleblower," said Julia. "By all rights, she should be rotting in a federal prison somewhere. It was a government contract she stole; government secrets. When they finally caught her, they charged her with treason."

"But she got off?"

"Not exactly. The trial collapsed. Something to do with one of the jurors communicating with the press. They had to declare a mistrial."

"And Trip got the code back."

"They never lost it. John Holland had made a copy: only one of them, but one he kept outside the office on his private system. I suppose he thought that some rules were worth breaking. They rolled out the algorithm here and in the States less than a month after she was first arrested."

"Is there an antonym of serendipity? Jesus."

"Though why they're focusing on policing outrage, rather than something to do with, I don't know, national security... that, I couldn't tell you. Perhaps outrage is a dry run for something else - something more serious, more substantial. Perhaps the algorithm is still in beta."

"All of this must have happened a while ago, right? I mean, the whole system's been up and running for, what, a year now?"

"It did. I remember following it all on news while my own... situation was ongoing. Her initial case was very drawn out. Took an age to get to trial. I assume the prosecutors involved needed time to gather their evidence."

Robin opened her mouth to reply, and noticed, to her acute embarrassment, that she'd edged closer to Julia as they'd been talking; had, without knowing she was doing it, laid her head back against the cushions and slung her legs across Julia's lap, with the result that they looked, to an outside observer, like a long-married couple, catching up on the couch after a day at the office.

Accelerated intimacy in action, she thought.

"Why is she here, then?" she said, swinging her legs back to the ground with what she hoped was some degree of subtlety. "How did she go from treason to... outrage, or whatever it is she's meant to have incited?"

"She was very polarizing," said Julia, adjusting her posture. "I told you I supported what she did; I still do. But a lot of people didn't, Americans especially. There's nothing quite like the word traitor to get the patriots frothing at the bit."

You got that right, she thought – remembering the red-faced man on the courthouse steps, the string of saliva hitting her lawyer's sports coat.

"I can't believe I haven't heard of her before," she said.

"You should turn on your television occasionally," said Julia, smiling. "And you're welcome to put your legs back where they were, unless you prefer them down there."

Robin blushed; felt the heat creep up her neck, onto her cheeks and forehead.

"Do you really think it's a coincidence?" she said, pulling her feet back onto the couch, onto Julia.

"That what is?"

"All of us and Vanderhalden."

"Vanderhalden? I don't follow."

"They own Trip. *They're* the dark money – *they're* where the connections came from."

Julia looked thoughtful for a moment. Then she smiled, ruefully.

"Of course they do," she said. "Makes perfect sense. I should have seen it before, really."

"You're not surprised?" said Robin.

"Perhaps not as much as I ought to be. I knew they had tech interests. And we all heard rumors about them and Trip, back when they bought us out. I just didn't put it together with the Medida purchase."

"Okay. Now you know for sure – *do* you think it's a coincidence?"

"The island and Medida? Of course not. I daresay it was all very deliberately orchestrated. Anything to swell the coffers."

"Not that. *Us.* All of us, now, being here on the island."

"What do you mean?"

"Sat pisses Vanderhalden off - she ends up here. Your lab runs into trouble and brings them a barrel-load of bad publicity - you end up here. Carol goes digging into their acquisitions - she ends up here. You can't need me to tell you there's a pattern there."

"Is that why Carol Bannister's here? Interesting. I thought perhaps she'd written something inflammatory in that column of hers."

There was contempt there, Robin thought. She wondered what kind of *column* it was that Carol wrote; what that column might have said about Julia, once upon a time.

"It can't be an accident," she said. "There's something more going on, something bigger."

"So you do believe in conspiracies," said Julia.

"I don't know. But three total strangers all get under the skin of the evil empire in completely different ways, and they all end up together in the same place, precisely because of that empire's technology... that doesn't feel suspicious to you?"

"It might, if it were only the three of us on this island. But it isn't. There are people here for all kinds of absurd reasons, all kinds of ridiculous transgressions, none of them anything at all to do with Vanderhalden. Unless you want to tell me that your friend Jack once set fire to their head office, or that cat in the dustbin belonged to John Holland and his wife."

"I don't know. I don't know what I'm trying to say. But there's something."

"I think perhaps..."

There was a flurry of noise outside: hoofbeats, a lot of them, pounding and clattering over the cobbles.

"Do you hear that?" said Robin, bolting up from the couch.

"I'm not deaf," said Julia, with a touch of the sharpness Robin had seen the first time they'd met. "Yes, I hear it."

"Should we go out there?"

"And fly headlong *into* danger?"

"What if it's Sat?"

"On horseback?"

The sounds intensified, suggesting movement almost immediately outside the door. There were voices now, too; low and murmured, indecipherable over the clatter of the horses.

"I'm going out there," she said, pulling on her shoes.

"Are you mad?" said Julia, tugging at her sleeve to spin her around. "Are you *trying* to attract their attention? Attract *Hampton's* attention, if he's there with them?"

"It could be Sat out there. I need to know."

"And do what? You can't go out there. He's already threatened you once - the *last* thing you ought to do is give him cause to do it again."

She stepped to one side, still holding Robin's sleeve, and then backwards, until she was blocking the door.

"Get out of my way," said Robin, grabbing at her arm for leverage.

Julia stared at her, open-mouthed; face flushed, somewhere between anger and frustration. They stood together in front of the door for perhaps half a minute like human statues frozen mid-way through a waltz: touching, not moving.

"I'll go," said Julia eventually; still watching her, still holding on.

"What?"

"Stay here. I'll go and see what's going on."

"I thought it was too dangerous?"

"It is. But whatever danger there is, it's likely greater for you than it is for me. Hampton doesn't care who *I* am or what *I* see."

The hoofbeats quietened - coming to a stop, Robin thought, rather than moving away.

"And if it's her?" she said, dropping her voice to a whisper. "If it's Sat, out there with them?"

"Then," said Julia, equally softly, "I very likely won't be able to do anything. But at least you'll know."

Robin looked back at her, wanting to argue. Nothing came.

"Move away from the door," said Julia evenly.

She stepped backwards, her eyes still on Julia - long, deep strides that took her across the room to the edge of the mattress. Watched her turn the door handle; watched her step out into the courtyard and close the door behind her. Then she listened, waited, counting breaths in fours and eights and sevens until the hoofbeats picked back up again, striking loud - unbearably loud - on the cobbles and then fading away.

One, two, three breaths and the door opened, just enough for Julia to slip back inside.

She looked pale, Robin thought; two shades lighter than she'd been even 10 minutes earlier.

"They have her," she said quietly. "I don't know how they got her, but they have her."

# CHAPTER 17

What did you see?" said Robin.

"They had her on the back of one of the horses," said Julia, unsteady. "I couldn't see well, but I think her hands were tied - there was some sort of plastic wrapping holding her wrists together."

"What was she doing out there?"

"She must have gone back to her flat for something. It looked as if they'd found her there."

"Was Hampton with her?"

"No. Just the island men. Three of them. But they looked organized. It seems safe to assume they were following his orders."

"Where did they take her?"

"I don't know."

"Well, which direction were they headed in?"

"I don't know! Away from the beach. Towards the village, maybe."

"If they're taking her to Hampton, he'll kill her."

"We can't be sure of that."

"I think it's a pretty fair conclusion, don't you? He's already made a bunch of other people disappear. Or if he hasn't, he's been covering up for whoever has. She was the one who *told* me that, for Christ's sake."

"I have to sit down."

"Sit *down*? Now? We have to move."

"To go where, exactly?"

"After them. After her."

"And what do you propose we do once we catch up to them? *If* we catch up to them. They have animals. Possibly weapons - I know for a fact that Hampton keeps a gun in his satchel. And even if he didn't, we're *prisoners* here. We have no way of getting off this island without his say-so. Think about it, please. We have to be sensible."

"We have a weapon, too. Or did you forget?"

She walked across to the closet; opened the suitcase and pulled out the cutters.

"You aren't seriously thinking about using those?" said Julia.

Robin drew out a backpack of her own from the back of the closet; the one she'd originally packed with the handful of books she'd chosen to see her through her sentence. It was bigger than Sat's, and sturdier; more camping equipment than accessory. Before now, she'd only ever brought it out for weekends in the mountains.

The cutters fit inside with room to spare. She slid her arms into the straps; tied the buckle at her waist. With the weight distributed, it was a lot less heavy than she'd been expecting. She'd be able to move in it, she thought. Maybe even move quickly, if she needed to.

"We have to be sensible," Julia repeated.

"You don't think we have an obligation to help her?"

"I think if we go charging in after her, there'll be consequences."

*So we should stop trying?* said David's voice in her head. *Just roll over and let them do whatever they want to us?*

"I'm going," she said, moving towards the door.

"I'm not," said Julia.

"You're not?"

"I'm sorry."

"Are you that fucking spineless now?" she said, her blood rising. "What happened to *you stay here, I'll fix it*?"

"My son," said Julia, not looking at Robin. "I can't do that to him. Bad enough that I'm here at all. I can't leave him without one of his mothers."

Robin looked over at her; saw the guilt radiating off her, the shame at having to make the decision. She felt her own anger recede, retract back into her veins.

"Lock the door behind me," she said more gently.

"You're going?"

"Yeah. But you don't have to."

"Robin."

Julia stepped forward, closing the gap between them.

"It's not safe," she said, reaching for Robin's hands.

"No," said Robin, letting herself be touched. "You're right. It's not."

She thought about running; taking off in the direction of the standing stones at a sprint, to try to make up whatever ground she could between her and the horses as they rode away. But as she walked out into the quad and saw the other riders, posted like Praetorian Guard between the apartments, she thought better of it, and settled into a slower pace, one more appropriate for an early-morning amble over the grassland.

They looked down on her as she passed them, faces hardening into contempt.

They're pissed, she thought. Even more than usual.

*Wouldn't you be?* said David's voice in her head. *They got colonized. They live under a fucking fishing net. And now they have to pull babysitting duty, too?*

When did you start talking to me like this? she thought. When did you start to colonise *me*, Davey?

She kept her head low, her hands in her pockets; trying to fade into the background, to seem too unremarkable to warrant close scrutiny, even with the backpack over her shoulders. She dropped her eyes to the floor; concentrated on her feet hitting the cobbles as she walked.

A few feet away, one of the apartment doors opened with a bang. She jumped, but didn't look up.

"Hey!" said Jack, from behind her. "Hey, Robin! Wait."

She turned around; saw him staggering towards her. He'd looked bad the last time she'd seen him; today he looked worse, as if he'd aged a decade overnight: the lines cutting even deeper into his mouth and forehead, the dark circles under his eyes turning the red of burst blood vessels. He'd slept in his clothes, the same ones she'd seen him in the day before.

Be casual, she thought.

*And get rid of him*, said David. *Unless you want to take him with you?*

"Hey," she said. "You just come from Bill and Carol's?"

"I was coming to get you," he said, lightly accusing. "You said you weren't going to go anywhere."

"I didn't," she said. "I've been in my room the whole night."

"But you're here now."

"I needed a walk. Walls were starting to close in on me a little."

He looked up and down.

"What are you carrying?" he said.

She changed course, leading them away from the islanders, out of earshot. She'd have to circle back to the standing stones, she thought, once she'd shaken him off.

"A change of clothes," she said quietly. "In case it rains. I got soaked to the skin last time."

"You shouldn't go out there on your own."

"It's daytime. It's fine."

She pointed upward - to the faint white-grey light streaming in through the mesh.

"Doesn't mean it's a good idea," he said. "We still need to be careful."

"I'm being careful. I swear."

"Where are you going?"

"Just... around."

"Want some company?"

"I'm good, I think."

He followed her anyway, trailing a half a foot behind her as she took a wide circle around the perimeter of the quad, eventually pointing them in the direction she needed to be moving.

"Where are we going?" he said suspiciously, once they'd cleared the quad altogether and were crossing the grassland - the outlines of the standing stones up ahead of them, far in the distance.

He's not leaving, she thought. And I don't have time for this.

*Do you trust him?* said David.

Yes, she thought. I mean, he's not of totally sound mind right now, and he thinks there's some kind of mythological monster chasing after him, and he's detoxing, and the sleep deprivation probably isn't helping his cause. But yes, I trust him. He has my back.

*Then tell him,* said David. *Who knows? He might even help you.*

"I need to go the village," she said.

He flinched, stiffened; twisted his body away from her, as if she were an electric fence he'd forgotten too late he wasn't meant to touch.

"After what we saw yesterday?" he said. "You can't want to do that."

"I don't *want* to," she said. "But I have to."

"Why? Why the hell would you *have to*?"

*Tell him,* said David.

"Do you know a girl called Sat?" she said. "Kind of young, lot of piercings, tattoo all the way up her arm?"

177

"You mean Sat Lakhani? The A-FECT girl? Sure. Everybody knows her."

Everybody but me, thought Robin.

"What about her?" he said. "What does she have to do with anything?"

"I think she's in there," said Robin.

"In the village?"

"Yeah. And not out of choice."

"Fuck. Someone took her there?"

"Yeah."

"Who? One of the island people?"

*You don't have to tell him everything*, said David. *Just enough. Stick to what you know, not what you suspect. You could still be wrong, right?*

"A few of them," said Robin. "This morning. Bundled her up onto a horse and rode off with her."

"Oh my God. Have you told somebody? Have you told Hampton?"

"No. I... I just saw it happen, out in the courtyard. I couldn't find him. I called out for him, but nobody came. And I can't just leave her."

I just lied to him, she thought. Lied to him outright.

*He'd understand*, said David. *If he knew the whole story, he'd be okay with it.*

"Fuck," said Jack. "He must be out on the mainland with the police, or something."

"Probably."

"Those bastards. They must have known he'd be gone when they took her. You know they hate us. I bet they've been planning it, picking their moment."

"I don't know," said Robin, honestly.

He stopped; seemed to think about something for a moment.

"Why didn't you tell me right away?" he said. "When I asked what you were doing before, you said you were out for a walk."

*He'd understand*, said David again, though she wasn't sure she believed it.

"There were more of them in the courtyard," she said. "Didn't you see them? Islanders, right outside the apartments, watching. I didn't want to risk saying something if there was any chance of them hearing it."

He chewed over the answer.

"Makes total sense," he said. "But I wish you'd come got me before."

"It just happened. Maybe 20 minutes ago. I didn't know *what* to do."

He pulled her in for a hug. It only exacerbated her guilt.

"We'll get her back," he said. "If Hampton can't help us, we'll work it out ourselves. I'll go get Bill and Carol, see if they can round up some of the other guys they know, and we'll go... storm the battlements, or something."

"No!" she said - quickly, too quickly. "We can't. You can't get them involved."

"Why not? We can't just go in there by ourselves. We'll need help. Backup."

"They're watching the courtyard," she said, improvising. "The islanders. We do that, and they'll notice. They'll know something's wrong. Nothing's more likely to tip them off than a big group of us heading up here together."

"Oh, man. You're right."

"And besides - we don't have time to go back. They have her now. We can't afford to waste even another half hour."

*That part's true enough*, said David.

"Okay," said Jack.

"Okay yes?"

"Yeah. But we're gonna need to be careful, going in there. They can't see us coming."

This isn't right, she thought. I'm putting him in danger.

*What's funny*, said David, *is you think he wasn't in danger already.*

In the end, there was no need for them to worry about being seen. The village was deserted: no people, no horses, no signs of life. And maybe *village* wasn't the word for it, she thought. The buildings - what buildings there were

179

- were arranged haphazardly; a thin strung-out line of them leading out to another section of beach, another stretch of sand and water ending in the familiar mesh of wire and beyond it, beating an arpeggio down on the metal, the frustrated waves of the open sea.

"Are you sure this is the place?" said Jack, as they followed the crumbling drystone wall past the first set of buildings - what looked like cottages, square single-storeys made of grey slate and another material, darker and rougher, one that made Robin think of charcoal and volcanic rock. The same light mist that speckled the other parts of the island hung in the air, wetting their faces, making the sloping roofs of the cottages glisten like seaweed on sand.

She imagined how it must look from overhead, caught up in the cage's mesh: like a scene from a snow globe, viewed through opaque glass.

"Positive," she said.

"Then where the hell *is* everybody?"

She shrugged, and they walked on, past other cottages and what could have been a stable block. There was hay on the ground, forming a rough winding path through the village, straw mixed in with a semi-dry clay that clung to their shoes. The air smelled worse here than anywhere else she'd been on the island - thick and animal, a concentrated version of the rotten meat-and-salt stink she'd noticed the first day she'd gone down to the beach.

The last building was different than the others: an unstable-looking wooden structure built on low-lying stilts. A house on legs – hammered into the sand, marking the space where land met water.

"That's not gonna stay up for long," said Jack, appraising the back of the building with a professional eye.

"Maybe it's meant to be temporary," she said.

They approached it cautiously, walking around to the front to take the ten rickety steps leading up to the entrance on tiptoes. There was no door, just a wide empty doorframe. The floorboards creaked and groaned underneath them as they moved inside.

"Nothing here," said Jack, taking in the bare walls and empty space. If it ever was anything, she thought - a storeroom, a prayer room, even a house - there was no way of deducing that *anything* from the evidence left in front of them.

"Looks like it," she said.

"We should probably... Wait, what *is* that? Is that blood?"

He followed his line of sight to an area of floorboard in the corner, one darker than the rest even in the grey island light, something red-black staining the wood in pools and spatters.

"It could be anything," she said, uneasily.

He walked carefully over to the staining; bent down and examined it, then licked his fingers, dipped them in the largest pool of colour, brought them to his nose and sniffed.

"It's blood," he said.

"How do you know?"

"Smells like iron and hamburger meat."

"Doesn't this whole place smell like that?"

He opened his mouth to reply, then stopped, angling his head to the side as if hearing something.

"Someone's coming," he said.

She listened; tuning into the rattle of approaching horses, of hoofbeats negotiating the dirt path, moving towards them.

*A whole pack of them, it sounds like*, said David.

There was another sound, too; something that sounded like wheels turning, a metallic clink of chains hitting hard earth.

"We have to leave," she said.

"They'll see us," he said.

"Not if we go now."

The sounds were growing; getting louder, closer.

*They're coming this way*, said David. *You're out of time.*

"Get back," she said. "Out of the light."

She ran across the room, cognizant of every footstep: every shudder of floorboard, every snap of shoe leather on wood. She unbuckled the backpack, laid it on the ground beside her and flattened her body – her back, her arms, the palms of her hands – against the wall immediately beside the doorframe; keeping her in darkness, out of sight, but affording her a view of the beach, the strip of sea.

Jack followed suit, coming to rest next to her against the wall, the tread of his boots loud enough to make her wince.

"What now?" he whispered, already breathing hard - out of fear or exertion, she didn't know.

"We wait. Maybe they're not coming all the way over."

*Sure they are*, said David. *Don't you hear that? They're already on the sand.*

Seconds passed, maybe a minute, the hoofbeats merging with the crack of the waves to form a single unbroken roar, and then she saw the riders: ten of them, at least, racing towards the water in an inverted V formation, the front two horses pulling behind them an open wooden cart that made her think of covered wagons and Amish buggies and 19th century agriculture, the technologies of other times and places.

The lead horses came to rest at the edge of the shore, bringing the cart to a stop behind them. Their two riders dismounted; walked across to the cart and pulled something free of it, a rectangular plywood box that seemed to Robin very like a coffin.

They hoisted the box onto their shoulders, pallbearer-style, and carried it down from the cart, bringing it to rest on the sand beside the water.

The other riders followed, jumping smoothly down from their horses and forming a loose semi-circle around the box.

Not one of the horses moved a muscle.

One of the pallbearers reached inside his jacket and brought out a ring of knotted green flowers, something like a lei or a skinny Christmas wreath, and laid it on top of the box. The second pallbearer drew back his shoulders, straightened his back and started to chant, a rapid string of guttural consonants in the island language that sounded, or so Jack had told her, a little like Icelandic.

Are we watching some kind of funeral rite? she wondered. Is this how they bury their dead? By sending them off into the water?

*Wouldn't get too far,* said David. *Not with all that wire in the way.*

The second pallbearer - the one she'd started to think of as the priest - stopped chanting. Another of the riders, seeming to take this as her cue, reached down and pulled the wreath from the box and laid it down on the surface of the water. Then she pulled back the lid of the box, and stepped away.

Two other riders stepped forward, raised the box a few feet in the air and turned it upside down, dislodging its contents into the water.

She was horrified, but not surprised to see that it was a human body, naked and stiff.

*Not just a body,* said David. *Look closer.*

"Holy shit, Robin," said Jack, voice straining under the pressure to stay quiet. "The body. It's Chuck."

He'd been cleaned, she saw; most of the blood was gone, although the wounds and bruises were visible even from a distance. One of his legs jutted out from his body at an unnatural angle, the fracture in the bone unhealed.

She thought she might vomit, or pass out, but in the end did neither. Instead she kept watching, appalled but hypnotized, entirely unable to tear her eyes away from the scene.

With the cage acting as a barricade against the waves, there was little tide in the enclosed area of sea. The body didn't drift far; just stayed, afloat, on the water.

The riders watched it. If they spoke at all, Robin didn't hear them.

And then the water broke.

When, later, she tried to describe it (even to herself), the best she could manage was: it parted. Seemed to split, somehow. And from the parting, from the place that wasn't land and wasn't water, *something* rose up.

Jack had been both right and wrong when he'd called it a horse. Like the statues in the chapel, it had the same shape, albeit drawn to a larger scale: the same thick, muscular body; the same four legs; the same long equine snout. But the proportions were all wrong, distorting the familiar into something entirely alien - the legs too long, the tail too thin, the neck too short, the cloven hooves more goat- than horse-like. Its pupils glowed red, the eyeballs bulging out from the sides of its head like the compound eyes of an insect. It was entirely skinless, red tendons and black arteries crisscrossing against blueish muscle and, in places, grey and yellow bone.

A human head and torso burst up from its midsection, bald and flayed, its eyes closed. Its arms, too, were out of proportion - too long and too thin for the body they grew from, trailing downwards, fingers scraping the surface of the water.

It smelled, she knew, like death; like brine, and rotting meat.

*The Nuckelavee*, said David.

It raised its head - the horse head - into the air and stepped forward, the water parting for it as it moved. When it came close to Chuck, it paused; looked down at the body with its insect eyes, tail swaying obscenely back and forth.

The riders waited, expectant.

And it kept walking: kicked the body out of the way (*guess it didn't want what's on the menu*, said David) and trotted forward onto the sand, towards the riders, who fell to their knees in what couldn't be read as anything other than supplication.

It ignored them; carried on walking, the same measured pace, past the cart and inland, towards the village. Towards her and Jack.

As it came closer to the wooden house, approaching it from a side angle that brought it into sharper view from her position by the doorway, it raised its head again, its wide nostrils flaring, and she was sure, somewhere inside her escalating panic, that it was *smelling* them, somehow, picking up their scent on the static air.

It turned its head to one side and fixed an eye on the doorway; on her.

"Run," she said to Jack, not bothering to lower her voice. "Now."

She unflattened herself from the wall; picked - with a presence of mind that would surprise her, later - the rucksack and the cutters up from the floor and sprinted down the rickety steps, hearing the wood splinter under her feet as she ran.

The thing - the Nuckelavee - was on her left, the islanders right behind it, so she went right, veering away from the village and down the beach, along the sand. Jack followed after her, keeping close, his breath coming harder than ever.

She was fast, she knew - had always been able to run fast, even as a kid, even when running fast served no practical purpose when all she wanted was to stay in her room with a bunch of old movies and a dog-eared copy of *Rebecca* - but the thing was faster, it had to be. She looked behind her, just for half a second, and saw that it was running now, too; not a full-blown gallop but a canter, closing the gap between them effortlessly, lazily.

It doesn't need to try, she thought. It has us; it's already won.

"We need to speed up," she said to Jack, forcing her muscles forward, straightening her legs to lengthen her stride.

"I can't," he said, barely able to get the words out.

He's not going to make it, she thought.

She turned her head again, another half-second, and saw she was right. His face was bright red; one of his hands was pressed against his chest, fighting off a side stitch or worse.

She looked up ahead; saw the sand narrow to a vanishing point as the path curved, a cluster of rocks, and something else, a collection of stone and brick - something, if she squinted, that might have been a building.

*There's an empty crofter's cottage*, Julia had said. *Out to the east.*

"There," she said, pointing at it, hoping he could see, would understand what she meant. That his muscles would respond to the presence of it, even temporarily.

She pressed harder; ran faster.

But not fast enough. She could hear it now, maybe thirty feet behind them, its strange hoofbeats bludgeoning the ground.

"I can't," said Jack again. And stopped running - falling to his knees like the riders, body bent in the same gesture of supplication, breath coming in rattling wheezes.

"Get up!" she said, screaming, pulling at his arms, kicking the sand out from under his legs.

And the thing moved closer; its own pace slowing, the insect eyes now regarding them with what might have been curiosity.

It knows it's won, she thought again.

"Go," said Jack, barely audible. "Robin. Go."

It was almost on them now, barely six feet from where Jack was kneeling. The stench of it was suffocating, unbearable, burning what little oxygen was left in her lungs to a crisp.

"Go," he repeated.

She saw it snarl; pull back its bloody lips, baring the razor points of its teeth. Saw it rear back on its hind legs, ready to strike.

And she ran.

# CHAPTER 18

**From:** l.webber@specialprojects.vanderhalden.com
**To:** c.lee@specialprojects.vanderhalden.com
**Re:** Salt Rock Construction Bids

Carl,

I'm reviewing the bids for the construction work on Salt Rock, and I've noticed that we're missing some paperwork.

Can you confirm that *all* contractors from *all* shortlisted agencies have submitted signed non-disclosure agreements along with their agencies' bids?

(And I do mean *all* contractors - not just the foremen and the project managers. We need everyone who's ever likely to set foot on that island under airtight NDA: every welder, every carpenter, every handyman. We can't afford loose ends here, as I'm sure you're well aware).

Can you also confirm that the schematics for the pen have been run past Legal? I trust R&D to do their jobs on design, but I'd like to be sure that our asses are covered on compliance.

Best,
Lucy

# SHIBBOLETH

# CHAPTER 19

Julia had never wanted children.

It wasn't a question of biology. Though she knew her mother's condition was potentially hereditary, she was reassured enough, having reached her 30s with no obvious symptoms, that her risk of passing it along to a genetic child was low, virtually negligible.

Nor was it really because of her upbringing, chaotic though it had sometimes been: she'd reached an agreement with herself, even before she left for university, that her adult life would play out as differently from her mother's as was humanly possible, that her thoughts and actions - her value system - would be governed by rationality and reasoned response, not superstition or impulse. Had she wanted it, motherhood might have easily been another differentiator - another showcase for her comparative stability.

But she didn't want it; had never wanted it. She had no objection to children in general; had found them perfectly pleasant in short bursts, at distant family get-togethers and daytime birthday parties (the volume of which inevitably increased four-fold with every year she aged). But she didn't yearn for them; didn't ache, or need, or any of the other florid verbs she heard thrown so casually around in magazine articles, films and television programs, and, to her ongoing disapproval, everyday conversation.

Grace had wanted them, though; had wanted them desperately. It was one of the unspoken conditions of their marriage: that they'd eventually have one, or two, or more. And Julia - though she'd never wanted, never ached - didn't feel so strongly opposed that she'd protested. She'd loved Grace, and children were never so frightening a prospect that she was prepared to go to war over them.

This was, she thought later, in all likelihood because she hadn't really believed that they would happen - that they *could* happen. She'd been 35 when they'd married, Grace two years older, and was aware - though at that point only in abstract terms - of the decline in fertility looking both of them in the face in the run-up to 40. So, even as she'd jumped through all of the relevant hoops - the counselling, the blood tests, the clinic appointments - it had never seemed quite real; never seemed as if a child - a flesh and blood thing - would ever result, anywhere down the line, from the gently-worded consultations or the needles in her arm.

When she was proven half-right - when one of the many tests revealed that Grace, at least, had scarcely any viable eggs left - she'd breathed a sigh of relief; had been attentive and supportive, said all the right things at all the right times, but inside had thought: thank God that's over.

And when Grace had turned to her over dinner the following evening, her face blotched and breath stale from a day and a half of crying, and said, at least we still have you, she'd made a conscious decision not to dwell on the implications. She was 37 by then: still young - still almost a wunderkind - by the standards of her industry, but surely old to begin the business of pregnancy.

*A steep drop after 35*, the obstetrician had told them a year earlier, pointing to the horizontal axis of the line graph he kept, she'd assumed for exactly this purpose, on the desk in his office. *Less than a 25% chance of a live birth thereafter, even with IVF.*

It wouldn't happen, she thought.

So, when the results of their very first round of insemination came back to reveal that she was, after all, 2 weeks pregnant, she refused to believe it. She'd wait, she thought, for a second test; a third.

Only once she'd submitted to an 8-week scan - once she'd seen the fetal heartbeat on the monitor, the look of absolute euphoria on Grace's face - did she begin to think: this may actually be happening, after all.

It was a terrible pregnancy.

The first trimester was nothing but nausea - not intermittent waves but a solid constant, shattering her concentration and depleting her energy. Throughout the second, she was physically better but psychologically worse, appalled at the changes to her body, petrified of the mood swings that sent her careering into rage or misery at the slightest provocation. By the third trimester, she was desperate for it to be over - for the child to be out of her, for the horror and discomfort of it all to reach its end point.

Her labor was mercifully short and, given the extended agony she'd been expecting, surprisingly bearable, even at its most painful. She didn't tear; didn't rupture her vocal cords from screaming; was calm and coherent, until almost the moment she delivered. Tom was a healthy and, as far as could be ascertained in the delivery room, reasonably content baby, and when they placed him on Julia's chest to feed, it was - as she'd hear later, again and again - the happiest moment of Grace's life.

Julia, by contrast, felt none of the elation she'd been told would surge through her in the immediate aftermath of birth: only exhaustion, and below it a growing unease at having committed to something so absolutely irrevocable.

She spent the first week of his life in a kind of fugue state, an unending cycle of feeding and changing and rocking unleavened by any sense of connection to the tiny stranger that clung to her, parasitic, all day and all night. If she was happy at all, then, it was exclusively due to the happiness that Tom had brought Grace - who, despite her own exhaustion, smiled beatifically through every nappy, every unexplained crying fit, every stream of milky vomit.

She wasn't going to be much of a mother, she thought, on their sixth night home. But perhaps that was alright. Perhaps Grace would be mother enough for both of them.

Then, on the seventh night, something changed.

She'd been watching television in the bedroom - a long-running American detective series she'd chosen in the hope that its many seasons might see her through the boredom of breastfeeding. Tom was asleep on her, his tiny mouth glued to her nipple. She'd let him rest there, fearful of waking him, until her calves began to cramp and the stabbing twinge of it forced her upwards, into an upright position on the bed - back resting against pillows, legs stretched out in front of her. For her own convenience more than his, she'd transferred him from her chest to her thighs and let him rest there, head against her knees, feet pressing into the new softness of her belly. As the program had progressed, one episode bleeding into another, she'd found herself looking down at him - watching him, taking in his squashed nose, his tufts of hair, the soft down he'd yet to shed from his cheeks and ears. Seeing him, in a way she hadn't previously.

And she thought: I belong to you. I may not want to, but I belong to you.

Things were better, after that. Not completely - she still found herself bored, and frustrated, and was more delighted than she'd dared to show when, after six weeks, she was able to leave Tom at home with Grace and return to the lab, to some semblance of adult normality. But better. Tom no longer seemed to her an alien species, an interloper in her home. He was her son, their son; they belonged to him, regardless of her regret, her nostalgia for the shape of her life before.

On Robin's sofa, the steady clip-clop of horses' hooves echoing around the courtyard outside, she remembered those first weeks: wondered, again, how it was that she'd come to understand him not as the product of a bad decision - taken half heartedly, disbelievingly - but as the basis for every decision she would ever make thereafter.

And wondered, also, what he'd think of her, when he was older; if he'd judge her, for the things she'd done, on the island and before. The things she hadn't done.

The things, as in this case, that she'd allowed to happen.

She thought of Robin, creeping down into the village, her absurd rucksack strapped to her back; completely alone, entirely outnumbered, archetypically heroic in her stoicism and will to self-sacrifice. Imagined how Tom - who worshipped Batman, Spiderman, the entire pantheon of comic-book supermen - might see her, if he knew.

She thought of herself: burrowed away in a locked room, weak and frightened, a slave to self-preservation. Felt her shame renew itself and expand, batter at the edges of the logic that said: it's more than a risk. It's suicide.

And then, not really thinking at all, she stepped out into the courtyard.

There were horses outside, as she'd expected: a dozen of them or more, each one with an islander on its back, strategically positioned in twos and threes across the concourse. A pair of them were virtually on Robin's doorstep; long-maned animals, eight feet tall and wide in the neck, their riders speaking softly together in the island dialect that was almost Norwegian, almost Gaelic, and that reminded her, so completely, of her mother.

She'd never learned it properly, the language that her mother had called *norn;* had never been taught it, or had it explained to her by either parent. Had heard it only in fragments; words and phrases peppering her mother's speech in times of particularly heightened emotion, their meaning something she'd teased out from the context of their use - though how accurately, she could never say. *Folekar. Mar. Rispa.*

She'd come to associate it, over time, with hysteria and superstition, with the nightmarish stories of the *pawbi* and the chaos it would bring, were it to get into the house - so strongly that she'd actively chosen *not* to learn about it, not to hunt down dictionaries or etymological catalogues or texts on its syntactic structures. Instead she'd left it alone; a half-dead, unreal thing belonging to the past, to the sea.

Hearing it again, within an hour of arriving on the island, had come as a tremendous shock, one it had taken all of her self-control to conceal from Hampton as he'd walked her across to her room - two of the island women following a few steps behind them, the rhythms of their conversation flowing over her and into her, reworking the few words she recognized (*kaldvard, hest, fremd*) into new patterns, unfamiliar arrangements.

With little else to occupy her, she'd got better at puzzling out others as the months had gone on, drawing on the same detective skills she'd deployed as a child to untangle the words for boat, food, cage; for cold, sunset, cramp. Just once, she thought she'd picked up a reference to the *pawbi*, from one of two teenagers charged with watching them at breakfast - both barely old enough to drive a car on the mainland, much less stand guard over a roomful of putative prisoners. The other teenager had glared at him, hissed a line of what she read as chiding invective through gritted teeth, and the both of them had fallen silent, exchanging barely another word for the next half hour.

More old wives' tales, she'd said to herself. Even here.

The men by Robin's door looked down, regarded her with the same blank contempt as always, then looked away again. She wasn't interesting, she thought; was neither a new face nor a known troublemaker, and as such was barely worth acknowledging.

One of them, the older and more weather-beaten of the two, leaned in to the other and said something, a smile curling at the corners of his salt-cracked lips. He spoke slowly enough that she could pick out one word in five - among them those she was reasonably sure translated as something approximating "home," "water" and "outsiders."

And then, still smiling, something else - something she thought might have been "body."

She kept her reaction in check, just as she had months earlier; her mouth still, her forehead relaxed. So long as she remained uninteresting, she knew, she'd be able to move around freely - no barriers raised, no questions asked.

They must have taken the girl to the beach, she thought - most likely the narrow strip of sand and seawater leading directly up to their village.

Though whether she'd been alive when she got there was another matter altogether.

She thought again of Robin, flying out of the door like a hurricane irrespective of the danger, and of Tom - of what she'd say to him about the choices she'd made on the island, if he ever asked. How she'd justify *this* choice, if she stayed.

She crossed the courtyard.

The beach circled the island; there were, she knew from months of casual reconnaissance, no checkpoints or barricades separating one point - one area - from another. She might, she told herself, very easily go out for a walk along one part, lose her way and end up, quite by accident, in a different part altogether. One stretch of sand, after all, looked very much like another.

She reached the grassland. Quickened her pace.

From their horses, the islanders watched her go.

In support of the story she'd already planned to tell - that she was out walking, completely innocuously, with no real destination in mind - she took a longer route around the island than was necessary. She passed the old crofter's cottage, which stood just as vacant as the last time she'd visited, its insides dark and derelict; a patch of rocks and beside them, a set of beach caves which - as one damp afternoon taking shelter from the rain had taught her - contained just about the only freshwater there was to find on Salt Rock.

The village, she knew, lay just past the caves, where the beach path curved sharply to the left.

She started to turn, to follow the path as it bent.

And saw Robin, racing towards her from around the corner.

She was moving fast, covering the space between them more rapidly than Julia might have been able to, were their positions reversed; her face, Julia saw as she came closer, speckled with exertion, her hair plastered to her cheeks with sweat.

"You can't be here," she said, breathlessness filing every other syllable to a punctuation mark. "You have to go."

She grabbed Julia's arms hard enough to bruise them, her thumbs pressing painfully into the flesh, then seemed to topple forward, her upper body lurching towards Julia's.

Julia reached out to catch her; felt her fall, just for a second, then readjust herself so that she was upright once again.

"You have to go," she said, still clinging to Julia.

"What's happened?" said Julia, feeling the first twinges of panic. "Is someone coming?"

"I don't know. I don't know. I've never seen... I don't know what it is."

She was crying, Julia saw. Crying, and terrified.

"What *what* is?" she said.

"*It*! We have to go!"

She grabbed Julia's wrist and twisted, pulling her body backwards, towards the cave. Julia resisted the motion, half-wrenching her arm from its socket in the process.

There was a smell in the air, suddenly. It made her think of butcher's shops in August; bluebottles roosting on hanging cuts of room-temperature pork and beef.

"It's here," said Robin, letting go of her arm.

*Something* loomed into view. Something so improbable that she found herself unable to perceive it as a cohesive whole; could hold it in her mind only in terms of its constituent parts. Something that shouldn't *be;* that couldn't exist in a rational universe.

It had too many limbs, was her first thought: the solid legs of a horse, albeit a bloody big one, and the thin arms of a man, far longer than they should be. Too many *bodies*, at that - its horse-like midsection supporting what could only be a human trunk and head, milky-eyed and hairless, the skull soft and malformed. There was a tail, anguiform and obscene. There were teeth, and lips, and an equine muzzle, darkly stained - like its red-raw human mouth - with what she took to be blood.

There was not a scrap of skin anywhere, on any part of either body.

She'd moved before she was aware of having done so; had grasped Robin by the hand and *pulled*, yanking her from the momentary torpor that had overtaken her at the sight of... whatever it was. And then they were running, Julia dragging her along by her fingers.

She didn't look back, but she could hear it: an animal snort of bafflement, then the thudding pulse of its narrow hooves hitting the sand underfoot, more slowly than she would have imagined, had she stopped to think about it.

The caves, she thought. They have shadows. Hiding places. And then, in an inner voice not entirely her own: it won't go in there. It can't.

They ran there at a sprint: Julia leading, Robin at her side and the thing at their back, always near but never quite reaching them, its stench clogging her lungs, coating the roof of her mouth.

She didn't slow even as they entered the first of the caves - kept running, pulling Robin after her, through ankle-deep puddles of mud and water, around rock formations that rose out of the wet ground almost to her thigh.

The cave was narrow and low but unexpectedly deep; it stretched back, she thought, perhaps forty feet or more, away from the beach and out, she supposed, towards the grassland.

She stopped only when the cave itself ran out; when there was nothing left in front of them but a wall of cold stone, solid and impassable.

"You've trapped us," said Robin. There was no accusation there, she thought; just despair.

"No," she said, and despite all the evidence to the contrary, she believed it.

The thing, whatever it was, was right outside now, its impossible body a grotesque silhouette in the cave-mouth.

"It's coming," said Robin, reaching for Julia's hand.

The thing snorted and pawed the ground - the gesture that felt to her both recognizably animal and entirely alien.

It took a single step forward, its forehooves splattering through the mud, the shallow water.

The water splashed upwards, into the raw meat of its belly. It opened its mouths and roared, the two noises harmonizing to create a sound like flint on metal.

Then, its red eyes never leaving them, it turned on the spikes of its heels and cantered away, back towards the village.

# CHAPTER 20

The water - that was what Julia remembered, when she looked back on it. It was everywhere: filling jugs and empty vases, buckets and washing-up bowls; arranged at every door and window, every gate and cat-flap. The taps had been left to run in the kitchen, the bathroom, the utility room; water overflowed from the bath and sinks, flooding the carpets upstairs and down.

(The water damage was significant, her father had told her, years later; the floorboards had swollen, the ceiling sagged, the plaster bowed in the hallway. It had taken weeks to repair it all - weeks of sleeping, all three of them, in a single room in a bed and breakfast, eating takeaway pizza and fish and chips with wooden cutlery for every meal, drinking cans of off-brand cola, doing her homework on her lap while the television blared in the background. It was an adventure, he'd said at the time, but it hadn't felt like one: she'd felt displaced, and guilty, complicit in their temporary ruin).

They'd sat cuddled together on the sofa, she and her mother, more buckets placed around them in a protective circle.

"It willnae come in," her mother had said, holding Julia tightly. "It bides in salt. It canna cross clean watter."

She'd meant the *pawbi*, though she hadn't said it outright, not then.

"How long do we have to stay here?" Julia had asked - conscious even at nine of the school she was missing, the lessons she'd need to catch up on afterwards.

"Until Sea Mither comes tae tak him back where he belongs," her mother had said.

The *pawbi* is real, thought Julia. And I am losing my mind.

She could still smell it - the lingering rotten-pork scent of it all over the cave, all over Robin.

Do hallucinations smell? she wondered. Are they more than visual, more than auditory?

"Do you think it's gone?" Robin said.

"I think so," said Julia, and then thought: there's absolutely no way I can know that for sure.

"It killed Jack," said Robin, flatly. She dropped the rucksack to the floor; sat down where she stood, where the water was shallowest.

"Jack was there?" said Julia, sitting down beside her. The groundwater sunk into her trousers; into the hem of her shirt. It was cold; would get colder, she thought, the longer they stayed in the cave.

"He came with me. To the village. And I didn't... I should have sent him away. He shouldn't have been there."

"Been where? In the village?"

"At the beach. There was some sort of... I don't even know what it was. Some kind of ritual. And then it came out of the water."

"That... animal? It came from the sea?"

Robin shrugged. Her eyes were glassy, unfocused; she was in shock, Julia thought. Perhaps they both were.

"It started chasing after us. We were running, but Jack can't go fast, you know? And it was catching us up, so I tried to go faster, but he couldn't keep going, and he fell down, and then it... oh, Jesus, Julia. It ate him. It fucking *ate* him."

She pictured a man on the sand, bent double with cramp and exhaustion, and the creature looming over him, ready to pounce. Could imagine it all too easily: the first blows landing from its hooves, then its elongated arms, then the rip of the man's flesh as both sets of teeth - the human and the animal - tore the muscle from his neck and shoulders as efficiently as a lion shredding the carcass of an antelope.

"What does that?" said Robin, staring blankly at the rock wall ahead. "What kind of thing *does* that?"

"The thing tae ken about the *pawbi*," her mother had said, using its name for the first time, "is tha it canna bide on the ground in summer. It's a winter beast. It comes in the autumn, when the nights are lang, and it leaves in spring. Sea Mither maks sure of it."

"What's Sea Mither?" Julia had asked, hearing the roar of the tap-water flowing from the kitchen.

"The Mither of the Sea," her mother had said. "The one who looks eftir us. Who keeps the ill things locked up under the mar."

"But not in the winter?"

"No in the winter. In the winter she needs tae rest, tae rekiver. And that's when the *pawbi* sees his opportunity. Tae come out fae the sea and walk about. Which is why we need this watter. Tae keep him out, keep him awa fae us."

"I think it killed Chuck, too," Robin said. "Or the island people did, maybe. I'm not sure."

"Chuck?" said Julia. "What do you mean?"

"They had his body. The island people. They'd done something to it - washed it, cleaned it. They were using it in the ritual, the one that Jack and I saw on the beach. I think they were... Oh, God. I can't do it. I can't think about it."

"What were they doing?" said Julia, holding both of Robin's hands in hers.

"That *thing* - I think they were feeding it. Like a zookeeper sliding a bucket of raw beef out to a lion – like that. Like Chuck... his body... like he was meat."

"What happens if it finds us?" Julia had asked, out of curiosity more than any belief that what she was hearing was real, was something that really *was*.

"It willnae find us," her mother had said, kissing the top of her head.

"But hypothetically," she'd said, trying out a word she'd learned the day before, enjoying the feel of it on her tongue, "what would happen?"

"Hypothetically? It wud eat us. Baith of us, where we sat."

"Do you think it's gone?" said Robin again.

"Yes," said Julia, with more certainty than before. "I'm sure of it."

When her mother had gone to the kitchen to make her a sandwich, her bare feet thudding wetly across the waterlogged Lino, Julia had snuck into the hallway to call her father - anxious all the way through the call that the still-running tap-water would leak down from the ceiling and electrocute her as she held the handset.

He came home from work immediately; packed Julia into the playroom with a pile of her books and turned off the taps and called the doctor, who arrived 45 minutes later - Julia could see, from the top of the stairs - with a black leather medical case and a grimace on his tired face. He'd patted Julia's father on the shoulder sympathetically; slipped a square white card into his hand and told him to call the number on it. That it was time.

She stayed that night, and the two that followed, with her aunt - a no-nonsense woman with five large dogs but no children of her own, who'd fed her and bathed her and taken her to school on time, but otherwise left her to her own devices.

On her fourth afternoon there, as she was settling down for dinner, her father had appeared on the doorstep. They were moving into a hotel for a while, he'd said; just until the house was cleaned and ready to be lived in again.

He'd hugged her, and told her he loved her, then sent her to sit in the car while he spoke to her aunt, who had seemed - as far as she could tell - very disapproving of the hotel idea, and possibly of her father in general.

"Please call me if you need me," she'd said to Julia as Julia had left, patting her stiffly on the shoulder.

Julia had nodded, and said thank you, and that she would.

Her mother had been waiting in the car. She'd looked tired, colorless, but had smiled when Julia had climbed into the back seat beside her.

"I've missed you," she'd said, the thick accent of a few days earlier mellowed to something softer and lighter.

"I've missed you too," Julia had said. "And I think I hate dogs."

Her mother had laughed, just for a moment.

"I'm sorry about the house," she'd said.

"Daddy says we're going to a hotel," Julia had said.

She'd looked out of the window then; seen him mouthing thanks to her aunt on the doorstep, drawing her into an awkward embrace.

"We are," her mother had said.

She'd leaned into Julia conspiratorially; lowered her voice, even though there was nobody else there with them in the car.

"Don't worry, though," she'd said. "There's running water there too. We'll be safe."

"We should leave," said Robin abruptly, getting to her feet in the pool of water.

"Just now?" said Julia, alarmed. "Wouldn't you rather wait a while?"

"The island people saw us - me and Jack. They're going to be looking for us. You don't think they'll find us, if we stay in here?"

Julia had no reasonable answer to that.

"Where do you want to go?" she said.

"I don't know. We have to get out of here. Not just *here* - the island. We can't stay. Not now."

"What about Sat?"

Robin's face hardened.

"If they took her," she said, flat resignation creeping back into her voice, "then she's dead already. There's nothing we can do."

"Let's say that's true," said Julia, not entirely sure that she thought it was. "How are we supposed to leave this place? It's an island. There's one boat a day, in and out, and we're literally caged in. It's not as if we can swim for it. Especially not if that... *thing* out there is in the water."

Robin shuddered.

"I'm not going out there," she said, wrapping her arms around herself protectively. "Not in the water."

She looked, Julia thought, somehow younger and smaller than she had earlier that morning - as if the things she'd seen had knocked years off her, not added them.

"It's alright," said Julia, reaching for her hand again. "Nobody's asking you to do that."

Wait, she thought. Wait a second.

"The islanders," she said slowly. "They don't know I'm with you, do they? They only saw you and Jack."

"I guess," said Robin.

"Then we can go to my place - to my flat. Nobody will think to look for you there, not immediately. And it's warm there - dry. We can rest until we work out what the hell it is we're going to do."

Robin's expression stayed frozen as the words sunk in. Then she smiled, a tiny spark of animation returning to her face.

"Okay," she said, squeezing Julia's fingers in hers. "Let's go."

She was astonished that they weren't seen on their way back to the apartment blocks. They'd tried to run, at first, until Robin's exhaustion, her wet clothes - and, perhaps, the weight of the rucksack she refused to leave behind - combined to slow them down, making anything faster than a brisk walk impossible.

There was nobody around, on their beach or the grasslands - no islanders, and no other prisoners. The smell of the creature that had gone after them - what she'd begun to think of, though she wasn't ready to say it aloud, as the *pawbi* - was less pronounced than it had been, less suffocating.

"It must be back in the water," Robin had said, her head pointed very deliberately towards the land, away from the coastline.

The guards and their horses were gone from the courtyard; only one was left, a young woman in a knitted jacket wearing the same sour expression she'd come to associate with all of the islanders. The other prisoners, she assumed, were off eating lunch, or possibly dinner - she'd lost track of the hours since they'd entered the cave. The copper-mesh sky - and the ubiquitous grey clouds behind it - made it impossible to count time with anything like certainty.

Only Carol Bannister and her partner were there, she saw - facing one another over a paper chessboard like something out of The Tempest.

She saw Robin first, and waved effusively - then, seeing Julia beside her, dropped her hand to the table and grimaced. In other circumstances it would have been comical.

"I don't know what to say to them," said Robin, clenching her teeth like a ventriloquist as she spoke.

"Say nothing," said Julia, under her breath. "But wave back. Put her mind at ease."

Robin waved, half-heartedly, but kept walking, away from them, in the direction of Julia's flat.

Carol frowned.

"Robin!" she shouted, her nasal voice ricocheting across the cobbles.

She stood up from her bench and strode towards them, uncharacteristically school teacher-like in a trouser suit and a pair of dark-rimmed glasses dangling above her chest by a spectacle cord.

("Stay calm," said Julia, looking over her shoulder at the island girl, who stared back at her - at all of them - but didn't move from her position.

"I can't talk to her," said Robin, biting her knuckle hard enough that Julia worried it might bleed. "Or to him. They'll ask me about Jack."

"We'll keep it quick," she said. "I promise").

"We wondered where you'd got to," said Carol, speaking directly to Robin and ignoring Julia altogether. "Jack went out to look for you this morning, and we haven't seen either of you since."

"He found me," said Robin dully.

"What happened to you? You're soaking wet."

She gestured behind her, a beckoning *come hither* flick of the wrist that Julia imagined was directed at her partner, the chubby academic with the little grey beard who liked to hear himself talk.

Robin hesitated. She was so obviously traumatized, Julia thought; it wouldn't take much to push her into catatonia, or a complete meltdown, right there in the courtyard.

There were hoofbeats behind them, suddenly; an animal ambling away from them, what Julia knew rationally must be the girl leaving, clocking out of guard duty. Robin reacted to the sound immediately, almost jumping out of her skin.

"We were down at the beach," said Julia, stepping in. "I dropped my book into the water, and Robin very kindly helped me retrieve it. Unfortunately we misjudged the depth somewhat, as you can see."

"And Jack was with you?" said Carol to Robin, suspiciously.

"Not then," said Julia, "no."

"Robin," said Carol, "is something the matter?"

"She's absolutely freezing," said Julia. "We both are. I for one was hoping to get out of these clothes and into the shower, sooner rather than later."

"I should shower too," said Robin, mechanically. It was as if, Julia thought, she was re-learning how to speak, to reassemble the units of sound into meaningful sequences. "It's cold."

"Come and sit down with us for a few minutes," said Carol to Robin. "Bill can go inside and make us a flask of tea."

"We really can't, I'm afraid," said Julia.

"Can't she speak for herself?" said Carol to Julia.

"She can speak fine," spat Robin. "And she doesn't want any of your goddamn tea."

Here comes the meltdown, thought Julia.

And then there were hoofbeats again, loud and fast, approaching from behind them - far more than just one set. This time Julia froze, fear and panic overwhelming her.

"They're coming, aren't they?" said Robin.

Julia couldn't speak; couldn't bring herself to turn around.

She didn't need to. The horses circled them, penning them in on all sides - five of them, she saw, including one belonging to the sour-faced girl in the knitted jacket.

The girl said something to another of the riders, a rapid-fire run-on that Julia couldn't begin to translate.

Another of the horses trotted forward to stand immediately in front of them, a fat tan animal with a vertical mane that stood up from its coat like a Mohican. Unlike the others, it was wearing a saddle, and on the saddle sat Hampton, his eyes unreadable behind mirrored sunglasses.

He was grinning; there was real pleasure in it.

"Well," he said, looking down at them, "here we are. And we didn't even have to send out a search party."

# CHAPTER 21

Hampton barked an instruction at the island men - a word that sounded like "fasten," and another that could have been "up." Two of the men dismounted their horses and edged towards her and Robin - warily, as if a more direct approach might startle them, cause them to bite or stamp or kick. They were holding, she saw, the same thin plastic material she'd seen wrapped around Sat's wrists that morning; might even, though she couldn't say for sure, have been the same men who took her.

"Hands in front of you," said Hampton.

She didn't comply, not exactly, but the position of her arms meant that she was easy enough for the men to restrain; to cuff. The plastic was tight across her wrists, inescapably binding.

Robin did better - pulling her arms up into a defensive position and dropping her weight down into her legs, resisting them.

Perhaps she *will* bite, after all, Julia thought.

It took both of the island men to get her into the handcuffs: one to hold her still, to keep her from lashing out, and the other to fix the cuffs around her wrists. She kept fighting them, even with the cuffs on, kicking at their shins and driving her arms into their chests, the points of her elbows into solar plexuses with a precision that was more than instinctive, and Julia thought again of Tom's superheroes, and of how he'd see Robin, were the two of them to ever meet.

"What the hell is going on here?" said a voice she half-recognized as Carol's garrulous boyfriend.

She looked behind her - saw that he'd shouldered his way between the wall of horses and into the melee, his dense brows beetling in confusion at the things he was seeing.

"Ask your lady," said Hampton. "I'm sure she can fill you in."

"Cai?" said the boyfriend, obviously baffled.

Bill, Julia thought; his name is Bill something. Bill the amateur mythologist. Bill the *pawbi* expert.

"I'm sorry," said Carol. She looked embarrassed, Julia thought; ashamed, even, her eyes refusing to look up and meet his.

"What is this?" he said. "What do I need to be filled in on?"

"He didn't know?" said Hampton to Carol, mirth still playing across his pale lips. "He really didn't know? Wow. You two really need to learn to communicate better."

To Bill he said: "She's been helping us out. Keeping an eye on things for us."

"Helping you out?" said Bill to Carol, incredulously. "You mean spying? You've been spying? Passing them information?"

"It wasn't like that," said Carol. She looked more than embarrassed now; looked broken, humiliated.

Julia remembered the columns she'd written for her paper during Julia's trial, and after; the headlines identifying Julia - every week, it felt at the time - as a mad scientist and a murderer, the Josef Mengele of British biotech. Remembered worrying how Tom would feel, when he grew old enough to search for her name in the archives, to understand what those headlines meant. And, despite the discomfort, despite the imminent danger, Julia found a certain dark satisfaction in the other woman's unhappiness.

"How was it, then?" said Bill. "Tell me, Carol. How was it?"

"I didn't have a choice," said Carol. "They own me. They've owned me since the day they came for me."

"What *they*?" said Bill. "Vanderhalden? You're not just spying for *him*, you're spying for *Vanderhalden*?"

He looked disgusted, Julia thought. Utterly repulsed.

"It's the only way they'll let me leave," said Carol. She was almost crying now - so bereft that Julia felt the stirring of something that might, in other circumstances, have grown into sympathy.

"So you're buying your freedom, is that it?" said Bill. "30 pieces of silver, and they let you off the island?"

"There wasn't any other way," she said.

Now they stared at each other across the courtyard: one distraught, the other horrified.

Hampton watched them for a moment - still grinning, obviously entertained by the drama he'd set in motion - then stepped in closer to her, to Robin. The island men, in turn, took two steps backwards, far enough away to accommodate his presence but sufficiently close to physically intervene, should Robin attack again.

"What's in the bag?" he said, pointing down at the rucksack Robin had dropped to the ground in the scuffle. "Mind if I look?"

"Fuck you," said Robin.

"I'll take that as a yes," he said.

He reached down and picked up the rucksack in one hand.

"Feels heavy," he said, shaking it experimentally. Inside, the cutters rattled together metallically. "Wonder what's in it?"

He unzipped the canvas top of the rucksack and dipped a hand inside.

"You know," he said, pulling out the cutters, "I used to have a pair just like these."

He opened the leather satchel on his hip and slid the cutters inside. They didn't fit, Julia saw; the length of both blades stuck out at the top, as long and sharp as they'd ever been.

"Think I'll keep hold of them for now," he said. "Boys?"

The island men stepped closer.

"Help me take these women here to my office, would you?"

It always surprised people to learn that Julia had never ridden a horse.

Her accent (cut-class Southern English, despite her mother's influence), her education (Home Counties day school, Cambridge, year abroad in Paris) and her income bracket (very high, until recently) all conspired to frame her as a horse person - a woman likely to have enjoyed many years of riding lessons as a child, a woman who may once have had a pony of her own, tucked away in a paddock somewhere in the Hertfordshire countryside.

In fact, she'd never liked horses - had found their size, their power and their well-documented volatility off putting, preferring to spend her weekends and school holidays indoors, surrounded by coding manuals and circuit boards and central heating.

Had she known, then, that her first foray into riding would come without a saddle, on the back of what she took to be a wild mare, handcuffed and tied by a thin strip of rope around her waist to a hostile stranger... then, she might have paid more attention. Might have taken in a lesson or two.

Horse riding, it seemed, was profoundly uncomfortable for the absolute beginner, even factoring the rope and handcuffs out of the equation. Her thighs ached - which she supposed made a kind of sense, since she was using them to grip the horse's body as if her life depended on it. Her back was sore, unused to holding the half-slumped posture that riding pillion on a live animal apparently necessitated; her lower legs, dangling down into nothing from a height of several feet, threatened to seize up, the tissues in them already beginning to twitch and contract.

She glanced over to her left, at Robin, and saw that she was faring slightly better - was managing to sit in an upright position, her eyes burning furiously into the upper back of the island woman in front of her on her own horse. Her clothes hadn't yet dried, Julia noticed - her jeans clinging damply to her calves, her shirt sticking tightly to the lean muscle of her midriff.

To her right rode Hampton, close enough to reach out and touch, if she'd had the inclination - the satchel (and inside it, the cutters) still slung around his neck, the absurd sunglasses still covering the top half of his face. It was, she thought, a ridiculously American affectation for a man she'd previously taken to be of Dutch or Scandinavian origin.

By comparison with the islanders, he seemed decidedly uncomfortable on his horse; was too stiff, all jerking movements and rigidity. She wondered how often he travelled around without his quad bike, and in what possible circumstances a horse might seem the more practical alternative. Or whether it was a stab at tribal affiliation – a way of signaling to the islanders that he was just like them after all, in spite of the masters he answered to, the weapon hidden away in his bag.

The strange geography of the island shifted around them as they rode, the cobbles of the courtyard becoming grassland, then sand, and finally - on the rocky approach to Hampton's office block - bare stone and salt-baked soil. Beyond the beach the waves, always angry, screamed louder than ever, hurling themselves against the cage; she couldn't see it, but she imagined the wire shaking, the higher reaches of the whole contraption rattling as the water hit, again and again and again.

Perhaps eventually it'll fall, she thought. It's only wire; only copper and aluminum, soldered together. It's not concrete. Enough pressure, and it'll break.

"Pretty loud out there, right?" said Hampton, staring ahead to the coastline.

"You know about it, I assume?" she said.

"About the water?"

"About the *pawbi*."

The man in front of her - her rider - turned around at the sound of the word; looked at her, surprised, then looked back at the path. Robin's rider turned too, her interest piqued. She was another teenager, Julia saw; dark-haired and wide-eyed and painfully young. She should be at home, Julia thought, or at college, or gorging on fast-food with friends at a burger bar somewhere. Not here, doing this.

"Surprised to hear you say that word," said Hampton. "Surprised you know that word at all."

"I have a very rich vocabulary," she said, adding another word, one she'd only ever heard her mother use in moments of anger or irritation. She'd inferred that it meant something close to "cunt" and something close to "motherfucker"; was spiced with a bitter, accusatory flavor.

The island girl laughed, then immediately covered her mouth in embarrassment. Robin turned to watch her, curious.

"Wouldn't think you'd know *that* one, either," said Hampton. "You're just full of surprises. But yes, I know about the... what did you call it, the *pawbi*? It's not easy to avoid. You should know - you've seen it. Or *she* has, anyway."

He cocked a thumb at Robin.

"The island boys tell me she had a very close encounter with it earlier. She and that friend of hers, the drunk. God rest his soul."

"Did it kill Chuck?" said Robin, daggers in her voice.

"It did not," said Hampton, mock-solemnly.

The face he'd shown them previously - by turns paternalistic and explicitly intimidating - was gone now, replaced by cold mirth, a cruel humor that she thought might be closer to the real man inside. He's laughing at us, thought Julia. And why shouldn't he? He's holding all the cards. He can do whatever he wants.

"Did *you* kill him?" said Julia.

"No," he said, seriously.

"Then who did?" said Julia.

"Let's just say," he said, lowering his voice, "that some of the island boys weren't so happy with what he was doing - what he was *trying* to do - with some of the other island boys. You know how they feel about outsiders. And outsiders like *that*... well, I bet you can imagine. They're not a very open-minded people."

Why, thought Julia, is he telling us this?

And then: because he can. Because we're not going to tell anyone. Because he isn't going to *let* us tell anyone.

"You knew?" said Robin, close to shouting. "When you saw me after I found him. When you came into my apartment and threatened me. You knew it was them?"

"Then?" he said. "No. I was as shocked as you were. It wasn't on my order. They went... well, they went rogue there. Left me to tidy up the mess. The good news is, I can guarantee you they won't be doing that again. They've learned that lesson."

Julia looked over at the island girl; she seemed frightened, now, her eyes fully on the road ahead, conspicuously avoiding her and Robin and Hampton.

They've certainly learned *something*, she thought.

"The police were never here, were they?" said Robin. "Everything you said, about calling them, sending them the body, bringing them out to the island to investigate... it was all horseshit. Another way to keep us frightened, keep us in line."

"You're pretty sharp, aren't you?" he said. "And you're right, obviously. The police have never set foot on the island, at least as long as we've been in charge. And before we were... hell, it was hardly even a place then. I can't see why *anyone* would have wanted to come out to look around, police or not."

"Do you even have a telephone?" said Julia.

"Strictly speaking?" he said. "No. I have a few other options, if I really need to get in touch with the mainland. But we're on our own here, more or less. You were right the first time," he added to Robin. "The cage *does* block phone signals. It's why your other little friend with the cellphone had to cut a hole in the fence and crawl through it. *Swim* through it, I should say."

There was silence between them as the implications of what he'd said sunk in.

*We're on our own out here*, thought Julia. It's the Old West, and he's the sheriff. Which means he's the only law in town.

"Chuck's body," said Robin eventually. "They took it, the islanders. They tried to feed it to that thing - the Nuckelavee. The *pawbi*. Whatever it is."

"It needs the meat," he said simply.

"I don't understand," said Robin.

"Sure you do," he said. "It's not that complicated."

"It needs to feed," said Julia. "That's what you're saying?"

He bent the hand closest to her into a finger gun gesture; pointed it at her and smiled, clicking his tongue against the corner of his mouth.

"Keep it fed, keep it happy," he said. "The locals understand that. Unless you'd prefer it came inland to look for something fresher?"

"It came after us," said Robin, venomously. "It got Jack. Even after they tried to feed it."

"It's always going to prefer live meat to dead. It won't bite the hand that feeds it - that's these guys," he said, indicating the islanders, "but anyone else who comes near it, they're fair game. You, your friend... even me. Which is why I never get too close."

Monster or not, Julia thought, it's a wild animal. And it's trapped in a cage. Of course it needs a steady food supply.

She looked up; saw, somewhere through the wire, a few faint streaks of late-afternoon sunlight emerging from the grey of the clouds.

It's still light, she thought. Because it's July; mid-summer.

*It's a winter beast*, her mother had said. *It comes in the autumn, when the nights are long, and it leaves in the spring.*

Which means, she thought, that it shouldn't be here now.

"Why is it still here?" she said abruptly.

"What?" he said.

"We're in July. Why hasn't it gone back...wherever it goes back to?"

"It lives here," he said, momentarily confused. "It's part of Salt Rock. *This* is where it goes back to."

He doesn't know about that part, she thought. He thinks he knows what he's dealing with - but he doesn't know that. Which means the islanders haven't told him everything *they* know. Some things, they're holding back.

"Does Vanderhalden know about it?" said Robin. "About the things it's been doing?"

"You should be careful, throwing that name around here," he said - half-casually, the threat implicit.

Julia looked right, then left, deliberately exaggerating each movement for his benefit.

"I don't think there are enough people listening to care, do you?" she said, fear and adrenaline - and the near-certainty that he had no intention of ever letting them free - making her bolder, less cautious than was probably prudent. "Answer her question. Do they know about the *pawbi*? Or is it your little secret, you and the island people?"

He lowered his sunglasses to the bridge of his nose; stared at her.

"You're a smart woman," he said. "Why do you think they bought this island? The weather?"

"They knew," said Robin.

"They've always known," said Julia.

"You know what the senior partners call this place?" he said. "Unofficially, I mean."

He was enjoying it, Julia thought - getting off on the process of revelation, of unveiling hidden truths to a captive audience he could be sure would never be able to tell. She wondered how long it had been since he'd had a conversation like this; since he'd been able to tell someone, anyone, about the things he'd seen, the things he knew, the things he'd done.

"I couldn't begin to imagine," said Julia.

"Oh, I bet you could," he said. "They call it The Bermuda Triangle. Things come here, and some of them just... vanish."

"Not things," said Julia. "People."

"Things, people... it's all one, isn't it?" he said. "It's all just problems to solve. Loose ends to tie up. Messes to tidy away."

"They send them here," said Robin. "The people who end up on the island... they send them here to die."

Julia considered what Robin was saying, what Hampton had already said, then thought of what she'd seen for herself in the last few months - of Sat, and Carol Bannister, and even Robin herself, and the dozens of other men and women she'd almost recognized who had had passed through Salt Rock in the time she'd been there.

"That isn't true, is it?" she said. "Not exactly. Not everyone is here to disappear. Just a few of us - a handful of agitators, slipped in among the others. The ones Vanderhalden find inconvenient."

Among the ranting drunks and the racists, she thought - the sex tape-makers and the activists, the wrong-place-wrong-timers and the kids too stupid or naive to keep their half-formed opinions to themselves, even when they knew that people were listening. They hide us here with them, in plain sight. Protestors. Whistleblowers. Scapegoats who wouldn't go down without a fight. The whole range of thorns in Vanderhalden's side.

And once we're here, she thought - that's when they make us vanish. They'll call what happens by another name - illness, early release, a tragic accident - so the others don't grow too suspicious, the short-stay guests who'll eventually go home to their family and their friends and tell them what it was like to live, even for a while, in an impenetrable bubble, an enforced state of suspended animation. So that those people - the shamed, the opinionated, the indecent - don't spend their first hours back on the mainland talking about the missing ones, the disappeared.

What, she wondered, does Hampton tell the families, afterwards? What will he tell *our* families?

Would he even be the one to do it? Or would it be someone else - some other spoke in the Vanderhalden wheel?

"That's us, right?" said Robin. "We're the inconvenient ones. You're going to make us disappear."

He didn't answer.

"And you don't think that anyone is going to notice that we're gone?" said Julia. "Our families? Our colleagues, our friends, our next-door neighbors?"

"Maybe they will," he said. "But the bigger question you have to ask yourself is: who's going to listen to them or care what they think? Everybody hates you people, back on the mainland. I mean, really hates you. You're about as likeable as war criminals. You think anybody cares what happens to war criminals, once they go to jail?"

"Not everyone believes what they read," said Robin, with real feeling. "Some people can still think for themselves, even with people like your bosses watching. Some of us see past outrage."

The idealism was really rather lovely, Julia thought; the kind of sentiment that, in another time and place, might cause her to melt a little inside even as she'd scoff at its naivety.

"Not enough of them to matter," he said. He wasn't grinning anymore.

# CHAPTER 22

What he'd called his office, she saw when they arrived, was really more of a jail: three old-fashioned cells with metal bars for doors, lined up side-by-side in a high-ceilinged holding room.

The doors of the first two cells were open. In both of them were a wooden-framed bed and sheet-less mattress with no dips or indentations; a free-standing sink, the stainless steel polished to a high shine; an open toilet, similarly gleaming. If anyone else had spent time there, she thought, they'd had the consideration to clean up after themselves.

Or, perhaps, they hadn't been there long enough to leave a mark on the environment.

Behind the closed bars of the third cell was Sat, laid out on the bed like a corpse, her eyes closed. Only the rise and fall of her chest under layers of tie-dye and plaid fabric assured Julia that she was sleeping, and not actually dead.

"You brought her here," said Robin, evidently relieved.

"Where did you think we took her?" said Hampton teasingly, the pleasure-grin back on his face. His fingers dropped to his satchel, to the flat surface of the cutter blades; reminding himself, she thought, that they were still there, that he had them back.

He nodded at the two largest of the islanders he'd brought inside with him, who moved into position - one beside her, the other next to Robin - and, without hesitating, dragged them by their arms into the empty cells. The bars closed behind them with the clink she'd anticipated, trapping them.

And as horrifying as it was, she thought, to be forcibly locked in a cell, there was something reassuring about it, too - some relief to be found, after months contained in a prison that purported not to be a prison, in the brick-and-mortar bars finally showing themselves, offering tangible proof that, actually, she'd been trapped all along.

"Make yourselves comfortable," said Hampton. "Let's go," he added to the islanders.

"You're leaving us here?" said Robin, as they flowed outside.

"Don't worry," he said, following after them. "It won't be for long."

There was a period, she remembered, when she thought she'd be going to prison - a real, traditional prison, one with heavy bolted doors and exercise yards and uniformed guards with keychains dangling from their belts. Sometime after the divorce, after she'd been removed from her lab and her job, between the corporate manslaughter trial ending and the media witch-hunt beginning, when it seemed entirely possible - even likely - that she'd be hung out to dry legally for the crimes of which she'd been accused, and not only in the court of public opinion.

She'd spent hours on the phone to her solicitor, an old friend and one-time girlfriend from university who'd been very kind and very understanding, but who had explained, more than once, that until charges were filed against her, there was very little to be done but sit and wait and hope for the best.

Julia's patience, never her keenest virtue, had frayed further in the waiting; her mind, usually occupied with some work problem or other, had turned in on itself, chewing over every possibility, every scenario. Eventually she'd become so anxious, so visibly preoccupied that Grace had intervened; had insisted on taking her out for coffee at a neutral venue that was neither her new flat nor the family home in which Grace and Tom still lived.

"This can't carry on," she'd said, through layers of irritability that Julia had never picked up on while they'd been married. "Tom needs you. And you're no good to anyone like this."

"I don't know what you mean," she'd said petulantly, stirring sweetener into her cup, avoiding direct eye contact.

"You know exactly what I mean. This worry, this self-pity. It's coming off you in waves. Tom can sense it, and it's starting to frighten him."

"I have a lot to be worried about, wouldn't you say?"

"And what's the use, exactly, in you sitting around the living room all day thinking about it? It isn't helping you. And it isn't healthy for him. It's making *him* worry."

"Stop."

"No. *You* stop. Whatever you might be caught up in, it isn't just about you. You have a child now. You're responsible for him. It's not alright to just... mope from sunrise to sunset and then drink yourself to sleep."

"A glass of wine after dinner is hardly a crime."

"He found the bottles, Julia. The empty ones under the sink. I had to tell him you were keeping them to make Christmas decorations."

She'd felt a stab of indignation at having been confronted - then a deeper swell of embarrassment, pulsing and oily in the center of her chest.

"I can't handle not knowing what will happen," she'd said, quietly. "I'm not very good at waiting."

"Then stop waiting," Grace had said, curtly - all business and practicality, no trace of compassion. "You like solutions, don't you? Invent one."

225

"How long do you think he's been gone?" said Robin.

"I couldn't tell you," said Julia. "An hour? Two?"

There were no windows in the holding room; no clocks on the walls. She'd taken to marking time with her stomach: she'd last eaten the evening before, and the extent of her hunger - latterly combined with a growing nausea - suggested that at least a day had passed since then.

It must have been longer for Robin, she thought.

They were sitting together on the floor of their cells - as close together, at least, as the bars would allow, legs stretched out and backs against the concrete wall.

Sat was still asleep; hadn't moved so much as a muscle since they'd arrived, from what Julia had seen.

"I don't think I've ever been this tired," said Robin, resting her head against Julia's through the bars.

"Then try to sleep. You should save your energy."

"For what, exactly? That long walk down to the beach before they throw us into the sea?"

She had no answer for that, and no plan to offer in response - no suggestions, no solutions.

"Is that what they're gonna do with us?" said Sat.

Julia looked across at where she lay, still flat on the bed, her eyes still closed.

"You're awake," said Robin.

"Not for long," she said. "I figure if I sleep for long enough, eventually I'll lucid-dream up some kind of way out of here."

"I thought you were dead," said Robin.

"Nope," she said. "Just, you know... on death row. Why are *you* here?"

"We saw something we shouldn't have," said Julia.

"That's, like, the crime of the century in this place. What did you see?"

"It's not important," said Julia quickly, feeling Robin tense up again beside her.

"Did they find the cutters?" said Sat.

"Hampton took them," said Robin. "When they found us."

"Well, that's inconvenient," said Sat.

"Just a little," said Julia.

"Did they tell you anything when they brought you here?" said Robin.

"Like what?" said Sat.

"I don't know. Anything."

"Lo siento, chica. I got nothing. None of them spoke to me, even while they were tying me up. Literally the only human interaction I've had the last few hours before you got here was with that island girl - the brunette chick who came in with you guys. And that conversation didn't exactly set my world on fire."

"The girl who was here before?" said Julia, thinking back to the dark-haired child on Robin's horse, the one who'd seemed so terribly young.

"That's the one," said Sat. "She was in here watching me for a while when they first brought me in, before a bunch of the other guys called her away. Guess they figured I didn't, you know, need someone meatier keeping tabs on me."

"What did she say to you?" said Robin.

"Honestly? It was kinda hard to tell. Their accents are pretty thick. I think it was something about food - bringing food around later."

Julia's stomach rumbled in response to the word; Robin's, she noticed, did the same.

She tried not to fixate on the promise of *later* - that there would *be* a later.

"Was that it?" said Robin.

"Pretty much," said Sat. "Except... I think she said something else, just before she left. Sort of mumbled it as she passed by the bars."

"What?" said Julia.

"*Sorry.* I think she said *sorry.*"

Inventing a solution, despite Grace's instructions, had proven impossible.

There was, however she'd looked at it, no way to think herself out of her predicament; no way to outwit (or even fast-track) the inner workings of the justice system.

Waiting, it had appeared to her at the time, really was the only option. And waiting was intolerable.

She resolved, therefore, to plan; to devise a contingency measure, one she could implement, should the worst happen.

("The worst," at that stage, had meant prison and all it entailed: financial crisis, professional ostracism, even physical threat. Her parameters for "bad" and "worst," she'd realize later, had shifted quite dramatically not long afterwards).

So, as much for her own peace of mind as much as for the practical benefit, she'd hired a prison consultant - a white-collar criminal turned entrepreneur, who specialized in helping middle-class women understand and negotiate prison environments.

"I don't know for sure that I'm going," she'd said, over the course of their initial, awkward telephone conversation. "I haven't been charged."

"But you think you're going to be?" the woman had asked, her brisk manner and rasping Afrikaans accent doing nothing to put Julia at ease.

"Yes," she'd said. "It's looking that way."

"Then let's work on that assumption," the woman had said.

She'd met the woman the following day, at a chain restaurant in Highgate, one sufficiently busy that Julia - her face now a known quantity, though not so known as it would become - would attract no attention.

The woman - Bettina - was nothing like Julia had expected, from the single image and brief biography that constituted the entirety of her online presence. She was older than her photograph by a clear decade, a lightning streak of Susan Sontag white cutting through her black hair. She wore a tailored suit and carried a calfskin briefcase. She might, Julia had thought, have been a high-end headhunter, recruiting Julia for a job in the City.

Until she'd spoken.

"That attitude isn't doing you any favors," she'd said, before Julia had even reached for the drinks menu.

"I'm sorry?" Julia had said.

"You look frightened. Ground-down. Like you can't even look at me in the face."

"It's been a difficult few months."

"Doesn't matter. You walk into any prison, anywhere in this country looking like that, and you're asking for trouble. Meek is weak. The girls in there, they aren't going to care that you've had a *difficult few months*. All they'll see is a rich woman who can't stand up for herself. You should just as well write kick me on your back."

She'd been angry - furious - but had tried to rein it in, to project at least a semblance of composure, if only to prove her wrong.

"I think perhaps this was a bad idea," she'd said, putting down the menu, preparing to leave.

"You don't want my help?" Bettina had said, barely acknowledging the change in temperature between them.

"I don't want to be insulted by a stranger over a lunch I'm paying for," she'd said, making none of her usual effort to keep the bite out of her words.

"There we go! That's the attitude we're looking for! You might want to tone down the haughtiness, but the anger, that's perfect. It won't make you many friends, but it'll get the other girls to back off."

"You want me to be angry?"

"I don't want anything. But I'm telling you that anger - if you control it - will serve you better on the inside than all that maudlin self-pity you brought in with you. And that the best time to start to channel that anger is now, before you go away. If you go away."

"Okay," Julia had said, settling back into her seat. "Let's say I believe you. What else do I need to know?"

They'd talked solidly for two hours, over three courses and two carafes of expensive water: about prison rules, prison food, prison bedding. About how to avoid fights, and when it might be beneficial to pick one. About how not to make enemies, without ever really making friends.

And they'd talked about the guards.

"You'll feel like they're out to get you," Bettina had said. "You'll think they're petty, and stupid, and in love with the power they have over you. And sometimes you'll be right: some of them are absolute bastards. But not all."

"So I ought to respect them?" Julia had said.

"Ag, no. They're not your friends, even the nice ones. And sucking up to them won't win you any points with anyone, screws or prisoners. No, all you have to remember about them is: they're just as stuck there as you are. It might not seem like it when you're lying there in your cell watching them finish their shift and go home for the night, but they are. A lot of them, they couldn't get into the police or the military. Becoming a PO is their last resort - they didn't choose it. But they need the money. So they have to keep working."

"Why is this important?"

"Because if you want to make it through your sentence with everything intact, you need to learn to live with them. Work with them. And to work with them, you have to understand them."

"And what exactly do I do with that understanding?"

"You use it. However you need to."

Hours passed - or what felt to Julia like hours, her nausea turning to outright sickness and a clenching stomach pain that doubled her over on the hard floor.

Robin dozed, hunger and exhaustion apparently lulling her to sleep.

Only Sat was fully alert, pacing up and down the length of the cell like a lynx in captivity.

"I thought you were busy dreaming up a way out," said Julia, through clenched teeth.

"Turns out it's kind of impossible to lucid-dream a key into existence. Which I figure is what we're gonna need to get out from behind these bars. If we *could* get out.... then, maybe, I've got something. The start of an idea, anyway."

"Something you'd care to let us in on?"

"I still need to work out if it's viable. So, not yet."

Julia rolled onto her side and rested her head against the concrete. More time passed - hours or minutes, it was impossible to tell. For a while she napped, a light half-sleep punctuated by dreams of waves and sand and copper wheels turning at the bottom of the sea.

It was the smell that woke her, the scent of cooking oil and fried meat puncturing the odorless sterility of the holding room.

She opened her eyes; saw the dark-haired island girl enter the room, a large serving tray in her hands, steam rising from the three overlapping plates on top of it.

Julia's stomach rumbled, an animal growl so loud that she struggled to understand how it had originated from her body. She looked over at the plates, her mouth watering involuntarily. In each one was a mass of bright yellow she identified as scrambled eggs; a pile of burnt shards she thought might be fried potato, and a thick slab of pinkish-brown meat that could have been beef or pork.

Except that you know it's not, she thought. There are no cows or pigs on the island. And you've seen steaks like that before, in France - you've *eaten* them before. It's horsemeat.

Her stomach lurched again, acid roiling low in her gut.

"Guess dinner's here," said Sat.

The girl laid the tray down on the ground, picked up one of the plates and walked across to Sat's cell. A small letterbox opening, evidently designed as a food hatch, cut through the bars somewhere around waist height; she pushed the plate through it wordlessly, directly into Sat's waiting hands.

Julia got up from the floor, her body aching, and pushed herself towards the bars, close enough to study the girl's expression - remembering the way she'd laughed when Julia had insulted Hampton, then immediately covered it up; the apology she'd (maybe, possibly) made to Sat earlier that day.

To work with them, she thought, you have to understand them.

And then: she's just as stuck here as you are. It just doesn't seem that way from this side of the bars.

"Help us," she said, piecing together the fragments of broken *norn* she hadn't spoken aloud since childhood. "Please, help us."

"They daena like strangers," her mother had told her once, describing her own family, the island where she grew up. "Tourists, ay - they like them, the money they bring in. But they daena like it when they settle, when they stay."

She'd been easy to talk to that morning, lucid and relaxed (and, Julia had realized afterwards, probably heavily medicated) in their newly-decorated living room, and Julia had found herself asking questions she'd never asked before: about her background, where she came from. About the grandparents Julia had never met.

"Like Daddy?" she'd asked.

"Ay, like Daddy. Only he ne'er really got the chance to settle. As soon as he got comfortable, my Da, your grandfaither... he had some things to say about it."

"What sort of things?"

"Just... things. Bad things. Like I say, they daena like strangers. Especially no strangers that want to marry their daughters."

"Is that why you left? So you and Daddy could get married?"

"That's one o' the reasons. No the only one, tho. I'd been wanting to get away anyway. I wasnae made for a place like Skerry Head."

"Why don't you ever go back? Bridget's granddad lives in Portugal, and they go there to visit him at Christmas."

"It's no so simple. Your grandfaither - he's no like Bridget's. If I were to gae back, he wadna want me to leave again. And if he were to meet you, he'd dae everything he could to get us to stay."

"Because he misses you?"

"Because the folk on Skerry Head... they daena like it when people leave, no when they're from there. No when they're *blood*."

She'd pronounced blood strangely, Julia remembered - as if she were quoting someone, as if the word itself were wrapped up in speech marks.

"Am I blood?" Julia had asked.

"For the islanders," her mother had said, "ay, you are."

"So they'd want me to stay, too?"

"Ay. You're my daughter. Which maks you one o' them."

It must be nice, Julia had thought at the time - to be part of something, always and forever, no matter what you do or say.

"But not Daddy?"

"No Daddy, no. Just us."

"Because we're blood?"

"Because the way they see it, we belong there, to the island. And when you belong somewhere... you never can leave it, no really. No even if you gae away."

"How do you know those words?" said the girl, in Scots-inflected English. "How do you know what they mean?"

She looked frightened, Julia saw; frightened and bewildered.

"It's my *tunga*," Julia said. "My speech. My language. From my mother."

"You're a liar," said the girl. "Your ma is no frae here. No frae the island."

"No," said Julia. "But near here. Very near."

(Robin had woken up, she noticed; was sitting up on the bed now, regarding Julia oddly, as if she'd never seen her before).

"Whair?" said the girl.

"Skerry Head," said Julia. "Another *øja*. The next but one along."

"Ay. I ken it. It isnae like here."

She shook her head and turned away from Julia, from the cell; bent down, picked up a second plate from the tray and passed it through the slot in the bars to Robin, who took it from her hands.

"Thank you," said Robin to the girl. She walked with the plate to a corner of the cell, closer to Julia; sat down on the floor and, with barely a moment's hesitation, dug into the food with her bare hands, grasping the meat between her fingers and tearing into it with her teeth until watery pink blood trickled down her chin.

("You know what that is, right?" said Sat, gesturing at Robin's plate. "That thing you're eating, you know where it came from? Where it, like, *must* have come from?"

"You think I care?" said Robin, chewing. "This may surprise you, but I'm not feeling so warm toward horses these days").

"I know about the *pawbi*," Julia said to the girl.

"Na, you daena," said the girl. "Mebbe you ken its name, but you daena ken *it*."

"That's not true," said Julia, desperately. "I know what it is. I know where it comes from. I know what it will do to you, you and your people, if you don't keep it placated. The only thing I don't understand is why it's still here.

It's summer time, isn't it? It should be under the water by now. Sea Mither should have seen to that."

("What is she talking about?" said Sat to Robin.

"You know as much as I do," said Robin, still chewing at the meat. "But I think maybe it's important").

"You ken about the Mither," said the girl, shocked.

"I know she should have come, and she hasn't. But I don't know why."

The girl laughed, a bitter cracking of her voice quite at odds with her delicate china-doll face.

"You no ken?" she said. "You mean to tell me aefauldly tha you no ken why?"

"I'm sorry," said Julia, "I really don't."

The girl laughed again; there was no joy in it, no happiness.

"It's *you*," she said, half spitting the words at Julia. "You, and her, and all of youse fastlanders. Youse and Vanderhalden."

She split the last name into its component parts, each syllable bringing home its foreignness, its *fastland*ness: Van-da-hal-den.

"What did we do?" said Julia, with growing horror.

"You kept her out," said the girl. "All of youse. You biggit tha big wire cavie all around the island, an' a hunder o' youse moved in under it, so the Mither canna get inside. An' if she canna get inside, she canna tak the *pawbi* awa. He's *stuck* here, you ken? He canna get out."

# CHAPTER 23

From what the girl was willing to tell her, from the things she learned later for herself, and with only a little imagination, Julia was able to understand how it had unfolded:

In the years before Vanderhalden, Salt Rock had been similar, at least superficially, to many of the other isolated islands that surrounded it: grey, and close-knit, and religious, and accessible only by boat. Its small population and unyielding geography meant that there were none of the quaint little shops or rustic bed and breakfasts of its larger and more populous cousins - only stables for the horses, and enough subsistence farming to allow the locals to feed themselves through the seasons. There were no cables or telephone lines, no digital coverage, no reliable source of electricity.

The lack of hotels and restaurants, and of any regular transport to and from the mainland meant that the tourist industry that flourished in Shetland or Orkney had never taken root on the island, while the marked absence of indigenous birds and interesting wildlife meant that it attracted none of the rangers, research teams or amateur ornithologists that flocked to Isle Martin or the Calf of Eday. Those few who did make it, from time to time, across from the mainland commented on their return on the strangeness of the place: the dearth of natural beauty, the unfriendliness of the islanders and their half-wild horses, the unpleasant taste that seemed to hang in the air and stick to the roof of the mouth for all the time one stayed there.

But, while it never thrived or modernized, Salt Rock survived, anomalous and unlovely - season upon season, year after year.

Until, one late September, Vanderhalden arrived.

They'd come by flying machine, six of them: fastlander men in thin neckties and summer jackets, bearing clipboards and handheld electronic devices, trampling over the grassland in their unsuitable shoes.

Who are you? the island elder had asked them in English, stopping them in the tracks on their way to the village. What are you doing here?

One of them, a slender man with oil-slicked hair and eyeglasses, had stepped forward and grasped the elder's hand; had shaken it effusively.

We're the new owners, he'd said. Happy to meet you.

They'd bought the island, they told him, from the government - which had come as a surprise to the elder and the other islanders, who'd never known the land was up for sale. Would never, even if they'd stopped to think about it, have conceived of the land - *their* land - as something that could be bought or sold.

The slender man had taken the elder by the elbow and guided him away from the other men, away from the helicopter and towards the water, where it was quiet.

I know this must come as a shock to you, he'd said. It's a lot to take in. But we want to do everything we can to make the transition easier for you and your community. We haven't come here to make enemies. We want to work *with* you.

The elder was shell-shocked - more confused than outraged, at least then.

We're on your side here, the fastlander had continued. This isn't about displacement. Not at all. We're here to *help*.

Help? the elder had said, finally finding his voice. What kind of help do you think we need?

There's no need to be coy, the fastlander had said. We've been watching you for a while now. We know about your problem. And I have to tell you: we might just have the perfect solution.

They'd known about the *pawbi* - the slender man, and all the other fastlanders too.

It's a son of a bitch, isn't it? the slender man had said. Turning up at your door whenever it wants, making trouble, demanding to be... taken care of. I can't even imagine the toll that must take on you, on all of you.

Ay, the elder had said warily.

It's unimaginable, really, the man had said. The choices you've had to make, just to keep it at bay. The sacrifices. What is it, a man a year? Two? A small community like this... that's a terrible loss. Just terrible.

The elder had said nothing. Even if the fastlander didn't know it, *he* knew - you didn't *talk* about the *pawbi*. Not outside, by the water. Not where it could hear you.

Talk was for later - in springtime, once the winter had passed, inside the walls of the chapel with the candles lit and the seaweed dried and burning. Then, maybe, you'd say its name. Beg that it would let you be for another season. Give thanks to it, and to the Mither, for stopping at just one body, one sacrifice. Pray to God, to whoever else was listening, that the next year would be the last - that finally, the *pawbi* would have taken enough, would have had its fill.

But what if I told you, the man had said, that you don't need to lose any more of your own? That we'd found a way to take care of things for you?

What the fastlander wanted, the elder had gathered, was to fill the island with mainlanders - criminals, no less.

They won't be dangerous, the man had said. We're not talking about *real* criminals here. Nobody will have robbed a bank, or shot up a post office, or sold heroin in kindergartens. Your people will be perfectly safe.

The elder had no frame of reference for *heroin* or *kindergarten*, but had kept his peace and let the fastlander talk.

But still, he'd said, they're not *good* people. Not like you or me. Which is why we need to segregate them - take them out of the general population and put them somewhere... else. Somewhere remote and out of the way. And Salt Rock... well, it's pretty damn remote, isn't it?

What does any of this have to do with the *pawbi*? the elder had said.

I'm going to be frank with you, said the man, because I think I *can* be. Men like us, leaders - tough decisions are what we live and breathe, am I right?

Ay, said the elder, thinking of the last ceremony, the body of his brother's son floating, cold and still, out into the water.

Then let me put it this way, said the man. These people, these... what do you call them, fastlanders? They're expendable. A few of them go missing from time to time, and nobody back home is going to complain.

Is that so? said the elder.

I think it is, said the man. And I think that, if you wanted to stop losing your men, your own family and toss a few strangers to the *pawbi* instead... Well, I for one wouldn't blame you.

It was a deal with the devil, the elder knew - one he would have found unconscionable even a handful of years earlier.

But a lot of hard time had passed him since then; had bruised and battered and buffeted him, torn threads from his heart and the lining from his conscience.

There are different kinds of devils, he'd thought. And *his* devil - the one he'd lived with for six decades - was surely worse than this fastlander man with his suit and tie and promises.

And these *other* people, these fastlander criminals - they were nothing to him. Nothing to any of them.

They scarcely mattered at all.

Here's what's going to happen, the fastlander had told him:

The prisoners would come to the island - just a few of them at first, and then more and more, under the guard of a warden handpicked by the man (or group of men) the fastlander called Vanderhalden from one of their mainland prisons. One briefed on Salt Rock and its backstory, its unusual condition.

Vanderhalden would build these prisoners a village on the other side of the island: somewhere for them to cook and eat and sleep, as far away as possible from the elder and his *folekar*, his people.

The younger and more able of the islanders would tend to the prisoners - would keep watch on them, stop them from roaming where they ought not to. Protect them from harm, where they were able.

And in exchange, every autumn when the seasons changed, the guard would bring to the elder and the *folekar* a prisoner for the *pawbi*. Another cold body, to offer up to the sea.

Only that wasn't how it went.

What really happened was:

The fastlanders left in their flying machine, leaving torn earth and sand clouds in their wake, and the elder told the others what Vanderhalden had offered him - what he'd agreed to. And though some of them had been angry (just as he'd expected) at the strangers appearing out of thin air to lay claim to their land, not one of them objected to the deal that he'd made on their behalf. To the prospect of keeping a husband or a brother or a son - or their very own skin – out of the sea when they or it might otherwise have been lost.

So, knowing what was coming, they waited for the prisoners to arrive.

For weeks there was nothing - no boat from the mainland, no flying machine plunging down from the clouds - and the elder began to wonder whether they would come at all.

And, as autumn drew closer, and the promise of the *pawbi* with it, he wondered whether he and the *folekar* might have to placate it as they always did, and always had. Whether he'd been a fool to believe that there might ever be another way.

By early September, with no fastlanders in sight, he'd begun to make alternative plans - asking for a volunteer among the oldest and the weakest men, the few without wives or children, steeling himself to send another of his own to be taken.

Then, with no warning or fanfare, more fastlanders came. But not the prisoners he'd been expecting.

Instead, they were *bygger* men, and many: men with tools, and metal, and sparking torches, with machines that lifted and bent and drilled holes in the sand, deep down into the seabed. They didn't talk to him or the *folekar*, or even acknowledge their presence; didn't offer explanations, didn't tell - or even hint at - what it was they were doing.

In a week, they'd built what looked to be a long, low wall of tight-weave metal netting around the island's perimeter, buried in the salt-sea away from the shore: some parts in shallow, some in deep, all running to waist height from the place they broke the surface of the water. It had seemed to the elder, although he couldn't say why, as if they were the beginnings of something; as if the *bygger* fastlanders were laying the foundations for some edifice, some iron Babel.

Another week, and the wall was higher, too high by far for a man to scale, and circling every bit of the island - high enough, he'd thought, to keep the *pawbi* out and away from them all.

And though puzzled by this new solution - which wasn't at all the solution that the slender man had offered him - the elder was happy. Perhaps, he'd thought, they were finally free; perhaps the *pawbi*, thwarted by the wall, would be forced out to other lands, to other shores.

The *bygger* men weren't finished, though. Next, they'd raised a dome to the top of the wall, adding great plates of woven metal piece-by-piece with their lifting machines until, on the 21st day of September, the wall had become a cage, blotting out the sun and looming high over the island like a second sky.

On the night of the 22nd day, the night of the equinox, the *pawbi* had come. And the elder had realized: the great metal wall hadn't kept the *pawbi* out at all. It had trapped it, like a wasp in a bottle.

It took one of the *bygger* men first, the one who operated the lifting machines - snatching him out of his tent as he slept, leaving nothing for the other men to find the following morning but a trail of bloody hoof prints leading out to the sea.

The other men had been frightened - had packed up their camp and sailed away to the mainland on the boats they'd arrived in, leaving behind their tools and their construction machines, the dense scaffold they'd built over the heads of the *folekar*.

The elder had been frightened, too - had spent long days and sleepless nights in his house by the sand, waiting for the *pawbi* to come again, waiting to feel the hot breath of its anger at having been walled in, kept from roaming the length of the sea and archipelago.

But the *pawbi* hadn't come back - not then. Instead, Vanderhalden had sent more boats from the mainland: some loaded with new *bygger* men, these ones in the island not to build but to reclaim the equipment left behind by the ones the *pawbi* had scared away; another holding just one passenger, the man the elder would come to know as Hampton.

The first prisoners were following after, Hampton had said; would be there on the island the next day, all being well.

Quietly, he'd said to the elder: tell me how many of them you'll need, when you'll need them, and I'll make it happen.

The elder had tried to tell him about the *pawbi*: that it was trapped now, stuck. That it wouldn't - *couldn't* - go away now as it had in the past; that it would stay with them, for all the seasons, as long as the cage above them held. Would take more, demand more. Wouldn't be content with just one offering a season. More than likely wouldn't wait for the offering to be given at all.

I understand, Hampton had said. I know it's been a problem for you here - that it's been haunting you. But hopefully now we can take a little bit of that pressure off.

You daena understand, the elder had said. The Mither canna come now. She *canna*.

Hampton had furrowed his deep brows, scratched his thick red beard.

It'll all be fine, he'd said, understanding nothing, the words pouring from him unthinkingly, automatically - soft soothing from a tired father for a bairn feared of the dark.

You don't need to worry anymore. We've got it covered.

# CHAPTER 24

**From**: c.lee@specialprojects.vanderhalden.com
**To**: l.webber@specialprojects.vanderhalden.com
**Re:** A Few Things

Hi Lucy,

Greetings from sunny Texas! Hope it's not too chilly out in the Bay Area.

Sorry to bother you while you're away, but a few things have come up on the Salt Rock front these last couple days and I wanted to see if maybe you had any thoughts?

So, here we go:

First... we've been getting some slightly frantic reports in from Security about unusual weather patterns in the area immediately surrounding the island. 'Tidal waves' was how one of the guys described it. Apparently this isn't normal at all for Northern Scotland, and none of the surrounding islands seem to be experiencing anything similar - the waters are pretty much calm most everywhere else you look.

We've got waves hitting the pen hard and fast, by all accounts, but we're not too anxious about structural integrity. That thing was built to last!

It's more that Security are concerned about the attention weather like this could attract to the project. Because the waves are *so* high, and the whole phenomenon is *so* uncharacteristic for the region, they're worried that it's the kind of thing that could catch the eye of the media. Local, obviously (which is less of a worry) but also national / international. Check out some of the aerial photos (attached) and you'll see what I mean. You can totally imagine something like this making the Weird News segment on NBC.

And what we definitely *don't* want is publicity!

Which brings me to the next thing: we're having some issues with one of the Red-Label inmates, Julia Mitchell. I've just heard that the NYT have been doing some digging around her case (or the case *before* her case, I should say - some corporate manslaughter thing, not the outrage trial). And it seems like they've found a few discrepancies - mostly to do with the testimony of a lab tech, who was pretty pivotal during the trial but who turns out to be, shall we say, not so reliable after all as a witness. The Times haven't quite got their ducks in a row yet, so nothing's gone to press - but it's going to be a tough story to kill, if and when it's ready, and I can already see where something like that might lead.

(We *definitely* don't want another Free Martín Lopez campaign on our hands).

I checked, and it looks like the Special Projects panel have a care plan in place for Mitchell... but do we maybe want to ask them review it, just in case? Would be good to minimize any potential blowback.

Finally: Deliveries & Logistics have raised a few red flags about Hampton Smit. Now, I know what you're going to say here - that he's a Human Resources issue, not one for us. But I figure, since the heads-up came from Peter and his crew, we might want to have him on our radar.

I'll forward on Peter's report so you can see for yourself - but Smit comes off as kind of a loose cannon. Very paranoid, kind of erratic. And if the Deliveries guys are seeing it (and they see him for a *very* small window), can you imagine what he's like the rest of the time?

I've been over his personnel file, and I totally see why HR think he's the right guy for the job. He's got a hella impressive record. (10 years working the SHU in Supermax! 10!)

But if he's not holding it together over there, then maybe we want to start thinking about some kind of retrieval and replacement strategy. If only so we have one. Better to have one and not need it than need one and not have it, right?

Anyway - let me know what you think, about this and the rest of the above. I'm on my cell all weekend, so call whenever if you want to talk it through. Would be great to hear your thoughts on how to move ahead.

Thanks,
Carl

# TSUNAMI

# CHAPTER 25

I t was probably night-time.

The island girl was long gone, the plates of food she'd delivered still in their cells. Robin had scraped hers clean; had cleared Sat's too, grabbing shamelessly at the new cut of meat through the bars the second it had been offered.

She'd felt ill, briefly, as the protein had hit her system, sick and light-headed - then unexpectedly wonderful, the temporary shot of euphoria inappropriate but overwhelming, as irresistible as a seizure or a migraine.

Now, with the food settled in her body, she felt energized and lucid - able to think straight for the first time in hours, maybe days.

Which, she thought, wasn't actually all that helpful, because even with clear eyes and a full stomach, she could see that they were screwed. Hampton had them, there was no obvious way out of the holding room - and if what the island girl had said was true (and Julia, with her insider knowledge and knack for hearing the meaning in the girl's dialect, had assured her that it was), then there was no use at all in looking to the islanders for help. Their fear would make sure of that - fear of Hampton, fear of Vanderhalden, fear of their goddamn *pawbi* most of all.

Hampton wanted them gone. Vanderhalden wanted them gone - wanted Sat and Julia gone, at least. And the *pawbi* was hungry, and pissed, and essentially unstoppable.

*Bullshit*, said David's voice, still in her head. *You* know *it can be stopped. You just heard how.*

By this Mither thing? she thought. What the hell good is that, if it can't even make it through the wire?

"You seem thoughtful," said Julia, from the cell across. She'd been sleeping the last hour or so, curled up on her bed, a curtain of hair across her face. Robin had watched her sleep, unthinkingly, for a little while, before she'd realized what she was doing. She'd stopped immediately then, embarrassed by her sentimentality.

"There's a lot to think about," she said.

"I'd say so," said Sat, still pacing the floor.

"How's that planning going?" said Robin, not intending the question to sound quite as pointed as it did.

"It's going," said Sat.

"In any particular direction?"

"I think maybe. It kind of depends."

"On what?"

"On whether we ever, you know, get out of this room. And even if we do... there are other factors to consider."

"Like what?"

"Like the depth of the water, wherever they take us. How fast metal corrodes in salt. Whether or not horses can swim."

"They can swim," said Julia. "Rather better than you'd think, actually."

"I can't, though," said Robin. "Not well, anyway."

"And I can't ride a horse," said Julia.

"Maybe I'll keep thinking," said Sat.

She was starting to get hungry again when Hampton opened up the holding room, two of the burly island guys from earlier stepping inside with him and the young girl following after, her eyes fixed to the floor.

He'd taken off the aviators and changed his shirt, she noticed, but the satchel still hung from his right shoulder, bisecting the fat around his belly. The cutters were still in there too, she saw, the outline of the handles bulging through the brown leather, though he'd managed to close the bag this time, enough to keep the blades concealed.

The landing gate must have stuck again, she thought. He must have needed to open it manually.

*It wouldn't take much*, said David. *Blades like that - they'd slice through wire like it was butter.*

There was something else at his hip now, too: a holster, made of the same leather as the satchel, apparently empty.

She looked down, and closer, and saw the gun was in his hand: a snub-nosed revolver, the pearl grip longer than the barrel, half-hidden behind the brushed denim of his thigh.

Will he shoot us first? she wondered. Put a bullet in us before he puts us in the water? Or is it just for show?

"Saddle up, ladies!" he said, with a smile like the Joker, all teeth and elasticity. "There's someone out there who really wants to meet you."

They rode to the beach the same way they'd come: on horseback, pressed against the bodies of the islanders in front. She'd wound up beside the island girl again, and the experience was exactly as uncomfortable as it had been the first time around - her head thrown back and forth with every step, her legs scrabbling for purchase on the horse's smooth hair in the absence of a saddle.

Emboldened by the gun and the presence of his island strong-men,

Hampton hadn't bothered to tie their hands, but still she was reluctant to use hers - to take hold of the girl's body, to use her waist for balance.

Julia seemed to be thinking something similar - her arms crossed firmly in front of her chest even as her shoulders bounced and rattled. Sat, conversely, looked intent on causing her rider as much discomfort as she was able without actually pushing him to the ground, grinding her forehead into the back of his neck and digging her elbows into his kidneys.

Hampton travelled behind them on his squat brown horse. In her mind's eye she saw the revolver in his hand; imagined it trained on the three of them as they rode, the hammer cocked, one finger on the trigger.

Maybe a bullet in the head would be better, she thought. Better at least than that *thing* breaking her skin with its teeth, grabbing her throat with its nails, driving into her body with its hooves and pulling her down into the sea.

This journey was short, at least, the horses clearing the path through the village from Hampton's office in a handful of minutes. Exactly as some part of her had been expecting, they came to a stop on the beach, beside the wooden stilt house she'd hidden in with Jack, before.

Behind the cage the sea roared, the waves more deafening than she'd known them; a hundred feet high, crashing against the wire with the weight of a tsunami, forcing a thousand tiny waterfalls of saltwater through the mesh.

*There it is*, said David. *Or there* she *is, I guess. On the outside, trying to get in.*

*Another push, and she might make it.*

There was someone waiting for them on the sand: an old man, older than any of the other men or women she'd seen on the island, his wrists loaded with wooden bracelets and long beard braided into an elaborate plait. He was holding something, something knotted, dark green and damp-looking, the strands of it stretched out between his open palms like a prize fish.

It's seaweed, she thought. A seaweed wreath, same as the last one.

A wreath for a sacrifice.

"And here we are," said Hampton, raising his voice over the sound of the waves.

He guided his horse around and in front of the three of them and the island riders, so that he stood between all six of them and the sea. He jumped down from the horse, and she saw that she'd been wrong about the gun; it sat in the holster at his hip, snug as a snail curled up in a shell, his fingertips lightly caressing the handle exactly as she'd seen him stroke the cutter blades on their way to the holding room.

*Now* he drew it, though. *Now* he pointed the muzzle at her, at Julia and Sat; at the islanders, by default.

What does he care if they're collateral damage? she thought.

"Time to get down," he said.

One by one they complied, sliding down onto the sand with varying degrees of grace. The islanders moved away from her, from Sat and Julia, in unspoken synchrony, out of the line of fire and toward the old bearded man and his wreath. The horses didn't move, not a hair or a muscle.

Hampton stepped around them again, keeping the gun on them - on all three of them - as he walked behind them, back towards the sand.

There was nothing between the three of them and the water now - the water and whatever was underneath.

Behind them, Hampton cocked the hammer, the click of it loud in her ears in spite of the crashing waves.

If he's going to shoot me, he's gonna have to look at me, she thought, and turned around to face him, the swelling water at her back.

Sat followed, then Julia.

Julia moved in close beside her; took her hand and held it, spreading warmth up her arm and into her shoulder.

Sat, to her surprise, did the same, stepping in to her left and taking Robin's other hand in hers, joining the three of them together like a row of kids in a schoolyard.

"Cute," said Hampton.

He shook the gun at them, urging them backwards and into the water.

"In," he said.

The old man laid the seaweed wreath down on the sand and backed further away from them, from Hampton. The island girl did the same; reached for the old man's arm and whispered something to him, then took another few steps inland, towards the village. After a second's hesitation, the two men moved to join them.

They know something's coming, Robin thought. They can feel it.

"Are you deaf?" he said. "I said go. Now."

The water roared again at their backs as another wave hit, shaking the cage, rattling the metal dome above them.

Hampton looked up, startled, momentarily lowering the gun.

Sat leaned in closer, pressing her head to Robin's, resting her bodyweight against Robin's shoulder, her legs seeming to give out from under her.

"When it happens, stay back," she said, directly into Robin's ear.

"When what happens?" said Robin.

The cage stilled, and Hampton seemed to compose himself, widening his stance and levelling the gun, steadying the grip with both hands.

"In!" he shouted. "Into the water!"

"What did you say?" said Sat, shouting back. "We can't hear you!"

Hampton took two steps forward, then another two, closing the gap so that there was barely the length of a person between them, the gun so close that Robin imagined she could see down the barrel, see just about every bullet in the chamber.

"I said get in the fucking water!" he yelled.

Yet another wave rose and landed, harder and faster than the one before, battering the cage, and the whole island seemed to shake, the metal screeching and shifting under the force of the water.

This time Hampton looked not just alarmed but genuinely frightened, staring up at the roof of the cage in horror.

He thinks it'll fall, she thought, watching him.

*Maybe he knows something you don't*, said David.

"Like what?" she said, aloud.

Julia turned her head towards her a fraction, confused.

*Like exactly how much pressure it can stand before it falls*, he said.

There was another screech of metal directly behind them, way out in the water, and Hampton's eyes widened, his elastic mouth puckering into an O of panic. He dropped his arm to his side, taking the gun with it.

And Sat ran at him - lowered her stance and charged towards him at a sprint. Her shoulder connected with his stomach, and her arms reached behind his knees, taking away his legs. He fell backward and she followed him, driving her own knee into his groin, her forearm into his throat.

His arm flailed, and the revolver dropped, out of his fist and onto the sand beside him.

Julia moved fast: let go of Robin's hand and darted forward and down, reaching into the sand for the gun.

Hampton grabbed her ankle, Sat's body still sprawled over his. Julia kicked out, then away; stamped down on his knuckle with the heel of her boot.

If it weren't for the waves, Robin thought, she'd have heard the bones break; heard the air leaving his body just before he screamed.

Julia stood up in the sand, the gun in her hand.

Robin looked over at the old man, the islanders. They weren't moving - were fixed to the spot, as still as their horses. Were staring not at Sat and Hampton, still fighting on the sand, or at Julia and the gun, but at Robin. Directly at Robin.

*At you, or behind you?* said David.

She turned around.

Far away from the shore, out where the sea met the wire, the waves were parting. And from the void between them, the Nuckelavee was rising.

# CHAPTER 26

J ulia had never held a gun before. It was a strange sensation: heavy and cold and *weighted*, powerful but not entirely trustworthy. Like holding the leash of a poorly-trained attack dog, she thought - one that could separate an intruder's limb from his body with its jaws, but that might turn in a heartbeat on its owner.

She clutched it between both hands; extended her arms and flexed, then raised it to shoulder height. Pointed it at Hampton, then at Sat, then at Hampton again.

"Stop," she shouted, as loudly as she could, dredging the breath from somewhere low in her stomach.

They looked up and saw her, and immediately stopped struggling - freezing in place on the ground, their legs still tangled together.

"Let go of her," she said.

Hampton loosened his grip on Sat's biceps; she broke free of his grip and stood, pushing up from her knees and straightening her back until she was half-upright.

She drew back her lower leg and ankle and kicked, the ball of her foot connecting with the meat of his testicles.

He cried out; rolled onto his side and balled up his body, protecting his head with his unbroken fingers.

"Bastard broke my ribs," said Sat.

She took in the gun; Julia's hands around the handle.

"You know how to use that?" she said.

"Not even a little bit," said Julia. "But I daresay I'll pick it up as I go."

She kept the muzzle trained as best she could on Hampton's midsection, trying not to imagine the blood flowing there, the organs held behind soft tissue.

Sat came up behind her; placed one hand over the top of the gun, a thumb on the catch at the top of the metal.

"You have to push this down," she said, depressing the catch. "And put your finger on the trigger."

Hampton rolled back around onto his back to watch them. His eyes were watering and his lip was bleeding, but he looked almost relaxed, she thought, lying flat out on the sand. But for the blood and the tears, the rips in his clothes and the swelling around his knuckles, he could have been a holidaymaker, unwinding on the beach of a chilly British coastline.

"If you're planning to shoot me," he said, "you'd better do it now. I don't think *he's* going to wait around."

He flicked his chin upwards, gesturing behind them, towards the sea.

"What *he*?" said Sat.

"Take a look," said Hampton.

I'm not going to move, thought Julia. It's a distraction tactic, the oldest trick in the book. I'll turn around, and he'll come at me - come for the gun.

She kept her head forward and the gun on Hampton, and let Sat do the looking instead - focused on the detail of her reaction to what she was seeing, watched her expression shift from confusion to shock to a commingling of fear and disgust.

"It's coming, isn't it?" said Julia, more to herself than to Hampton. "The *pawbi* - it's here."

260

Only its head was visible at first - its *human* head, the raw flesh and muscle seeming to form, to somehow *make itself* as it rose. The shoulders and arms came next, impossibly long and thin. Then the equine parts: the elongated snout, the too-thick neck and withers.

Robin watched it, hypnotized; oblivious, in the moment, to the gun and the fighting behind her, the storm building to a crescendo in the sea behind the cage.

She heard her name called, loud and then louder again; felt a hand on her body. The touch was enough to break the spell, and she spun around to face the beach, the village.

*Don't turn your back on that thing*, said David. *Remember how quickly it moves when it wants to?*

Julia was holding the gun, still - had it pointed now at Hampton, who lay belly-up on the sand, clutching his hand to his chest, satchel still around his neck.

Sat was closer - almost directly in front of her, a palm flat against the small of Robin's back.

"Time to go," she said.

There was something wrong with her, Robin saw; something subtly off about her gait, the way she was carrying her weight, one elbow tucked in tight to her side.

"Go where?" she said.

"Away. Anywhere. Anywhere not here."

Julia didn't need to see it to know it was coming, to smell it - salt and blood and rot, the butcher's shop stink of the *pawbi* rising out of the water.

I have a gun, she thought. If it comes close, I can shoot it - shoot *at* it. Hurt it, perhaps. Frighten it off, somehow.

*It's a monster*, said another part of her, one that was at once less rational and more swayed by the evidence of its senses. *A demon. Do you really think a bit of metal is enough to scare it away?*

"I can get you out of here," said Hampton, still on the ground.

"I very much doubt that," she said, keeping the gun on him, the weight of it making her shoulders ache, sending shooting pains through her wrists and forearms.

"You shouldn't. I got you the other things you wanted, didn't I? All those books your wife sent. I say what comes in and out of here, people included. Let me go, and I'll get you out too. Put you on the next boat back to the mainland."

The waves roared again; the wire mesh quaked, and the sea inside with it.

The Mither, thought Julia. She isn't taking no for an answer.

"I know you don't believe me," said Hampton. "But I'll do it. I'll open the door for you. Just let me go."

He was desperate, she thought; frightened and desperate. And why wouldn't he be? He could see over her shoulder; see what was coming.

"Stay where you are," she said, keeping her finger on the trigger, the tremor out of her voice. "Just stay where you are."

The horses were gone, Robin saw; the horses and the islanders, with only the old man and his seaweed wreath left behind on the beach.

Julia was closer to Hampton now, standing virtually on top of him. The gun was shaking in her hands.

*Go take it off her*, said David. *And do it quick, before she drops it. He won't lie there forever.*

"We need to leave," said Robin, from somewhere behind her.

Julia turned, and five things happened, all at once:

She saw the *pawbi*, out in the sea but rising - moving slowly towards them through the water, watching them through two sets of eyes, one animal and the other a warped facsimile of human.

She saw Robin beside her; was aware of Robin's fingers closing around her wrist, ready to lead her away from Hampton, away from the coastline and the *pawbi*.

She lowered the gun, just a fraction, so that the end of it was pointing downward, not out.

She felt Hampton wrap both of his legs around hers and pull her to the ground on top of him; felt his hand on hers, pulling the gun from her grasp.

And she felt her own fingers squeeze back against the trigger.

For a split-second, the sound of it was louder than the sea, louder than bombs - a shock rocket exploding into her eardrum.

The momentum forced her backwards, until she was flat on her back too, her legs caught between Hampton's, his thighs heavy against the bones of her calves.

Then there was another smell in the air, an extra layer added to the *pawbi*'s charnel reek and the momentary undertone of burning that followed the gunfire - fresh blood, sour-sweet and close, on her and around her.

She looked down at her hands, her body - saw the blood, seeping into her trousers and staining her shirt. Registered, in the absence of pain, that it couldn't be hers.

"You shot him," said Sat's voice, from somewhere nearby.

And then there were more hands on her, pulling her off and up and away.

He wasn't dead. Robin could hear him breathing; could see his chest rising and falling, his mouth opening and closing as he tried to speak.

The wound, as far as she could tell with Julia's body covering his, was in his abdomen, but there was no obvious hole: no clean through-and-through hole or tell-tale spatter pattern, just blood, pooling and seeping across his stomach, through his clothes, smearing itself across the brown leather of his satchel.

Julia, though also covered in blood, didn't look to be hurt, just dazed, and Robin felt relief even through her panic. The blood itself, she realized, was less shocking to her than it would have been even a week before.

*You're getting numb to it*, said David.

Maybe you're right, she thought. And maybe that's not such a bad thing.

She heard Sat tell Julia that she'd shot him, and then something else, something she couldn't make out over the roar of the storm. Saw Sat bend down, over Hampton's prone body; reach down further, still holding her ribs on one side, and pull the cutters from his bag.

Then another sound, coming from behind them: a whine and a snort and a scream all rolled into one, ground to a point just sharp enough to carry over the water and over the waves, the sound of farmyards and slaughterhouses, gallows and glue factories.

She looked back; saw it coming closer, almost onto the sand, its progress still slow but steady, unrelenting.

*And it's faster on land*, said David. *You've seen that for yourself.*

*You have to move.*

She took ahold of Julia, a hand under each of her arms, and dragged her up, away from Hampton's not-quite-still body and onto her feet. She collapsed against Robin, just for a second, then recovered herself and stood straight, though one hand still held tight to Robin's, the fingers trembling.

"The cave," said Robin. "We need to get to the cave."

"Is he dead?" said Julia, not looking down.

"No. But we can't take him with us."

A terrible understanding passed between them - *you're getting numb to it,* she heard David say again - and Julia nodded.

There'll be time later for guilt, Robin thought. But not now. Not yet.

They took off down the coast, away from the village and toward the empty cottage, the freshwater caves. Sat kept up, to her surprise; wincing and clutching her side, but matching their pace, the cutters tucked tight under one arm.

Another wave struck the wire, this one like a thunderbolt, and all three of them slowed down, looked up, and saw what could only be a panel in the dome of the cage fly loose - detaching from the wire and spinning out, away from the island and into the sea.

*It's happening,* said David. *The center definitely cannot hold.*

"Oh, shit," said Sat.

"Yeah," said Robin, her eyes still on the cage, the gap in the metal. "It's falling."

"Not that," said Sat. "*That.*"

She looked down, and saw what Sat was seeing: four islanders, men and women, riding towards them on their bareback horses, blocking the path to the cave. Each one, she saw, was armed: the men carrying hammers, the women what looked to her like swords carved out of rock.

"Other way!" said Julia.

She turned around, preparing to change direction, to sprint down toward the village, into the dead grass.

The Nuckelavee was on land now; was pawing at Hampton as he lay on the sand, sniffing and tearing at his body the way it had torn at Jack's.

There'd be blood on its snout, she knew; skin between its teeth.

*Don't think about it,* said David. *Just go. Now, while it's distracted.*

She broke into a sprint, veering left, pulling Julia with her toward the long grass.

Then saw what was coming from the grassland, from the village, and stopped dead in her tracks.

More islanders and more horses: twenty of them, maybe more, riding out to the beach in groups of three and four. Every one with a weapon: a sword, a knife, a hammer.

Coming for them. Closing in on them.

# CHAPTER 27

The riders and their horses were all around them now, coming in from all sides but the sea. And slowly: penning them in, not trampling them down.

They're driving us out, Julia thought. Us and the *pawbi* both.

In among the hard island faces she spotted the girl from the holding room - impassive now, her fingers tight around a dagger that seemed to be made entirely of stone. The old man from the beach rode beside her - his horse markedly larger and more powerful than the others, but no weapon at all in his hands.

The elder, she thought.

The girl saw Julia seeing her, but didn't look away.

"Please," said Julia, directly to her in the broken *norn* she'd used before. "Please, let us out."

"We canna," said the old man in English, his dry sandpaper voice carrying over the distance, over the crashing waves. "The *pawbi* kens you now. He'll ha gotten your scent, all of you. If he daesna get you, he'll follae you back - whauriver you gae, ontae the holm. We canna let that happen."

"It already has Hampton!" shouted Robin. "It has him right now!

Whatever sacrifice you think it needs... it's already been made. It doesn't need us too."

The old man shook his head.

"It daesna maiter," he said sadly. "He kens you - you've been promised to him. And he willnae let up. Willnae let go."

He tugged on the reins and the horse moved forward, slow and steady. The other riders followed suit, equally slow but unstoppable, an impenetrable wall of muscle and bone driving them backwards along the beach, towards the water.

Towards the *pawbi*.

They rounded the corner, where the coastline curved, and it came back into view: still kneeling over Hampton's body, its animal legs bent, its human head and shoulders upright and turned away from them, seeming to look out across the sea.

The cage rattled again as another wave landed, what felt like the strongest one yet - dislodging a second wire panel from the top of the dome.

It fell down rather than out this time, breaking the surface of the water close to the shore, and the *pawbi* startled, its equine head jerking up from the body and its forelimbs drawing back in the sand.

It's afraid, she thought. Not of the cage but of what's outside of it. Of the sea - the Sea Mither.

And then she knew - what would have to happen, and what they'd have to do.

# CHAPTER 28

The water was warm - that was the first thing that struck Robin as she waded in. Warm like a hot tub; warm like blood.

It shouldn't have been, she thought. The air outside was cool, the sunlight exposure minimal through the damaged cage - there was nothing to heat it up externally. But nevertheless, it was warm - the heat of it massaging her legs, drawing the stiffness from her muscles.

*It's coming from underneath*, said David. *Not from outside - from* under *the water. Can't you feel it?*

It wasn't deep. Barely reached her waist - even as she moved further out from the shore, away from the sand and towards the wire.

Maybe I'll get lucky, she thought. Maybe it's shallow all the way out.

*I wouldn't be so sure*, said David. *Take a look beside you.*

She looked to her immediate right, at Julia - who was swimming, not wading, her face half-immersed in the water as her arms and feet propelled her forward. Then further right again, at Sat - who *was* wading, exactly as Robin was, one arm clutched against her damaged ribs while another held the cutters, keeping them at shoulder-height, above the surface.

It's deeper in the center, she thought. Shallow around the edges and deep in the middle.

*That's where it lives*, said David. *Underneath. In the deep.*

She craned her head backward, toward the coastline. *It* was there on land, still; still bent over Hampton, its hybrid body turned away from them as it fed.

We've got time, she thought. Not much, but some. Enough, maybe.

It started; jerked again, the way it had when the second chunk of cage had fallen. Twisted itself around and fixed its eyes on her. On all of them.

*No*, said David. *You're wrong. There's no time. Not now.*

We have to cut the wire, Julia had said, leading them down to the coastline. Break it open and let the water through.

Haven't you seen what's outside? Sat had said, hanging back, one eye on the Nuckelavee. We can't swim through that. It'll crush us.

And I don't swim, Robin had thought, but had let herself be led into the water.

We won't be trying to get ourselves out, Julia had said. We'll be opening a door. To let the Mither in.

And what if the cage falls in? Robin had said. That'll crush us, too. And not just us – everybody.

We're not trying to take the whole thing down, Julia had said. Only a section of it. Enough for the water to come through.

You really think this thing is gonna hold up, whatever we do? Sat had said.

But Julia hadn't answered her.

Sat reached the wire first, in spite of her injury - Robin held back by her fear of the open sea, Julia by the depth of the water she was navigating.

Robin saw her raise the cutters, press them against the metal - and then pull back, letting one hand fall from the handles, the blades dip into the water.

"I can't do it!" she shouted back at them. "They won't cut!"

Julia accelerated, her breaststroke changing to a rapid front crawl that drove her forward, through the deep water, to the place where Sat was standing.

Robin sped up too, her tentative steps becoming a faster walk that made the upper layer of the sea part on either side of her - looking behind her every few seconds, tracking the Nuckelavee's progress.

It was moving towards them now, quickly, both heads lowered as it accelerated away from Hampton's body and into the water.

*There's no time*, said David again. *Whatever it is she wants to do, she needs to do it now.*

The problem was leverage, Julia saw as she approached the cage. With her ribs cracked, Sat didn't have the strength to close the blades together - couldn't exert enough force to slice through the wire with them, despite their sharpness.

"You have to cut here," Sat said, pressing the cutters into her hands, gesturing to the line where one area of wire met another. "Where they soldered the panels together. It's weak. Won't stand up to pressure."

Julia hesitated, the weight of the cutters pulling down her arms, tugging at the tendons in her neck. She looked back to check on Robin; saw that she was safe, still upright, still treading through the water.

A wave slammed against the mesh, as high and strong as the previous set - rocking the structure and showering them with seawater.

It's now or never, she thought.

She pulled the handles of the cutters apart, the motion requiring enough

271

force for her to understand immediately why Sat had found it impossible in her current condition, then forced the tip of one blade through a gap in the wire, more or less in the spot that Sat had indicated. She squeezed the handles together, feeling the effort in her back and shoulder-blades, and the wire tore - just an inch, but enough for her to force more of the blade into the hole and repeat the action.

"Keep going," said Sat. "It won't take much."

She squeezed a third time and the wire ripped again.

"Now cut horizontally," said Sat. "Along the line. It'll go quicker."

She followed the instruction and cut again, along the seam where the cage's foundations met the wire panels that formed the dome. Two more cuts and a panel fell away, flapping down into the water, letting the sea outside pour through - colder and fast-moving, the current almost knocking her down into the shallows.

"It's working!" she said, elated.

There was a sound from behind her - a voice that she thought might be Robin's, shouting things she couldn't hear, words that scattered like raindrops into the rolling thunder of the Mither's storm.

Then another sound, something like a howl, sharper and much louder, and a smell - a smell she recognized, thick and fleshy and iron-rich. A death smell, the smell of the *pawbi*.

Then a splash and a spatter, the plunge of hooves on liquid. She felt a rush of air as *something* rose up behind her - and a blow like a metal bar against her lower back, driving the air from her lungs and forcing her forward into the water.

It wasn't slow this time.

It slid through the water with the litheness of an eel, the focus of a great white shark - its horse-head lowered, its human torso flattened against its equine body like a jockey urging its animal on to the finish line.

It knows what it wants, she thought. Maybe it really has gotten our scent.

For a few moments she was still, torn between racing forward toward Julia and turning on her heels, back to the shore, to take her chances with the islanders, their weapons and their horses – her indecision paralyzing her, rooting her to the spot.

It moved closer - gliding through the deep center of the enclosure, as close as Julia had been to her a few minutes before - and she squeezed her eyes tight: waiting to feel its teeth at her throat, its hooves striking at her face and body.

But nothing came.

She opened her eyes, and saw it was moving forward, still - towards Julia and Sat and the wire. Ignoring her.

It doesn't want me, she thought. Why doesn't it want me?

*Because it knows,* said David. *It's more than just some dumb animal - it can* think. *It knows what they're trying to do out there. And it wants to stop them.*

"What am I supposed to do?" she said out loud.

*You know the answer to that,* said David. *Or do you want to pretend you don't? Are you still spineless, even after everything that's happened?*

The anger caught alight inside her, and something else with it - something bigger than anger, something darker and more incandescent, something that rose up from inside her like a chemical corrosive, burning her chest and spilling out into the air, into the open water.

"I was never spineless!" she yelled. "I might not have done things your way, but what I *did* do wasn't wrong! And you know what happened the one time, the one single time I *did* do it your way, I *did* try to be like you? I wound up here, in the goddamn mouth of hell. Because your way wasn't smart, David! All it did was get you buried in some secret prison somewhere, or shut up in a hole in the ground. So don't call me fucking spineless!"

There was silence for a second, the space inside her head quieter than it had been in as long as she could remember.

She looked up ahead, and saw the Nuckelavee charge. Saw Sat crouch down against the wire in an airplane brace position, her body sinking low until the water reached her throat, her chin. Saw the Nuckelavee drive its thick animal skull into Julia's body. Saw her fall, her hand still wrapped around the handles of Sat's hedge cutters.

It's going to kill her, she thought. Kill both of them. Then it'll come for me.

She looked down at her feet, and saw that she'd already started swimming, propelling herself forward just below the surface of the shallow water - as fast as she could manage, toward Julia. Toward the Nuckelavee.

Julia could move her legs.

Her kidneys burned and the tissues around them were agony, but she could move her legs, wriggle her toes. Which meant, she reasoned, that none of the vertebrae were broken - that no permanent spinal damage had been done.

If she were anywhere but underwater, she thought, she might play dead: close her eyes, still her body, hold her breath and hope that the *pawbi* would lose interest, would move on to fresher meat, more interesting prey.

But the very real prospect of drowning made it impossible. And fresher meat, in this case, meant the bodies nearest to her. Meant Robin.

She raised her head out of the water, just a fraction.

The *pawbi* had its back to her again - its heads and upper body turned to face away from the wire, its forelegs drawn up into a striking position.

She raised her head higher again, edging her nose and lips out of the water like an alligator in a swamp, and saw why.

Robin was crawling through the water towards her - or perhaps towards *it*, her trajectory placing her directly in the *pawbi*'s path.

And it was watching her - not striking, not moving.

It's confused, she thought, and was reminded of the opening moments of a bullfight - the bull's dazed bewilderment, seconds before it ploughed forward to tear at the matador's innards with its horns.

Robin picked up speed, lowering her head, seeming almost to dive at the patch of water directly in front of the place where *pawbi* stood - and then abruptly changed course, veering off to its left just as quickly, keeping to the shallows, away from the center of the water.

The movement seemed to spur the *pawbi* into action, and it took off after her, its equine body breaking through the water in a canter, then a gallop.

At that pace, she thought, it would close the distance between them in half a minute. Less.

"What the hell is she doing?" said Sat, pulling Julia to her feet.

"She's drawing it out," said Julia, not quite believing what she was seeing. "Luring it away from us."

She half-swam, half-jogged through the shallows, the Nuckelavee at her heels. It was faster than her, she knew, in the sea as well as on land - and she was struggling to keep up her pace, her thighs and stomach protesting as they forced her body on against the weight of the water.

If she carried on straight, she knew, she wouldn't have a hope. It would catch her in a heartbeat.

Changing direction seemed to throw it, though. For every turn she made, it seemed to need a moment to regroup - to work out where it was in relation to her, to reorient and reposition itself so that it was facing her again before it charged forward.

She hit the cage and turned again a quarter way, pushing through the water, back toward the shore.

Cut the wire, she thought. Just cut the damn wire.

"What are you waiting for?" said Sat, pointing down to the cutters Julia still clutched in one of her hands. "Finish it!"

Robin was further away from them now, leading the *pawbi* back towards to the beach, zigzagging left and right, up and down.

She'd bought them some time, she thought. Not much, but some. If she could keep it up, they had perhaps a minute.

She raised the cutters to her chest, her back screaming in protest with every inch; pulled apart the handles and thrust the blades forward, sideways, into the hole she'd made in the mesh.

And cut.

Sat was right, of course: the soldering was shoddy, the metal damaged from the storm and - she imagined - the prolonged exposure to seawater.

The wire parted, and the hole in the cage grew longer.

She stepped forward, and forward, cutting as she went, and the hole became the length of a table, then the length of a car.

Seawater rushed through, a river of it, streaming in and out and down, raising the water level to her ribs, then her breasts.

A wave landed from the outside, and the cage shook everywhere: the dome, the wire, the foundations. More panels fell from the sky into the water, one almost grazing her shoulder as it landed.

A secondary tide burst through the hole she'd made, knocking her off balance.

"How much more?" said Sat.

More, she thought, getting back to her feet. As many as it takes.

She had to keep turning - it was the only way to keep it at bay, to keep herself from getting caught.

She made it nearly onto the sand, the Nuckelavee so close she could smell it, and spun back around, back toward the cage in a wide circle that took her back up through the shallow water, away from the depths in the center.

Julia was cutting into the wire, up ahead, Sat just at her shoulder. They'd made progress, she could see; some of the panels had come away, exposing the sea - the *real* sea - outside and beyond it, miles into the distance, the dark outline of something that she couldn't let herself believe might be the mainland.

There was something else, too - a tide, an undulating wall of water, endlessly high and unnaturally blue, sections of it visible through the gaps in the wire, not quite breaking through.

The Sea Mither, she thought. She's here.

Julia cut again, opening up more of the cage, carving a longer wound through the guts of the mesh.

And from just behind her, the Nuckelavee struck. Brought a hoof down onto the side of her head, her face, slicing the skin and shattering her cheekbone, bringing her to her knees in the water.

She must have screamed, because Julia and Sat both turned to look at her - were close enough that she could see their reaction to the thing that loomed over her.

She stared up at it - the bloody lumps of flesh that formed around its body, the impossible red eyes, the long nightmarish hands reaching down for her. It reared back; exposed the raw tissues of its belly, the needlepoints of its teeth, and she tensed herself for the second strike: the fingers gouging into her, the teeth biting and rending.

Another wave hit.

This one was different than any of the others that preceded it. Stronger, yes - strong enough to rip more panels from the cage, to shake them back and forward like a lobster cage in the ocean. But targeted, somehow; focused.

It landed low on the wire - smashing in through the gap that Julia had made, scattering more panels, blasting a hole the size of a house through the metal.

A burst of saltwater flew into her eyes as the wire broke, hard and painful as ice pellets, and she squeezed them shut on instinct; opened them, and saw more water sweep in, a rising tide of it. Saw Sat's head disappear under it; reappear again, closer to the shore, then vanish under the surface.

And Julia nowhere at all.

The Nuckelavee threw back its head and roared, and still the water poured through, seeming to gather height and speed as it moved inland.

The wave that it formed rose above her; towered over her, a cobra ready to attack.

The Nuckelavee roared again; turned its impossible body around in the water and ran, away from the tide.

But there was no hope of outrunning it.

The wave grew and grew, rising and expanding, changing shape - becoming less a tide than a hurricane, a spinning vortex of liquid energy moving inland, onto the island but somehow leaving her unscathed as the storm it brought raged around her on all sides.

In its center, the water swirled and tossed and rearranged itself into something that might have been a woman's face, ancient as the sea and creased in anger.

It caught the Nuckelavee perhaps six feet from the shoreline - collapsed almost on top of it, sucking its body in and then down, suffocating it under a thousand tons of water, pulling it back from the island and out, away.

The cage was a burst dam now, she saw - shaking and unstable, its total collapse a matter of *when* not *if*.

And through the ruins of it, the water flowed in - thick and fast and heavy enough to bury an island.

# EPILOGUE - 1

The rescue crew arrived just after lunch.

From the air, the island had seemed impossible to navigate at ground level: a relief map of stone and water, displaced sand and cross-hatched metal.

They'd brought the copter down to land on the most stable piece of ground they could find, a strip of parched grass and soil far from the beach, one that looked as if it hadn't seen daylight in a long time but that was - remarkably, under the circumstances - free of seawater and debris.

All of the survivors, they'd been told, had been evacuated already - vanished away to the mainland by other men in other machines.

Civilian teams, the Pilot had told one of his Crewmen after the briefing. Contractors. They'll have had the poor sods back under lock and key before you can say *private prison*.

What about the islanders? the Crewman had asked. What did they do with them?

They took them too, the Pilot had said. Any that were left.

Their job, in this instance, was less *rescue* and more *salvage* - picking up the pieces, tagging the bodies for collection. They'd been told to expect the worst, chaos and carnage and death.

The landscape didn't disappoint.

They split up into pairs: the Pilot and his First Crewman heading down to the beach, the other two on their way to the higher ground where - they'd been told - the blocks of flats still stood.

Rather them than me, said the First Crewman. Do you know how many flats they built on here? That's a lot of rubble to sift through.

They saw their first two bodies out by the shoreline, lying side-by-side on the sand: an old man, bits of metal and seaweed tangled in his long beard, and a young girl, dark-haired and fragile-looking, about the same age as the Pilot's daughter. There were no obvious injuries on either of them, and not so much as a scratch on the girl, despite the heavy wire panels strewn around the both of them - panels, or so they'd been told in the briefing, that had fallen clean out of the sky when the Faraday Cage had caved in.

Bloody stupid idea in the first place, the Pilot thought. Who in their right mind would build something like that in a place like this and expect it to stay standing?

They logged the bodies as drownings, and moved on, up and along the beach.

The next body wasn't a person but an animal - a great black horse, one of the biggest the Pilot had seen, its coat saturated, its belly distended. Saltwater, the Pilot thought. Another drowning.

"Poor thing," said the Crewman, bending down to stroke its soaked mane.

The Crewman liked horses, the Pilot remembered. Took his kids riding at the weekends.

"Real shame," said the Pilot. "They'll be some live ones, though, too, I expect. They're tough animals, horses."

As if to prove his point, a second horse ran at them from behind - a chunky chestnut thing, equally wet but very much alive, galloping out to the water.

"Log that, would you?" said the Pilot. "Any that are left, we'll have to get them airlifted out when the time comes."

The fourth body was in a far worse state than the first three.

It was definitely male, that much the Pilot could tell, densely-bearded and thick around the gut. But though it couldn't have been in the water longer than a day, it looked well on its way to decomposition.

Must be the salt, thought the Pilot.

Its face was grey and shriveled, and some animal or other had been at its hands, stripping the skin and flesh there down to the bone. One of its feet was missing, torn off at the ankle. Above the beard, its face was a horror show: cheeks gored and both eyes gone, scraps of scalp hanging down on its forehead, the red hair still attached to it.

"Log it as an unexplained," said the Pilot. "The coroner can sort it out when they take it back to the city."

"Will do," said the Crewman, looking green about the gills.

He'll soon learn, thought the Pilot.

They walked for another half a mile, dodging wire and debris, logging bodies as they came upon them: horses and humans both, though none of them in so bad a way as the footless man. All of them were locals, to the Pilot's eye, men and women - all dressed in thick coats and animal-hide hats of the kind he associated with farming communities and rural isolation. All of them had drowned.

"What do you think they were doing out here?" said the Crewman.

"Couldn't say," said the Pilot.

"And why didn't they go inland when the storm came? I can't understand it, not when all the prisoners made it to shelter."

"Almost all," said the Pilot.

"Still," said the Crewman. "It makes no sense."

He was a sensitive soul, the Pilot thought. And a thinker, too. They'd have to do something about that, if he stayed on with the team.

They kept walking, following the curve of the beach past a cluster of rocks and a small stone outhouse that he was amazed was still standing, until they reached a set of low-lying caves poking out into the sodden grassland up above.

And a sound coming from inside the first of them: the echoes of something like a voice, soft and murmuring.

"It's like the apocalypse, isn't it?" said the Crewman, each word a booming thunderclap in the Pilot's ear.

"Quiet!" hissed the Pilot, pressing a finger to his mouth for emphasis.

He crept to the opening of the cave, keeping his footsteps as light on the sand as he was able.

Careful now, Jim, he thought. You don't know who's in there. All this was a jail until yesterday.

"What are you doing?" said the Crewman.

"There's someone in there," said the Pilot. "Maybe more than one someone."

There was movement from inside the cave; a splash of water and the slow, wet tread of feet on damp ground.

"Stand back," said the Pilot, ushering the Crewman behind him, reaching into his kit bag for his torch.

A girl appeared in the mouth of the cave - another young one, only a few years older than the dead one on the beach, this one soaked to the skin and half-naked, her eyes and cheeks hollow, tattoo ink snaking up and down the blue-brown skin of her arms in elaborate patterns.

She walked towards him slowly, limping, holding her belly on one side.

"Are you with Vanderhalden?" she said, her voice weak but recognizably American.

"We're Search and Rescue," said the Pilot. "We're not *with* anyone."

"We've come to help you," said the Crewman.

The girl looked them up and down with naked suspicion.

"So you're *not* Vanderhalden?" she said.

"Cross my heart," said the Crewman.

He unzipped one of the pockets of his jacket and pulled out his ID badge, the lanyard damp but the laminate protecting the photo from the elements.

"Here," he said, handing it across to the girl. "See."

Idiot, thought the Pilot.

The girl studied the photo for a drawn-out second, then turned away from them, back towards the cave, the badge still in her hand.

"You can come out," she said. "It's not them."

Two more women limped out of the cave, older than the girl but just as wet and bedraggled. One of them was injured, the Pilot saw - leaning on the smaller, darker woman next to her for support as she walked, one half of her face black with bruises and her right leg obviously broken.

The Pilot pulled a foil blanket from his bag, stepped forward and wrapped it around the shoulders of the injured woman.

"Thank you," she said, not letting go of the other woman's arm. She was English, well-spoken; a world away from the tattooed American.

"Did everyone make it out?" said the woman next to her - another American, the Pilot noted, a deep gash cutting into one of her cheeks.

"We can talk about that on the way back to the mainland," said the Crewman, handing her another blanket.

"Just tell us," she said, refusing to take it.

"Almost all of the prisoners were accounted for," he said quietly. "But the islanders..."

"They're dead?" said the Englishwoman.

The Pilot, more used to bad news and grieving relations than the Crewman, took the reins.

"Most of them, yes," he said, firm but kind. "I'm very sorry."

Something passed between the three women - a look the Pilot couldn't read, couldn't begin to understand.

Very carefully, still taking the brunt of her bodyweight on one arm, the older American turned to look the Englishwoman in the eye.

"You think it's over?" she asked gently.

"For now?" said the Englishwoman. "Yes."

The older American nodded; cupped the unbruised side of the Englishwoman's face with her free hand and kissed her, lightly, on the lips.

"Okay, then," she said.

She turned to the Pilot.

"We're ready," she said. "Take us back."

# EPILOGUE - 2

**From:** l.webber@specialprojects.vanderhalden.com
**To:** c.lee@specialprojects.vanderhalden.com
**Re:** Project Phoenix - Newfoundland / Fox Point

Carl,

Just heard your news. Before you go, could you forward me the original scout's report on Fox Point (Newfoundland) if you still have it?

We're scoping out potential sites for Project Phoenix and it seems, from memory, like it could be a good fit.

Best of luck with the new venture.

Lucy

# ABOUT THE AUTHOR

TC PARKER is a writer and researcher based in the fox-ravaged wilds of Leicestershire, where she lives with her partner and two extremely energetic children.

The author (as Natalie Edwards) of the *El Gardener* series of feminist heist books and (as TC Parker) of the upcoming novel *A Press of Feathers,* she's been a copywriter, a lecturer and, very briefly, an academic; now she runs a semiotics and cultural insight agency by day and dreams up horror and crime fiction at night, when the kids are asleep.

Visit her online at www.tcparkerwrites.com

Printed in Great Britain
by Amazon

47707181R00165